HE PLAYED A LONE HAND—
AND HE PLAYED TO WIN

White Moon Tree learned early that he had what it took to come out ahead when he bumped heads with the best five-card-stud players in the Montana Territory—a razor-keen mind, iron nerve, and lightning reflexes.

Those same qualities stood him in good stead as he built a private cattle kingdom in the great Montana grasslands, where only the strongest could survive the blaze of range wars and the rapacious sweeps of rustlers.

But now he was tested anew . . . as he had to track down a gang of killers before they killed him . . . as he had to juggle his feelings for beautiful wildcat of a woman and a properly lovely female rancher . . . as he had to save his brother from enemies closing in on him . . . as he had to be a man worthy of the ancient traditions of a noble tribe and of the father who had showed him what a man should be. . . .

WHITE MOON TREE

WHITE MOON TREE

Paul A. Hawkins

A SIGNET BOOK

SIGNET
Published by the Penguin Group
Penguin Books USA Inc., 375 Hudson Street,
New York, New York 10014, U.S.A.
Penguin Books, Ltd, 27 Wrights Lane,
London W8 5TZ, England
Penguin Books Australia Ltd, Ringwood,
Victoria, Australia
Penguin Books Canada Ltd, 10 Alcorn Avenue,
Toronto, Ontario, Canada M4V 3B2
Penguin Books (N.Z.) Ltd, 182-190 Wairau Road,
Auckland 10, New Zealand

Penguin Books Ltd, Registered Offices:
Harmondsworth, Middlesex, England

First published by Signet,
an imprint of Dutton Signet,
a division of Penguin Books USA Inc.

First Printing, January, 1994
10 9 8 7 6 5 4 3 2 1

 REGISTERED TRADEMARK—MARCA REGISTRADA

Printed in the United States of America

To my wife, Ann,
who also plays a mean game

ONE

July 1882

Most people called him Moon, the second son of the breed Ben Tree, who owned one of the largest ranches in the Montana Territory. His close-knit family, however, still referred to him as White Moon, his given name among the Absaroke or Crow Indians with whom he had lived most of his life. After White Moon and his older brother, Benjamin One Feather, had arrived to share in the family ownership of the giant spread in the beautiful Gallatin Valley, their given Crow names had proved to be a bit incongruous in the white man's society. So they resorted and made do with what many people around Boseman City usually called these two well-versed young men—Moon and Young Benjamin. They had been at the ranch over a year now.

After the beginning of the demise of the buffalo herds on White Moon and Benjamin's native land in the Yellowstone, the tribe of Man Called Tree had slowly disintegrated. Many of the villagers forced to new homes on the great reservation were living the usual life of reservation lassitude in meager comfort, accepting the food supplements supplied by a benevolent government, the same government that for years had attempted to tear apart their culture. Ben Tree, or Chief Man Called Tree as he was known by the various tribes, long ago had foreseen this slow, insidious destruction, the inevitable consequence of civilization's encroachment upon the Indian's West.

Through homesteading, politics, and a great sum of money that he had both earned and inherited from a prosperous freighting business during the great migration years, he established the Tree ranch in 1868 and hired capable men to manage it, all in preparation for his family's future in the white world. The future of the West, as he envisioned it, was beef and horses. And this had come to pass. The Tree ranch holdings now encompassed twelve-thousand deeded acres of choice range land and watershed. With the great unceded portions of the distant Yellowstone rapidly diminishing to the realm of range cattle and the plow, White Moon and Benjamin One Feather, their freedom harnesses and tribal friends disappearing, had finally moved to the Gallatin and taken up their inherited duties. Their great father and beautiful mother continued to live in isolation on a large homestead in the Stillwater Valley.

For White Moon, the duty on this particular day, was working on the upper range above the hot springs' line cabin with Zachary Hockett and Willie Left Hand. Willie, a breed of Salish origin, and a bachelor, had been working for the ranch six years, while Hockett, an ex-army lieutenant, had arrived four years past. Hockett, married to a young Nez Perce named Two Shell Woman, lived with her and their four-year-old son Joseph in the line cabin, a one-room bunkhouse now converted into a three-room home. The three men were riding near the north end of the property bordering open range this afternoon in July when, in the distance, White Moon saw for the first time in his life a band of sheep grazing up near the edge of the timber. And this was the day that he was to meet Divinity Jones, another first in his young life.

After exchanging surprised glances, the drovers reined over and headed up toward the sheep to investigate, searching ahead for signs of a herder. White Moon, who spoke English, thanks to the literacy and tutelage of his father, finally said to the others, "Now, what do you suppose this fellow is doing bringing those woolies up this way? Old man Stuart's going to have a conniption when he hears about it. By jingo, he hates those fuzzy critters." Moon's reference was to Adam Stuart, a neighboring rancher who shared part of the big open range with the Tree ranch.

"He'll be sore, that's what," Zachary Hockett said. "But there's no markers on this land, so whoever's up here has his rights, too, just as on this side, it's our problem, not Stuart's. We'll just tell this herder to move on up the canyon."

With some annoyance, Willie Left Hand spoke up. "I told Mr. Clay one of these days we was gonna have to put wire and a gate up here. Ain't no way a man can know where the hell he is. Wire'd keep Stuart's stock where they belong, too. If old man Stuart wants the free grass, he can herd his cows over from the other side of the ridge, stedda letting them mix in with our critters all the time. Just makes work double later on, sorting 'em out this way all the time."

"I see somebody," White Moon said, pointing.

"A wagon?" Hockett asked, obviously puzzled. "A covered wagon?"

Willie Left Hand laughed derisively. "That's a sheepherder's outfit, you damned fool. Hell, I sees those things down south of here couple a times on the drives to Utah. Even got a cooking stove inside. See there, that little old stack sticking up? Bunk in that contraption, too, regular moving cook house, it is."

Frowning, elevating his nose, White Moon said, "I smell those sheep; all the way over here I can smell them."

"Yep," Willie Left Hand chuckled, suddenly becoming the authority on sheep. "Right peculiar smell they has, and they crap just like a big old jack rabbit, eat the grass, weeds and all, just like a jack, too, right down to the nubbin. Oh, I sees these critters before, but not up in this country. Lots of them coming in other side of the big mountains. Come winter, they's all gone far south.

Trims them up, they do. Come spring and the grass is up, they moves them back to the high country again."

As they approached the wagon, a lone figure attired in baggy pants and a large denim jacket stepped out from behind it. None of the three men could make out a face because of a huge, weather-beaten hat hiding it, but they clearly saw the double-barreled shotgun protruding from the great gathering of sleeve. This made Willie Left Hand grin. He said aside, "Looks like one of them damned scarecrows the sodbusters use to keep the blackies outta the grain. Now, look at that, would you!"

A former cavalryman, Zachary Hockett reacted a little less lackadaisically. He knew all about weapons, and a shotgun at close range was nothing to trifle with, not in his manual of arms. "Jesus, it's a kid aiming that thing at us!" He abruptly reined up, and held out a protesting hand. "Hey," he shouted, "put that thing down! We're coming in to talk and mean you no harm. Go on, boy, ease off, you hear?"

A small voice came back. "State your business and don't you come any closer, either."

"Aw, now," Willie Left Hand said, slowly dismounting, "if you touch that buster off, it mos' likely'll knock you on your ass, kid. Just put it aside. Hell, we're just looking for a few strays, that's all, cows from down below, always sneaking off on us in the timber up here to get away from the skeeters."

"Ain't no strays here."

White Moon, frisking the campsite with his quick, dark eyes, saw two mules grazing nearby, one pony, and hanging on a rear wheel of the wagon, a man's coat. His first thought was that perhaps another weapon was close by, probably aimed right at their heads. It was almost a certainty that there was someone else with this outfit. He said easily, "Where's your folks?" Then edging toward the wagon, he added, "You're not alone up here, are you?"

"My paw's up there with the dogs," the youth said, nodding. "We got strays, too."

"Well, how about your mother?" Moon asked. "She hiding in there?"

"Ain't got no maw. She's been dead for four years now," was the reply. "And don't you come up here. That's far enough, mister."

"Well, you shouldn't go letting your stock go wandering back there," White Moon said, motioning toward the adjacent woods. He stopped to stretch out his nearly six-foot frame, casually removed his hat, and swept away the perspiration from his forehead. Except for his black hair and dark eyes, he had the features of his famous father,—angular face, straight nose, the identical chin with a small cleft in the middle. And there wasn't the trace of a hair on his smooth, olive-skinned face. "There's all kind of critters in the timber there," he went on. "Killed a grizzly right about this spot last week. Ate up one of our cows plenty good. Six feet high, at the least. Claws on him three inches long. Bad medicine, I'll tell you that. Why, one of those woolies wouldn't amount to no more than a hotcake for the critter." Moon's jaw suddenly dropped and his eyeballs went white. *"Ikye!"* he shouted out in Absaroke. "Look there, boys, there's one of them now!"

Even Zachary Hockett and Willie Left Hand, both of whom had been duped by White Moon too many times, took a quick look. So did the youth with the shotgun. But before anyone saw the great phantom bear, Moon Tree had leaped headlong five feet and wrested away the gun. Flattened out next to the wagon was the young boy, scratching at the grass, cursing, and trying to retrieve his great hat. Only it wasn't a boy. It was a young woman, her blondish hair tumbling crazily in all directions and her steel-blue eyes spitting sparks. She came up flailing her arms like a molting goose, spewing a string of curses that would have put a muleskinner to shame.

"Jesus!" exclaimed Hockett, "she's a woman!"

"More wildcat," opined Willie Left Hand, hopping quickly to the side.

"Well, what the hell did you think I was!" she screamed, wiping at a grass smear on her chin. "You think I'm some kind of a monkey in the medicine show? You dumb bastards!" With her fingers crooked like claws, she shouted, "Get back or I'll scratch your goddamned eyes out!"

White Moon, with a wry smile, flipped out the shells from the shotgun and tossed it back to her; she snatched the weapon in mid-air. He said, "How were we to know what you were, that garb you're all decked out in?" He stared down at her feet and grinned. "Those clodhoppers you got on, those trousers, big enough to—"

She made one angry swipe at his legs with the barrel of the shotgun, but Moon Tree deftly leaped away, laughing. Thrusting her chin out, she cried, "What the hell you expecting I'd be wearing out here in this shitty place, a getting-married dress? You dumb bastards are all alike, drinking, chewing, never paying no mind to nothing." Suddenly, she sat on the grass, wildly beat her hands up and down, and started bawling, great tears dribbling down her cheeks, leaving shiny little trails across her dirty face.

For a moment, the startled men just stood there quite helplessly, and stared disbelievingly at this bizarre sight. "Oh, Jesus!" Zachary Hockett finally mumbled. He kicked his boot out at White Moon. "Look at what you've gone and done. Damn it, maybe she just doesn't have anything better than what she's wearing. You've offended her, got her all riled up."

"Well, I'm sorry, miss," Moon Tree offered lamely, trying to suppress a smile. Never in his life, even among angry squaws, had he witnessed such a crazy performance, from venomous bravado to a frazzled fit of weeping, almost within the flick of an eyelash. It was beyond him, all women were beyond him, always trying to get under a man's skin or give him an itch.

Hockett shot him another dirty look. "Oh, shut up! Get her on her feet, damn it. Help her up and let's get out of here. Jesus!" When White Moon, fearful of putting his hand into a nettle patch, hesitated and shrugged, Zachary Hockett cursed again. "Oh, hell, get out of the way." Bending over, he put his hands under the young woman's armpits and heaved her to her feet. He pulled off his bandanna and gave it to her. "Here, wipe off those tears," he commanded. Snatching away the red scarf, she promptly blew her nose, a very loud honk, bringing another smile to White Moon's usually solemn face. "What's your name?" Zachary Hockett asked.

"Divinity," she said with a final sob. "Divinity Jones."

And in the next few minutes Divinity Jones wove an amazing yarn for the men, laced with colorful invectives: how she and her father, Burleigh, had run their two hundred sheep all the way from the Idaho Territory up into the Madison Valley and had crossed over to the Gallatin. They were making a circuit for the Coombes Livestock Company, now planning to head west and graze the band back through the Beaverhead and then on home. Two dollars a day and grub, boasted Divinity, handsome wages. A rancher down near the Targhee country had already rousted them once, had even threatened to kill their two sheepdogs. Coyotes had stolen at least a half dozen of the lambs, and at one time it rained for three straight days, miring their wagon in the mud. Their extra mule was stolen, probably by wandering Bannack Indians. The mosquitoes had been ferocious and now the deer flies were beginning to hatch. She allowed that it hadn't been a pleasant trip. Besides all of this, Divinity said her paw was a drunk. There wasn't much Zachary Hockett, White Moon, or Willie Left Hand could do about her plight except stare at her sympathetically. This young woman was no more than eighteen years old.

Presently, Burleigh Jones made his appearance, riding in, followed by six sheep and the two dogs. The dogs chased the sheep back toward the main band, and Burleigh, a ring of froth around his whiskered mouth, went straight for the water bucket. He took one dipperful, drank only a teaspoon or two, gargled once, and spat disgustedly to the side. "Bad stuff," he said. "Bad stuff." Eyeballing the three visitors, he settled in on the closest, who happened to be Moon Tree. "Don't tell me," he asked forlornly, "we's on your land, ain't we?"

"No, sir," White Moon replied. "No, this is open range. 'Course, with those woolies, you aren't too welcome with all of the cattle in the neighborhood, and our neighbor over the ridge ten miles or so, he'd take exception to this, I'm certain. Fact is, you sort of surprised us. First time we've seen sheep this far north. Private land is half mile below here, markers out."

Burleigh, the exact counterpart of his daughter in dress, pointed to the west. "Heading that way tomorrow, anyhow. Yep, back around the horn." He sized up the drovers again, one by one; this time he chose Zachary Hockett, who appeared to be a tad more white than White Moon or Willie Left Hand. "Reckon you're the ramrod, eh? Wouldn't happen to have a touch of whiskey, would you?"

"Nary a drop," Hockett said. "Sorry."

"Sorry, shit," groaned Burleigh Jones. "I'm the one who's sorry. Little green feller with a big red nose lives in my belly. Thirsty little bastard, he is. Been naggin' the hell out of me for at least a couple days now. Reckon he's about done in till I swings by the diggin's."

Divinity, slumped disconsolately against a wagon wheel, glanced away, a forlorn look on her tear-stained face. Hockett gave her a friendly tap on her droopy hat and tried to put some cheer in her. "You take care, hear?" he almost whispered. "Things will get better."

And Moon Tree, mounting up, said woefully, "Sorry about jumping you that way. Those shotguns aren't much for welcoming, you know."

Divinity Jones simply waved him off. "Goodbye, stupid."

The three drovers turned and slowly rode away without so much as a backward glance. But they all were sharing thoughts about the Jones family encounter. White Moon spoke up first. "I've never seen my brothers look as poorly as those two. The Great Maker of Everything, Akbatatdia, must have been looking the other way when they passed through the gate, ei?"

Zachary Hockett agreed. But he had made an observation, one that went deeper than dress and grime. "That young woman would be downright pretty if she could afford to take care of herself, get some of that money her old man wastes on whiskey. She has a lot of grit in her, too."

"*Ei*," smiled White Moon. "Most of it on her face and tongue. Whoeeee, Divinity Jones."

The housewarming at the new home of Young Benjamin and White Crane was underway later on this same July day, a few friends from Bozeman City and Adam Stuart's spread in attendance. The big log and frame structure had been built several hundred yards above Benjamin's brother-in-law's place, adjacent to Six Mile Creek. It had one long porch across the front, a large parlor with a rock fireplace, a spacious kitchen, and three bedrooms. Unlike James Goodhart's home, in which water came into the kitchen by a gravity-flow pipe from the creek, Young Benjamin had built his kitchen over a hand-dug well, and a cistern with a shiny red handle pumped water into a huge basin. White Crane, the slender, pretty wife of Benjamin, was several months pregnant with her second child. The first-born being Thaddeus, a three-year-old named after the elder Ben Tree's wealthy father, who had been killed by outlaws on the old Oregon Trail back in 1852. Though most of the family was present this late afternoon, Ben Tree and his Nez Perce wife, Rainbow, were at their home in the shadows of the Beartooth Range, ancient grounds of the Absaroke whom he had led for so many years. This mountain home was midway between the Tree ranch to the west and the Crow reservation to the east.

Most of the conversation at the housewarming concerned the news of the Northern Pacific railroad's extension of track westward up the Yellowstone River to Bozeman City. This, of course, was beneficial to the ranchers now multiplying in the great basin country, who were to have better access to the lucrative cattle markets of the Midwest. And it was Ben Tree's idea to capture more of this market by establishing a central shipping point somewhere along the Yellowstone, thus eliminating the arduous month-long drives to the railheads in Idaho and Utah. The cattlemen far to the east were already moving stock south by rail from the Dakotas, some of it even dressed and packaged. It was time to firm up the Montana Territory's market with an operational base within a reasonable moving distance, and Ben Tree had suggested investing in a stockyard and perhaps a packing plant on the Northern Pacific line. Claybourn Moore, his long-time ranch foreman, had already approached several ranchers about the venture, including Adam Stuart. Most of the men were enthusiastic but without adequate funds to become partners. Presently only Stuart was still talking business, and his voice wasn't too loud. Ben Tree, however, had promised Claybourn Moore that one way or another, he was going to conclude his enterprise before one of the British cattle companies expanded in this direction. Several of the English lords now appropriating much of the unceded range were building up herds by the thousands in the Judith Basin country, all the way east to Miles Town.

While some of the evening's guests continued talking about cattle and the brisk business in horse sales, the women were busy bringing out huge portions of food to the makeshift plank tables spread out under the long porch. Finally Benjamin One Feather, holding his son, Thad, made a short speech, then invited his friends to take up their plates and begin helping themselves. A smattering of applause here, then his invitation was quickly accepted, and before long, everyone had found a seat either in the shade of the porch or beneath the huge cottonwoods fronting the new house. White Moon and the Hocketts and their son sat on blankets under one of the trees, and soon were joined by Melody, the five-year-old daughter of James Goodhart and Little Blue Hoop. Melody doted on her Uncle Moon, followed him like a camp puppy, rode in the saddle with him when he was around the corrals, and sometimes called him in for a good-night kiss if he wasn't in the bunkhouse playing poker. Moon had another admirer present, too, Jessie Stuart, the daughter of rancher Adam Stuart. But Jess was no little girl. She was eighteen, had the same large dark eyes as her mother, Ellie Stuart, was slim, slightly buxom, and displayed two dimples when she smiled. And this was quite often, particularly when she was around Moon Tree. She liked this handsome young man of dry wit and humor who always made a lot of people laugh and smile. In the bygone days in the Crow village of Man Called Tree, Moon's brothers had come to identify him closely with the Trickster, Esaccwata, the legendary Old Man Coyote, the perpetrator of humorous tricks. Adam Stuart, along with his daughter, thought Moon Tree a suitable catch, despite his half-Nez Perce blood, but Adam's wife, Ellie, was apprehensive about a possible mixed blood union. Moon's addiction to gambling was somewhat disturbing, too.

Jessie Stuart wasn't dissuaded in the least by this dim maternal appraisal. After all, in the spacious Gallatin Valley, there weren't all that many eligible bachelors around, and those few who were, usually owned nothing more than their horse and saddle, not exactly a prosperous out-look. Jessie was on the wide porch steps, seated with Young Benjamin, Lucas Hamm, owner of the largest mercantile in town, and James Goodhart. Her eyes were constantly drifting over to the cottonwood grove where Moon Tree, Melody in his lap, continued to eat and talk with Zachary Hockett and Two Shell Woman, who was often just called Shell. Jessie hesitated to join them because of a language barrier. Moon and Two Shell Woman held some of their conversations in Nez Perce. Both Shell and White Crane were embarrassed by their English deficiency. When the conversation became one with a series of accompanying gestures, Jessie Stuart had difficulty following. She thought it amazing that Moon Tree spoke Crow, Nez Perce, and English equally well. It would have been more convenient for her purposes if he used only the last.

Zachary Hockett, who like Benjamin One Feather possessed the eyes of an owl, was silently amused as he observed this small flirtation, and not for the first time. Jessie Stuart had been out on the range more than once with Stuart's drovers, including her brother, Ed, and often sidled up near White Moon to pass a few words. On occasions when Moon hadn't been among the outriders, she made her usual inquiry as to his whereabouts. This always prompted some hearty teasing back in the bunkhouse where White Moon lived with the other drovers, Willie Left

Hand, Robert Peete, and Peter Marshall, "the Quiet One." Nodding toward the porch, Hockett said to Moon, "Why don't you do something about that girl, damn it? You two have been playing cat and mouse for six months now. I should think in this amount of time you could come to some kind of mutual agreement, some romance even."

White Moon, gnawing on the last of a chicken leg, flipped the bone at one of the ranch dogs. "Bad medicine," he replied casually. "You want me in your boots, ei? I have plenty trouble around here with critters, more than enough without getting myself tied down with a filly like her. No, I do all right by myself, no woman to tell me what to do."

"But she's a good-looking woman," Hockett replied.

"Ei," agreed White Moon. "Plenty of spirit under those petticoats, too, but if I claimed every good-looking pony I ever saw I would have a hundred."

Two Shell Woman, listening intently, picked up part of this short dialogue, and she frowned at her husband. She said, "You want him toss blanket, no good. Maybe he no have heart song for woman. Bad, bring plenty pain in heart for woman. You hear me, I know woman inside me." And she reached over and pinched Zachary Hockett on the thigh. This short declaration had meaning, and both her husband and White Moon knew the subtle inference. Long ago during the Indian wars, she had saved Hockett's life, nurtured him to health from a bullet wound, only to fall hopelessly in love with him. Separated by the events of those tragic days, she thought she was never to see him again, bore his child, ultimately took haven at the ranch during the Nez Perce war. That he had returned a year later searching for her was the miracle in her life, her gift from the Great Spirit. But her heart had ached for many moons before this came to pass. She knew about pain.

Zachary Hockett tried to explain. "I didn't say anything about him tossing the blanket with her, damn it. I was just saying he ought to get together with her a little more. She's taken a shine to him, understand. Makes big eyes."

"No business you, my man," Shell said, wagging a finger of warning. Then in Nez Perce she told White Moon, "You listen to his words, and you'll find big trouble. If you make a child and don't love her, this is bad with these white people. You must get married or run away and hide somewhere. Maybe our people don't care, but her father would be plenty angry with you, my brother, maybe shoot you between your legs where this trouble all began. *Sepekuse,* so be it. I have spoken enough about this."

Zachary Hockett looked curiously at Moon, "What's she saying now?"

White Moon said solemnly, "Says that old man Stuart's liable to shoot my balls off one of these days if I'm not careful."

"Oh, Jesus!" moaned Hockett in frustration. "How'd we get into fornication! I never even suggested this 'tossing the blanket' crap. She's putting words into my mouth again."

With an indifferent shrug, Moon said, "Human nature, I suppose, one thing leading to another." He gave Hockett an impish grin. "She's just not forgetting what you put into her on that pack trip back to the fort that time. Boom, boom." And when White Moon translated this fully, Two Shell Woman giggled. "Plenty good," she replied with a small blush.

"Oh, oh," Zachary Hockett suddenly mumbled, and the others looked up in unison to discover the exuberant and pretty Jessie Stuart approaching to their side, holding her arms open to Melody Goodhart. As she embraced the child she said, "May I join you? The men are over there talking business again, saddles this time. I figured you people were talking about something more interesting than tack, at least."

"Welcome, Miss Jessie," Hockett answered, getting to his feet.

"Oh, do sit down," she protested. Holding Melody, she gracefully tucked in her dress and sat beside them, smiling at Two Shell Woman. "How are you, Shell?" she said. "You look so nice, your dress, and your pretty hair all swept back. Ah, but you always look this way. Someday I'm going to steal those pretty earrings."

Two Shell Woman returned her smile and politely replied, "Hallo, thank you. Happy I see you." She turned to White Moon, as usual, and said a few words in Nez Perce, and he, as usual, uttered a quick translation. "She says when you get some holes in your ears, she'll give you some earrings, be happy to. Makes them out of quills, shells, and beads."

"Holes like me," Melody Goodhart said, tilting her head, presenting an ear resplendent with a tiny gold ring.

"Will it hurt?" Jessie asked Melody.

Melody answered, "I don't know. Uncle Moon says I came this way. A fairy spirit gave me these. I kept them."

Jessie Stuart, giving Melody a hug, looked over at Moon Tree. "I never knew you told fairy tales, only tales. And where have you been this past week? Working or playing cards?"

"Riding up the far end with Mr. Hockett," Moon said. "That's his country up there, and I just follow orders."

"Evenings, too?" she asked slyly. "Night riding?"

"Some of the boys been trying to get even," he admitted. "I have to give them their chance. Hard to walk away a winner in the bunkhouse, not like in town. Big difference when you play with fellows you work with. That's fun. In town, it's mostly business, stakes are higher and you never know who's your friend."

The talk then wandered, and near dusk, Lucas Hamm and Willie Left Hand struck up their fiddles in the big parlor of the new home. Young Benjamin and White Crane had only sparingly furnished the house, so there was very little furniture to move. One carpet and two huge buffalo robes were pulled away, and soon most everyone was taking a turn at the circle two-step, French jig, and a schottische or two. Both White Crane and Two Shell Woman finally threw off their white woman's footwear and danced shoeless. While this was amusing and rather fascinating to several of the guests, it didn't faze Jessie Stuart. She dared to join them, and amid a few surprised stares she went waltzing away across the shiny new floor with Zachary Hockett. As they swept around the room, she asked, "What am I going to do about that man? He sees more in a deck of cards than he does a woman. I am a woman, don't you think? Too brazen for him?"

"Oh, he sees you," assured Hockett. "He's just a different cut, that one. He watched both his sister and sister-in-law fetch men, knows how you women operate. Refers to Benjamin and James as 'goners' now." Zachary Hockett chuckled. "He puts me in the same catagory, too. He doesn't want to get trapped that way. I'd say give him some time. Let the cream settle and one of these days he'll come around to lick the topping. I think you're too much of a woman to be denied. I reckon you overwhelm him a bit. But you're sure right about the cards. He has an affair going there, calls her 'Lady Luck,' and she takes up a lot of his spare time."

Her eyes gleamed and she said boldly, "If ever I get hold of him, I'll make him forget 'Lady Luck' in a hurry."

Zachary Hockett smiled inwardly. This, undoubtedly, was what young Moon Tree was worried about, a woman of desire and ambition who would put a snug halter around his handsome face and inhibit his new-found avocation. And as Hockett made a graceful sweep, turning Jessie on her pretty toes, there in the open doorway suddenly appeared the bedraggled Divinity Jones, mouth agape, her floppy hat down around her ears, staring directly at him. "Jesus!" exclaimed Zachary Hockett. He abruptly dropped his arm from Jessie's slim waist. "It's Divinity Jones!"

"You know that person . . . ?" Jessie's words dribbled off at the unexpected spectacle. She had never seen such an unkempt woman.

"Sheepherder's daughter," said Hockett. "Met her and her old man today on the high line." Suddenly the fiddles screeched away on discordant notes, and Willie Left Hand let out a long moan. "What the hell . . . ?"

Then from the silence, the hushed whispers, Divinity Jones announced: "My paw's dead. Kilt. Drovers, five of them, they kilt him. Noplace else to go but here . . ."

Claybourn Moore moved up quickly beside her, followed by White Moon. Moon said to the foreman, "This is the one I was telling you about, sheep, up above the line cabin. Her name is Divinity."

"What drovers?" Claybourn Moore asked her. "What the hell happened?"

Shoulders sagging helplessly, Divinity Jones replied, "Drovers pushing horses. They comes right through our sheep, yelling like crazy men, chasing their shitty horses. I was at the crick fetching water, and I hears some shots. I comes up and sees this black-whiskered bastard riding 'round our wagon and waving his gun. Then they all went riding hell-bent over the hill. I run up and my paw is dead by the wagon, dogs just sitting there by him moaning like."

Jessie Stuart slid a chair under a wavering Divinity Jones. Clay Moore asked her the location of the wagon and she said just over the ridge from where she had seen the three drovers earlier in the day, near a creek and some rock spires. Her father had thought it best to move on after the encounter with the Tree ranch cowboys.

Young Ed Stuart spoke up. "That's Finger Butte where she means. Hell, that's over on our side, twenty miles from here. Damnation!" He stared across the room at his father. "Hey, Pa, ain't we got horses up that way?"

"Forty or so head," Adam Stuart acknowledged. "Mostly mares and colts. Do you reckon . . . ?"

Clay Moore said, "You bet I reckon, Adam. Horse thieves, and I'd say that was some of your stock. Those fellows ran into the old man probably by accident. He got a look at them and paid the price, didn't know what the hell was going on."

At this moment, Divinity Jones simply fell from the chair and collapsed in a heap at the feet of Zachary Hockett. "Oh, Jesus, she's fainted away!" he yelled. "Get some water." Benjamin, pushing several people aside, lifted the young woman into his arms, and followed by White Crane, carried her away to one of the back bedrooms.

By then Clay Moore was in action, ordering Moon, Willie Left Hand, and Robert Peete to start riding for Finger Butte, allowing that the rustlers were leaving a well-trodden trail, and one that he knew White Moon was capable of following in the darkest of night. Adam Stuart, who had arrived at the party in a buggy, told young Ed to latch up and ride with the Tree ranch drovers. In the meantime, he and his wife and daughter would stop in town and advise Bill Duggan to get some deputies out by first light. This amused Moon Tree, and pausing at the porch steps, he winked at Jessie Stuart. Then, over his shoulder, he said, "By dawn we'll probably be to hell and gone, Mr. Stuart, somewhere over in the Madison country. If Duggan's boys come, tell them to bring some grub, ei?"

At the corral, Clay Moore had a few last words for White Moon. "Zachary and Pete Marshall will be up there in the morning to look after those damned sheep. Wrap the old man in some blankets and we'll bring his body down here, do him up proper-like. From there, God only knows." He grasped White Moon's arm. "And for crissakes, be careful, son."

Back at the house, the guests were beginning to leave, everyone discussing the strange turn of events, such a bizarre conclusion to a housewarming. Molly Goodhart, now supervising the care of Divinity Jones, fed her some of the food from the evening's feast. In between a few grateful sobs, the frazzled young woman devoured it all. And staring wide-eyed from one passing benefactor to another, she was unable to comprehend any of it. These were grand surroundings, but strangely, most of these people looked like Indians, some lighter than the others. A few even talked in a language that she had never heard before. And the women were wearing such beautiful clothes, the kind that she had only seen in the fancy stores once long ago in Ogden. How could this be? How could they be so rich when she, a white, was so poor? The Shoshoni and Bannack she often saw in the Idaho Territory lived in tepees and sod shacks. They were just as poor as she was, certainly dressed no better.

"Are you ready for a good hot bath?" she heard the kind older woman asking. "Make you feel better before you go to bed."

Divinity Jones's eyes widened in further amazement. "Who are you? You some breed Injun, too, like the rest?"

Molly Goodhart laughed heartily. "Molly's my name. Yes, I'm part Absaroke. Oh, gracious, we have all kinds here at the ranch, some Absaroke, a few Nez Perce, and Willie, he's part Salish."

"You mean to let me stay here tonight? In this place?" Divinity asked, bewildered by all the attention. "What about my paw up there, all dead and cold?"

"The men folks are looking out for all of that," Molly soothed. "Ei, you stay here for tonight. Tomorrow they'll decide what to do about all of this. No worry now. Take bath, go to bed. Get you some clean clothes, too. Store man is going to send out some things for you first thing in the morning."

Divinity Jones's blue eyes clouded with tears. "I'm pretty shitty, ain't I?" She stared down at her tattered trousers, her oversized boots. She shrugged forlornly. "Feller laughed at me today, you know. Said he was sorry, but I reckon he had reason to laugh." And as Molly led her away to the great tin tub in the kitchen, huge tears rolled down Divinity's cheeks and melted away in the dust of her faded jacket. In her bitter little world someone in a better world had given her a spoonful of kindness.

TWO

Dawn came, streaks of rosy crimson piercing the skies over the distant Land of the Smoking Water, and the four drovers found themselves, as White Moon had surmised, high above a sheltered draw on the east side of the Madison Valley. It had been almost fifty miles of tracking. Down below them, tucked into a high bank among the sage and juniper, was a small cabin, a trace of bluish smoke coming from a tin stack perched at the back of the sod roof. There was no doubt in Ed Stuart's mind: at least half of the horses in a nearby corral were mares and colts, and they belonged to Stuart's Lazy-Bar-S ranch. Had Moon Tree and his three cohorts arrived a day later, the horses would have been gone, on their way to the Idaho and Oregon territories for sale, their brands neatly blotted over with another mark. Stuart's brand, a simple /S, was one of the easiest of all to obliterate. Only the misfortune of Burleigh Jones, and his daughter's resulting alarm, had enabled the ranch hands to discover the stolen stock. If the thieves hadn't stumbled upon the unfortunate sheepherder, most likely it would have been a week or two before the Stuarts even knew their summer-range horses were missing, and after that lapse of time it would have been far too late to do anything about it.

Crouching in the brush, White Moon had carefully glassed the area, trying to determine how best to retrieve the horses without getting shot. Divinity Jones had told them that there were five men, but presently Moon could only spot three saddle horses. These were apart from the stolen stock, in a small corral near the squat cabin, their saddles straddling the stringer poles. This left two riders unaccounted for, and White Moon, after a brief discussion with the others, concluded these men probably had ridden on to another location, or were patroling the area nearby. If the latter was true, this made the immediate situation more hazardous. "We have a choice," Moon finally said. "We can stay up here and wait until they come out to start rubbing out those brands, or we can flush them out. Now, if we do this, it might cause a problem, shooting and all. No telling where those other two are."

Willie Left Hand suggested moving in, surprising them. "They's probably just sitting 'round drinking joe, or frying up some fatback down there." He grinned at Moon Tree. "I'd kinda like a swig or two of hot joe right now, anyways, even some of their grub. Take everything they got and leave 'em high and dry."

"Stale coffee," said Robert Peete. "Most likely just the dregs from yesterday. Make your hair stand on end, Willie, cut the grease right out of it." Peete pointed below and frowned. "No, ain't enough cover for us to go sneaking in on them like Injuns . . ." He smiled faintly at White Moon and Willie. "Meaning no offense to you boys, of course, and if we got ourselves in that opening there, we'd be sitting ducks."

"Well, it's for certain," Moon Tree put in, "we have to get a little closer than this. Almost a two-hundred-yard shot from here. If we rile those boys, they're going to come out loaded for bear, fighting mad, I suppose."

"Better'n getting your neck stretched." Willie Left Hand grinned again. "Reckon ol' Duggan and his boys are on the way? Maybe we could keep 'em penned in there until he shows."

White Moon merely sniffed, and gave Willie a sidelong, disapproving stare. "Last time you were out on something like this, I recall you were riding with Duggan. Ei, you arrived a day late. Benjamin and his Crow brothers had finished off those rustlers and were on their way home. You remember that, don't you?"

And Willie Left Hand did remember. So did Ed Stuart, who was also along at the time, almost four years past when cattle from the two ranches had been stolen by four men and herded east toward the Crazy Mountains. The thieves had also rousted several of Benjamin One Feather's Crow along the way, stolen their rifles and ponies, only to be tracked down later. In the ensuing fight, the thieves were killed. Both Willie Left Hand and Ed Stuart had been in the trailing posse that arrived twelve hours too late. "Well," said Willie lamely, "we got the critters back, anyways."

Moon, nodding toward the rising sun, said, "I figure if it's taken us most of the night to get here. That should make Duggan's arrival about suppertime, and I'm not about to sit around here all day eating jerky. We have to move, and plenty soon, too."

Peete, now using the binoculars, said, "Activity down there. Someone's coming out the door . . . just one. Looking around a bit. Now he's going over to the side. Oh, oh, all he's doing is shaking the dew out of his whistle. That's all, just taking a big leak, the bastard."

After another short conversation, White Moon took the binoculars and sized up the small cabin again. Not wishing to wait any longer, he finally turned and addressed the other three. "I have an idea. We'll have to spread out, get in a little closer, ei, then flush them out. Now, I think I can sneak around that back side from the draw, get in back of the place and come down on the damned roof . . . plug up the smoke stack. That'll bring them out, and—"

"Man, you're crazy!" Ed Stuart said, cutting him

off. "They'll come out and pot you before you can get back up the hill. No, that's piss-poor, Moon, piss-poor. Shoot fire, we have to come up with something better than that."

Self-assured, Moon Tree answered, "Won't go that way. I'll head right for the corral, jump in with those ponies. They sure as hell won't go shooting in there, not after trailing those nags this far. Besides, that's up to you fellows. When they come out, I figure you should be able to dust at least a couple of them, maybe save my butt. Have yourselves another housewarming."

Robert Peete threw up his hands in surrender. "What the hell, why not? This is what we came for, ain't it? Nobody said it was going to be a Sunday-go-to-meeting. Come on, let's get on with it. Time we get home, it'll be dark as sin, just time for supper and a few hands of stud."

"Right," agreed Moon, moving away. "Good idea there, anyhow."

With a grin back at the others, Peete said, "Figured that'd get his ass moving."

While Willie Left Hand crawled cautiously down the edge of the hill, using the small juniper clumps for cover, Robert Peete and Ed Stuart followed White Moon for about fifty yards, then cut off toward the bottom of the ravine. Within ten minutes, they saw White Moon easing down the little knoll behind the cabin. Shortly, he appeared at the edge of the roof where the logs butted into the rocky hillside. Crouching, they watched Moon carefully cat-paw toward the rusty stack, the blanket suspended on his rifle barrel, and moments later, they saw him drape it over the vent. But then, to their utter astonishment, there was a sudden swoosh of smoke and dust, and White Moon dissolved like a ghost. The back section of the roof had caved in. At this point, the scene suddenly became one of mad confusion. The door flew open and two of the rustlers bounded out, one at the ready with a rifle, the other snatching at his trousers, trying to fasten his suspenders, clumsily because he was brandishing a revolver at the same time. Willie Left Hand, startled by Moon's swift vanishing act, came bouncing down the hill from his cover and immediately drew fire from the rustler with the rifle. The bullet whined by, taking a shred of Willie's duster with it. There was no second shot. Robert Peete, from the other side, blew the man over with his Winchester, and the second rustler simply threw his pistol in the dirt and quit dead in his tracks, hoisting his arms high. Meantime, both Willie and Ed Stuart ran up and stationed themselves to either side of the cabin door. "Moon!" Willie shouted. "Moon, you all right? If you ain't, that buzzard in there with you is a dead man."

A few anxious moments went by, then there were several loud coughs, and White Moon appeared at the door, a small cloud of smoke following him. His face was streaked with black, a layer of soot covered his denim jacket, and he emitted several more wheezes. "I'm all right," he finally whispered. "Alive, if that's what you mean."

Willie Left Hand gawked, then broke out in a spacious grin. It was truly spacious, as two of his front teeth were missing due to a long-ago brawl, and since he was self-conscious about this, his usual smile was about as tight as a banjo string. "Damned if you don't look like one of them cotton-pickin' darkies I seen once way south of here," he said. "You ain't no breed, man, you's a bogeyman, for sure. Black Moon, that's what. Not a lick of white in you, ol' Black Moon."

"Burned my butt on that joe you were figuring on drinking," growled Moon, with a scowl. He had his rifle in one hand, the other was clasped to his wet backside.

Ed Stuart, carefully peering inside the dark, smoke-filled cabin, asked "Where's the other one? Heard two shots."

"Dead, I expect." Wiping his face with his bandanna, White Moon added, "Damned lucky he missed me. He got off the first round just as I came up off the floor. By all rights I should have a hole in me somewhere."

"Reckon he just couldn't see you." Willie smiled. "They say that's the way those darkies used to get away in the black of night. No one sees them that way." He clucked his tongue, staring in at the gaping hole in the roof. "Boy, that ol' ceiling sure went in a hurry, eh?"

"Who's that one?" Moon asked, glumly pointing

at the captured drover sitting disconsolately to the side. Robert Peete was nearby, his rifle over his shoulder, he, too, smiling at White Moon's black makeup.

It wasn't long before they knew the rustler's identity, and all of his companions as well. His name was Gabe Arbuckle, and he quickly professed innocence when confronted with the killing of Burleigh Jones. This, he claimed, was the decision of their leader, Dupee Clancy. Clancy thought the sheepherder had gotten too good a look at him, so he rode back and shot him in the head, not once but twice. This disclosure brought swift reaction from the usually stoic and placid Moon Tree. Outraged, he lashed out with a boot and kicked Gabe Arbuckle in the ribs, sending him away crawling in the dust. "You bastards killed an old man who was doing nothing but moving through the land, just looking for a place where he could get away from white trash like you. By jingo, when we get back, it'll serve you right if the people swing you on the nearest tree." Gabe Arbuckle wasn't aware that a second witness had been nearby, the sheepherder's daughter who had come up out of the shadowy bushes of the creek.

Willie Left Hand and Ed Stuart, standing to the side, were exchanging surprised glances. The mention of Dupee Clancy brought a few excited words from both of them. Young Stuart turned back to White Moon and Peete. "You know who this Dupee fellow is, don't you? He's the brother of that Jim Clancy, one of those rustlers Benjamin killed over in the Crazies that time. Thought he had cleared this country."

"Same one, all right," Willie said emphatically. "He was out to shoot Young Benjamin some time back, figuring it was a payback. Dupee Clancy, same feller, for sure. Now, that's a caution, ain't it?"

Moon Tree, after hearing this, looked angrily down at Gabe Arbuckle, who now had some pain in him along with his despair. "Where is this Dupee? Where did he go?"

"Expect me to peach on him more?" Arbuckle asked. "After you done kicked the shit out of me, you expect me to peach on ol' Dupee?"

Peete interjected, "Might save you from a rope. Little information just may save your sorry skin."

Gabe Arbuckle's brows lifted hopefully. "You mean they'd go easy on me? Maybe the jailhouse and no rope?"

"That's possible," said White Moon.

Arbuckle swung his arm around and pointed south, and began squawking like a split-tongued crow. "Went to Idaho, place down below ol' Fort Hall, place we make the sales. Making a deal for the horses, and another fifty head we've got stashed other side of Bannack. Figure we'd move these ones here over to the other place tonight, till you fellers showed up. Have nigh onto seven thousand dollars coming from those horses, and nary a hitch. You spoiled a good game, and Dupee ain't gonna like it when he finds out. Now, there's other deals we're onto, too, I can let you in on some of these. Anything you might want to be knowing, I'm obliged to tell you. I sure ain't looking to meet my Maker so quick-like, you know."

"Who's the other man?" asked White Moon. "There were five of you. Did he go with Clancy?"

Surprised, Arbuckle looked up quickly at White Moon. "How'd you know that? That's Arvis James, ol' Arvie. How'd you know there was five of us?"

"You left behind a witness" was the reply. "A young woman, Divinity Jones. Leastways, I think she's a woman. She got a good look at the Clancy fellow when he was by the wagon, saw you boys riding away."

"Damnation!" exclaimed Arbuckle. "We didn't see no woman! A wild card in the deck."

"Ei, real wild, mister," White Moon said with only a thread of a smile. "More than you know."

Meantime, Willie Left Hand had discovered a well-stocked larder in the cabin, and prior to their departure for home the men had a good breakfast, including fresh coffee boiled over a fire by the corral. Once away with the pony herd, they headed down the Madison River, striking northeast near the Red Bluffs. At this juncture five riders appeared, led by the Bozeman City constable, Bill Duggan. Behind him were Adam Stuart and three men who had been deputized as a posse. Stuart, watching his mares and colts trot by, was delighted, more so when all the drovers hove into view. Luckily no one had been injured, a great relief to the rancher. But Bill Duggan wasn't all that happy, particularly when White Moon told him that two of the rustlers, Dupee Clancy and Arvis James, had escaped, and two others were dead and unburied at the cabin site. Once again, it was a fruitless and unnecessary ride for Duggan, the rustlers being dispersed and shot up by one of the Tree boys. However, Duggan found some solace in taking charge of Gabe Arbuckle. He and one of the deputies rode off with the prisoner to the Virginia City jail. There was some additional compensation for the constable. He would get the credit for recovering the stolen horses the gang had hidden above Bannack.

A few miles further down the valley, Adam and young Ed Stuart turned the horses north toward their property and gave White Moon a friendly wave. Not long afterward, the two remaining deputies parted company, heading east toward town, and as Robert Peete predicted, it was getting on toward sunset when the three Tree ranch drovers arrived at the big gate leading into the main building. James Goodhart, Benjamin, and Claybourn Moore were near the big corral when the men came riding in. Several of the small children came rushing out, following the horses, gleefully shouting at Moon. Clay Moore was relieved to see his three men back, but not too surprised to hear about the horse-stealing ring led by Dupee Clancy. The proximity of its operations disturbed the foreman. Apparently, rustling was now spreading down from Rocky Point, a nefarious outpost on the Missouri river beyond Fort Benton inhabited by outlaws of all sorts. The newspaper in Virginia City was reporting how swift nighttime forays were becoming a regular occurrence in the upper Missouri basin. These were not haphazard affairs but well-executed strategic excursions led by organized outlaw bands that were moving stolen stock into Canada, the Dakota Territory, and sometimes as far south as the Wyoming cattle country. In a land so vast, there wasn't enough lawmen to stop the depredations. Consequently the battle against the rustlers most often fell to the ranchers, who were often as badly outnumbered as the territory authorities. Of course, this wasn't all that alarming to White Moon and Benjamin One Feather. In their days at their father's village on the Yellowstone, they had stolen many ponies from the Sioux, Cheyenne, and Blackfeet. It was a game of coup, played by all the tribes. A man with many ponies was rich and prestigious. But those days were finished, and in the white man's new society, a great pony thief wasn't rewarded with kudos and praise songs. He was hanged.

As far as Clay Moore was concerned, this latest episode was too close to home, and as the drovers put away their tack in the big shed, he began outlining a few precautionary measures he soon planned to put into effect. First, he was going to move most of the horses into the lower pastures nearer the ranch headquarters. Others, he would range up the Six Mile bottom. Then, taking some of Willie Left Hand's advice, Moore said he intended to do some extensive fencing on the deeded upper ranges. This, he told the men, wouldn't be jackpoles but the newest type of fencing available, barbed wire, a costly venture but well worth the expense. Moore, with a smile, said to Willie Left Hand, "It won't eliminate all of the outriding, Willie, but it'll sure make it a lot easier. At least, our critters will be where we want them. Just have to keep our eyes peeled a bit more when we have them on the free grass during the good months."

None of the men had much to say about Moore's plans because barbed wire was something they had only heard about, news filtering up from the Texas Panhandle. And there was little reason to question their foreman. With the blessing, and sometimes guidance, of Ben Tree, he had made the ranch a profitable operation despite the keen competition now underway in the Judith Basin. No one doubted his ideas, not for a moment. After the last saddle was racked, they all went back through the corral.

The news of the raid on the rustlers' cabin already had come up to the ranch houses. Josh, Moore's young boy, had rushed away to tell his mother, Ruth, and she, along with White Crane and Little Blue Hoop, met the men as they were coming through the poles. Molly Goodhart stuck her head out of the kitchen at the bunkhouse and told the drovers their supper was almost ready. But before Moon, Willie, and Peete could turn away, Melody Goodhart ran up holding the hand of a winsome, young woman, and she cried out happily, "Uncle Moon, see my new friend!"

The new friend was Divinity Jones, her blonde hair immaculate and swept back into a neat bun, her tanned face shining brightly against the last flickering rays of sunlight. She wore new riding boots under a denim skirt, and her white shirt was accented by a double-string of Absaroke beads, red, white, and blue in color, these undoubtedly a gift from White Crane. The drovers were dumbfounded at this miraculous transformation. Their faces showed it, and this brought a few smiles from the women who were looking on.

Willie Left Hand stretched his neck out like a turkey, and he finally said, "Lordy, Lordy, is that you, Divinity? Lookee what they went and done to you!" He sniffed at her suspiciously and grinned widely enough to expose his fractured teeth. "Put some of that sweet water on you, too, damned if they didn't."

Melody said proudly, "Her name is Divinity Jones. She came to visit me with Uncle Benjamin."

"You look nice, Miss Divinity," Moon Tree managed, but weakly. He was abruptly conscious of his own trail-worn appearance. Some of the soot from the rustlers' stove still mingled with the perspiration on his forehead and cheekbones, and a dust ring circled his mouth. He suddenly remembered Zachary Hockett's words upon the hill, how this woman might be attractive under that tattered clothing and the grime on her face. Luckily, Hockett and Two Shell Woman weren't around to give him an elbow in the ribs, along with an "I told you so." Like a small crab hunching back into its shell, White Moon mumbled, "Yes, ma'am, you look plenty good, right ladylike."

There wasn't much of a smile on the renovated face of Divinity Jones, however. They were going to bury her father in a pine box the next morning, a sad occasion regardless of how nice she looked. Another thing, this Moon fellow in front of her was one of the drovers who had laughed at her on the range the day before, the very one who had leaped upon her and disarmed her. Nevertheless, she did owe some gratitude to his kin, the ones who had befriended her, especially his brother and sister-in-law. She responded kindly, acknowledging Moon Tree's compliment. "I don't look shitty no more, anyways. Got me some clothes, your kinfolks did, and I'm obliged, truly am." Little Blue Hoop, standing nearby, giggled once.

"Yes," said Moon, "I can see the difference, all right."

"Fancy pants and the trimmings, too," she went on. "Got me two dresses, pretty stockings that goes all the way up to my crotchie. Hell, yes, real bloomers, too, like I never seen before, white ones with little ol' flowers, real ruffles . . ."

Molly Goodhart's voice came from the bunkhouse again. "Come and get it, boys."

Thank God for that, and White Moon gladly started backing away. "Yes, ma'am, glad they took care of you . . ."

"You shoulda killed all of those sons of bitches," Divinity Jones said, acid suddenly creeping into her thin voice. "Filled their assholes with lead, the lot of 'em."

"Oh, we tried to," Moon said. "Maybe next time we'll have better luck. Ei, we'll get the men who killed your father, don't worry about that." He shrunk away, following the soft chuckles of Robert Peete, who like Pete Marshall never had much to say but always carried a twinkle of amusement in his squinty eyes.

Then Willie Left Hand took one last glance over his shoulder. "Anyways, she looks a whole lot better, eh?"

The three dairy cows were milked by Molly Goodhart early the next morning, and then she tended her big garden for a while before frying up a batch of hotcakes for the bunkhouse crew. This was the day of the funeral for Burleigh Jones, bringing all of the ranch work to a standstill. By nine o'clock, the women and children, along with the bereaved Divinity Jones, had gathered themselves into two wagons for the half-hour ride into

Bozeman City where the small church and ceme-
tery were located. All of the men were mounted
except Peter Marshall. He was staying behind to
watch over the property. Zachary Hockett and his
wife and child, who had ridden down from the line
cabin, were waiting on their ponies near the main
gate. A few words were exchanged, and the proces-
sion moved on toward town, led by Claybourn
Moore and Young Benjamin. Moon Tree, attired in
his fine gambling coat, white shirt, and black string
tie, brought up the rear, riding beside Willie Left
Hand and Robert Peete.

A few people from the small congregation were
already present when the clan of the Tree ranch
arrived. Moon was surprised to see Jessie Stuart
and her mother, Ellie, and he stopped outside the
church and briefly talked with them, felt embarrassed when Jessie impetuously toed up and
kissed him on the cheek. She told him that the
breath had gone out of her when her brother, Ed,
told them about the fight with the rustlers, and
how Moon Tree had almost been killed. He expressed gratitude that they had come, in fact was
surprised to see anyone except the preacher and
Lucas Hamm, who was to play the violin. No one
even knew the deceased, Burleigh Jones, a wandering sheepherder who probably could have
counted his lifetime friends on one hand. For
young Moon Tree and most of the Tree ranch
mourners, this was a new experience. None of the
Indians had ever attended a white man's burial

ceremony, and as they found seats on the long, hard benches, they stared expectantly at each other, awaiting some clue that might dictate propriety on such an occasion. None was forthcoming, so they sat silently, watching the man in the black suit at the front of the church. After meditating like a medicine man, he made a long prayer. Only Young Benjamin and Moon, along with a few others, said "Amen." A woman standing to the side sang a sad song about the heavenly gates, and Lucas Hamm played his fiddle, but no one offered up any death chants or strong medicine to keep away the evil spirits. Finally, when the preacher talked briefly about the late Burleigh Jones who gave up his soul to the Great Spirit, Divinity, her blonde hair covered by a black shawl, leaped up and shouted, "Hallelujah, praise the Lord and us creatures!"

Some of the men carried the pine box out the door, and everyone gathered around the grave site in back. A few women came by and tossed dirt on the box now below, the small pebbles clattering against the planks, some rolling away like marbles. Melody Goodhart and her grandmother, Molly, put a bouquet of wild flowers by the mound of earth. Then everyone walked away, Divinity Jones weeping, wedged in between White Crane and Little Blue Hoop.

Once back at the ranch, some of the people came and offered condolences to Divinity. Moon Tree and his family were thankful that she said nothing more than "thank you," plenty thankful that she made no further references to the "dumb bastards" who had killed her father. For Divinity, this had been a wonderfully impressive funeral. Although she didn't exactly express it this way to Moon Tree, he understood her heartfelt feeling of gratitude. It was far more than she had expected for a "no-account old bastard like him," for after all, he was her only kin, even though he wasn't much of a paw. She told Moon that when her maw had been put under, only she, her paw, and two other herders were present, and no one sang or prayed. "They just layed Maw in the hole and covered her. A pretty damned shitty way to treat my maw."

All those at the repast seemed to enjoy them-selves, and ultimately some of them became in-volved in a discussion as to what was now to become of Divinity Jones. Her band of sheep and wagon had been brought down to one of the up-per pastures. She herself had already decided that she was going to complete the grazing circuit and take the band back to the Idaho Territory and on to Utah. Of course, it alarmed a few of the women that one lone female would even attempt such a long journey, and they quickly informed their men about this frightening decision. No one at the ranch would be so callously indifferent as to let Divinity wander off by herself, not after what had happened to her poor father. Indeed, Claybourn Moore agreed sympathetically this did present a problem, but he had no immediate solution. After all, the sheep belonged to the Coombes people, not the Tree ranch. This was their responsibility, not his. He suggested that maybe a telegraph message could be relayed through Virginia City, that someone might ride up and take charge of the band. This idea had a good ring to it until Divinity Jones spoke up in her usual emphatic manner. "Shit, no, I can't do that. I'll lose my year's wages we's got coming when we gets back." This declaration put a damper on Moore's suggestion, and once again left the matter hanging. It seemed as though Divinity Jones was determined to make the journey by herself.

When Molly, later that day, suggested to Claybourn Moore that he send one of the drovers along with Divinity, he only laughed incredulously. "Now, who in the hell would I send?" he asked with dismay. "Not one of those boys would take on those woolies, not to mention that woman. No one's going to volunteer for this kind of work, I can tell you that. Time he got across the Beaverhead, he most likely would be turning bald traveling with that little wildcat."

"Well," huffed Molly, "wouldn't hurt to talk to them, suggest helping her a bit."

Claybourn Moore futiley replied, "They'd think I'm some kind of a Judas, that's what they'd think. Or plumb crazy. Besides, with the hay coming in, I can't be sparing any of the boys, anyhow."

Molly Goodhart, a glint of victory in her dark

eyes, placed her hands firmly on her hips. "Now, look here, Mr. Clay, that's no problem. Any of us women can handle a stacker team, one of the rakes, and we'd be glad to if it meant giving that little girl a hand."

This left Moore at the end of his rope. He sensed that the women were already working in collusion, and now Molly had backed him into a corner. He finally threw up his hands in surrender. "All right, all right," he said wearily, "I'll ask. Mind you, I said ask."

As anticipated, the drovers greeted Claybourn Moore's proposal that afternoon with an assortment of amused smiles and downright indifference. Herd Sheep! No one volunteered to accompany Divinity Jones. Willie Left Hand, with his cracked grin, said that he would rather waltz a grizzly across the Beaverhead, and the Quiet One, Peter Marshall, whittling a whistle, just wagged his head and frowned. Moon Tree and Robert Peete, calculating odds on poker hands, kept right on calculating, oblivious to Moore's quiet appeal. It wasn't until Molly Goodhart appeared on the scene toward suppertime that the matter of Divinity Jones received some real attention. She gently chastised the four men for their lack of charity. It wouldn't hurt any of them one lick to take three or four weeks of their time to help a stranded woman get back home and collect her wages. In fact, she considered this a noble gesture, and slyly, one worthy of culinary reward, such as a fresh pie every week for the drover electing to guide Miss Divinity. Though this stirred mild interest, still no one put a foot forward to accept the bribe, for this was a sure sign of weakness and probably cause for ridicule. Who wanted to admit he had been putting his stomach before his heart? It wasn't until they were eating that an honorable solution was found. Molly came to the table with four straws tucked into her fist, and she announced that the man drawing the short one would be the volunteer. She said that failure to select a straw was a clear indication of a man without courage or conviction, and absolutely heartless. They grudgingly drew, and when they measured the small pieces of broom whisk, everyone's eyes turned on Moon Tree.

He shrugged fatalistically, flipped the tiny stick over his shoulder, and continued eating—even with his appetite suddenly gone. What else could he do? This wasn't a happy occasion.

Bright and early the next day, he began packing an extra pony, deciding that as long as he was committed to playing sheepherder for the next month at least, his stomach would get some satisfaction. In the old days with his red brothers, he had survived many days on jerky, pemmican, and flatcakes, along with some fresh meat shot on the prairie. The ranch larder, however, offered a great variety of foods, and with Molly's blessing, he stacked up on corn syrup, flour, bacon, canned milk, beans, potatoes, coffee, and an assortment of tinned goods. What staples were in the barrels of Divinity Jones's chuckwagon he had no idea, but he certainly wasn't taking any chances, not after that first meeting with her and the late Burleigh Jones. It was highly probable that their staples compared favorably with the clothes they both wore: meager and in short supply.

When Claybourn Moore arrived at Young Benjamin's new home this same morning to tell Divinity Jones about the latest arrangements, her initial reaction was one of great relief. She was mighty obliged, everyone was so goddamned friendly, looking out after her and all, and she just felt like pulling her tits and squealing. Clay Moore hastily assured her this wasn't necessary. He and the Tree family were more interested in her safety than in any such display of exuberant, joyous jubilation. Some of this uninhibited joy dissipated when Divinity discovered that her companion-herder was going to be Moon Tree. He was the one who had bamboozled her with his shitty trick about the grizzly bear and made her eat grass when she went ass-over-teakettle by the wagon. He was a mite too fancy for her taste, too, like one of those high-falutin studs always prancing around with their tails up in the air, paying no mind to nothing. However, she kept this bit of animosity to herself, rationalizing that she was damned fortunate to get any help at all. These funny people, Injuns and whites all consorting like one big happy family, had buried her old man, given her new clothes, and made her welcome in her greatest moment of misery. Hell's bells, why should she bitch now about who was going to help her herd a band of crapping critters? Granted, this Moon Tree fellow might be kin of the devil himself, but he was a damned site better than that rascal Willie, with the teeth missing. Why, that little peder didn't have manners at all, couldn't even spit straight.

Sometime later, a small crowd had gathered by the foreman's house to bid Divinity Jones farewell. She was a fine-looking woman mounted on a rather sorrowful-looking pony. She wore riding pants, her new boots, and a fancy hat, the brim pinned nattily up on one side by a beaded Crow buckle. Her blue eyes were misty. She gave Melody Goodhart a hug and a kiss, saying, "You're a good little girl, best damned pal I've ever had, for certain." Mounting up, she waved around to all of the others. To White Crane she said, smiling down on her, *"Aho,"* the Absaroke word of thanks she had heard so often in Young Benjamin's new house. White Crane had given her beads, a brush for her hair, soap and a little bottle of sweet water, had told her about the new underclothes, how to care for them, and how she should keep herself clean by washing every day. Divinity said to her, "I'll remember you, Miss Benjamin, I sure will, by Gawd."

"Ei," White Crane said back. "You remember always be good wo-man, plenty good, make you happy," and she pressed her long fingers to her lips in a farewell kiss.

With White Moon riding beside her, she waved a final time and rode up through the shade of the cottonwoods toward the upper gate. Behind the fence sheltering Molly Goodhart's garden stood the last remnants of Divinity Jones. Willie Left Hand, retrieving her discarded clothing, had erected a scarecrow, partially hidden under her faded, tattered hat. Yellow straw tumbled crazily down over the shoulders of the old denim jacket. Divinity Jones eyed it critically and looked over at Moon Tree. "Pretty damned shitty, ain't it?" She smiled.

Moon Tree wasn't about to answer this question, but he whispered to himself the white man's final word, "Amen."

THREE

Moon Tree was a soft-spoken, patient, and often-humorous young breed who had proved himself many times in Indian country as a coup counter and reliable trail runner. Though he hadn't achieved the reputation of either his father, Man Called Tree, or his brother Young Benjamin, both known to be deadly marksmen, his abilities in this direction were never challenged. Just the mention of the name Tree was usually enough to bring mellowness to any cantankerous person who entertained thoughts of contesting him. Over the years on the frontier many legends were born, and they shrouded the Tree men like a mysterious cloak, some of the tales true, others fabrications, but it was almost a certainty that anyone who crossed the clan always drew swift and unforgiving retribution. It was told that the white man who murdered Ben Tree's first wife, a Crow maiden only seventeen years old, was crucified on a corral down at Fort Bridger; that the killers of his father and brother were all tracked down and one was

even scalped alive; other men who came to seek
out Ben Tree were never seen or heard of again.
These were old legends. Young Benjamin's exploits
were more recent: avenging the killing of James
Goodhart's father; dragging a Sioux warrior to
death behind his pony; slaying four cattle thieves
in the Crazy Mountains. That he had helped
White Bird's Nez Perce tribe escape to Canada
during their wars with the troopers, the government had never been able to prove.

White Moon, however, had gained his reputation in another direction: poker. In the saloons
from Virginia City to Butte and over to Bozeman
City and Helena he became known as "Red Man,"
the silent son of Ben Tree who sometimes appeared at a big game with Sad Sam Courtland,
one of the best poker players on the frontier. Sad
Sam had taken Moon Tree under his wing the
previous year, realizing that Moon's uncanny ability at swift mathematical calculations of odds was
a gift to anyone who had such a penchant for
poker. And the fact that Moon Tree had ice in his
blood and an expressionless face made Sad Sam's
instruction that much easier. He told Moon one
night after a successful foray in Virginia City that
Moon was a natural, one born for the scientific
approach to cards, not just an ordinary gambling
man. Sad Sam Courtland disdained the term
"gambler." He preferred to be called a card player,
because only the foolish ones who constantly
flirted with Lady Luck were gamblers. In his opin-

ion, truly good card players never gambled. A touch of instinct and luck, along with blessed science, were the ingredients that he said constituted the makings of a good player.

Instead of sharpening his mind for an evening around the felt table, the Red Man, Moon Tree, on a pleasant afternoon in late July, was helping herd a band of two hundred sheep across the mountains. Worse yet, his companion was a young illiterate woman who couldn't get through one sentence without using the word, "shit," or some variation. By nightfall, he would be stranded next to nowhere in a mobile shack covered with canvas, listening to a reedy prattle of nonsense, or luckily, hearing the distant howl of wolves or coyotes, sounds he once enjoyed. Whatever had he done in his young life to deserve this fate? One thing, he had gambled. There sure as hell wasn't anything scientific about drawing straws, three to one odds, and he'd come up a loser.

He had, at least, picked up two new friends, Salt and Pepper, the Collie sheepdogs, fairly intelligent beasts who for some reason already were loping up to him, cocking their heads and awaiting his commands. All he had to do was point and yell, "Bring 'em 'round" or "go fetch," and off they ran, nipping heels.

Toward dusk, Moon pulled up in some benchland not far from the Madison River. Because of the wagon Divinity Jones was driving, he had to pick his way carefully, always searching ahead for the best passage, particularly when he had no established trail to follow. The river was off in the distance several miles, and below him, a small willow-lined creek. Moon thought this was a good place to stop for the night, and in the morning he could find a shallow to run the sheep across. To his recollection, remembering his trip with Benjamin when they fought Colonel Red Nose Gibbon's troops in the Big Hole, this was the only river of consequence he would have to ford. Willie Left Hand had told him that once beyond Virginia City he would strike Ruby Creek, and by following it to its headwaters he would cross into the Idaho Territory near the Red Rocks. This was somewhat the same route that they had taken a year ago on a cattle drive to Utah, but as a drover, he hadn't paid too much attention to particulars, instead following Claybourn Moore.

After supper, Moon kindled a small night fire beside the wagon. Two of the bell ewes were hobbled and a small tinkle occasionally drifted up from the nearby bottom. The two sheepdogs, Salt and Pepper, had curled up off to the side of him where he was stretched out on a blanket, his head resting against his saddle. But the sheepdogs weren't napping. They had their eyes on him, had already accepted him as their new master. On the step of the wagon, Divinity Jones was watching, too. She hadn't accepted White Moon as readily as the dogs, but she had some new thoughts about him. At least this Moon Tree fellow was a mannerly son of a bitch. He hadn't talked much all day, but he had thanked her kindly for the supper she had whomped up, damned good vittles, some of that tinned beef he had brought along, good biscuits and pan gravy, and fried spuds. He had fed the dogs the leavings, and that was probably why they were lying there by him with those shit-eating grins on their faces. For a change, she felt pretty damned good herself. She finally said to Moon Tree, "Those old boys kinda taking a shine to you, ain't they?"

White Moon's lids fluttered. "I've been around dogs all my life," he replied lazily. "Always had a dog or two back in the village. Some of them were good hunters, others just plain old dogs. Never saw anything like these two before. Ei, they're plenty smart with those woolies."

She studied him a moment or two. He never talked about his past, nor did any of the women she had met at the ranch. She only knew that at one time the Trees had lived in a great village far to the east. Even the woman they called Molly had been there. Of course, she knew that Hockett fellow had been an army officer, and Molly did tell her about him, how he had met his wife during the Indian wars, how he had been shot and that Two Shell Woman had saved his life.

Divinity Jones asked Moon, "How come you talk so damned good, anyways? You and that brother of yours. Where'd you get your learning if you been living like a regular damned Injun all your life? That sister of yours, Blue, why, she talks up a storm, too."

"My father taught us," Moon Tree said. "*Ei*, we had books, learned to read and write, do some figures. Benjamin was the smart one, though. Never could get enough. Myself? Sometimes I fell asleep. My father said anyone without learning in the white man's world would be lost in the crowd, plowed under just like the land." He gave her a wan smile. "Of course, in those days we never thought the land would ever be plowed under. Who could believe what he had foreseen? He still has great medicine, knows plenty before it even happens."

"I reckon your old man is right," Divinity said. "I ain't had a lick of learning. My old man never did nothing all his goddamned life 'cept herd sheep, never learnt me nothing, either. Hell's bells, look at me. It's his goddamned fault, you know. I ain't worth a shit, either." She sighed longingly. "Never was one of those schooling places anywheres close. Never stayed around too long, anyways, always moving here and there. Had a couple of dresses once when I was a little bitty old shit, but I got too big. My ass stuck out and they went to rags." She stopped to pat her legs, then smoothed a hand over her skirt. "First time I ever had new duds like this. Saving all that other good stuff, packed it away in my box. Maybe sometime I'll get me to a dance like that one you was having the other night." Then she laughed at herself. "Shit, listen to me going on this way. Why, I can't even dance, don't know how."

"Maybe you could learn a few of these things," Moon Tree suggested, but then wondered why he had said such a thing. "Get around some people. You know, listen and watch. That's the way our women are learning their English. Can't do all of this overnight. Takes some time and effort to be ladylike."

"Ain't no one around my parts," she answered pathetically. "Nearest place is thirty miles, Yankee Flats, one old store, a rooming house and a watering hole for the no-accounts. Never see a soul up our way, 'less someone comes looking for a drink of water. Derby Flats, they call our place. My paw's shack. Damned old homestead ain't worth a shit. Ground's all sour. Grows a few spuds and damned poor hay. Big ol' spring, though, lotsa water. Reckon it's mine now. Way out on the lonesome, it is." Divinity Jones heaved back and stretched. Contemplating the lowering sun, she said, "Oh, I'd like to be one of those fancy ladies, all right, walking right nice down the boardwalk carrying me one of those parasols, have all the fellows looking at me, thinking about how'd they'd like to get in my crotchie. Shit, I'd just keep on walking, taking my time, you know, picking out the best of the lot." She looked away wistfully and sighed again. "One of my dreams, that's all, Mr. Moon. Paw always said I should get those crazy notions outta my head and tend to my business.

Said daydreaming gives you the worms, he did."
She glanced down at Moon Tree, who had a lazy
smile on his dark face. "You believe that shit . . .
worms? Lordy, what a notion!"

"I think your father was a ring-tailed rounder,"
Moon said. "Probably did the best he could.
Didn't know anything about bringing up a woman,
making a lady out of her."

"A lady!" scoffed Divinity. "My paw didn't know
nothing about nothing, only them shitty sheep,
that's all. Hell's bells, he couldn't even pee
straight. Sure as hell, I'd 'spect to be a lady living
with that old bastard. Hah!"

Moon came up on one elbow. There was absolutely no way he could find comfort in the cool of
the evening listening to this continuing lament.
He glowered across the small fire at Divinity Jones
and said testily, "So you have a dream or two, ei?
Well, by jingo, you can't go through life just
dreaming. Maybe you will get worms, for all I
know. Serve you right. But I'll tell you this. If you
want to be a lady, you have to start some place,
and the best time and place is here, and right
now—"

"Now?" Divinity Jones interrupted. She leaned
toward him curiously.

"Now," Moon Tree replied. "For one thing, you
can start by putting a harness on that tongue of
yours, stop cussing all the time like one of those
dumb muleskinners. You are a caution, Miss
Jones, a plenty big caution if I've ever seen one in

my life. Ei, you beat them all, bad medicine. Why, you're worse than a trooper, the way you carry on. Never, never, have I met anyone like you."

Divinity Jones's lower lip fell into a pout. She swallowed once, and big tears swelled up in her blue eyes. "I'm . . . I'm a caution? You mean, I talk bad? Is . . . is this what you're meaning?"

"Oh, Lord," moaned White Moon. "Now, don't go making one of those fits again. Last time you did this, Mr. Zachary went and blamed me, and I got kicked in the shins." Gently protesting with his hands, he tried to explain. "What I'm trying to tell you is that some of the words you're always using just aren't proper, especially for a woman. Now, if you really want to be acting like a lady, you'll have to stop saying 'shit' all the time. Ei, and some of those other words, too—'bastard,' 'son of a bitch,' 'hell,' 'god damn it.' And it's not nice to be talking in public about a man's peder, either, no matter how he's using it."

Divinity sobbed once, then caught herself and mumbled a few unintelligible words.

"Don't do that," Moon Tree said. "Stop it."

"You made me," she said, dribbling away a tear.

"Well, I'm sorry, but we have to start somewhere, damn it!"

"You said 'damn it'! Right then, you said it!"

"A slip of my tongue." Moon Tree sighed.

Divinity, dabbing at her eyes, said, "Well I don't talk different. I sure don't. Everyone I knows talks just like me. No one ever said I talked bad 'cept you."

White Moon, already exhausted, said imploringly, "Can't you see, Miss Divinity, that's the problem. You've never been anywhere but that jack-rabbit country you're talking about ... this what's-its-name—"

"Derby Flats," she said.

"Derby Flats, yes," Moon Tree went on, "and most likely, the lot of them down there couldn't tell the difference between a thunder mug and a milk pail. Good grief, woman, how would you expect to learn anything different among a batch a men like that? No wonder you talk like they do. If you go denning up with a pack of wolves, you end up howling like a wolf, smelling the same way, too."

"I don't smell no more," she said quickly with a smug look on her pretty face. "Got me some fancy soap from Miss Benjamin. Sweet water, too."

White Moon sighed in exasperation. "By jingo, I didn't say you smelled, only used that as an example of how people get to be the way they are."

"I'm going to wash every day, just like Miss Benjamin says," Divinity Jones added. "My crotchie, too."

Cringing inside, Moon Tree bolted upright. "And that's another thing," he said with a moan of frustration. "A woman doesn't go around talking about her crotchie, as you call it. That's plenty personal to a woman, something she keeps secret, all to herself, understand? If Akbatatdia wanted your crotchie to be something public, he would have put it out where everyone could see it, maybe hung it from a scalp stick."

Divinity giggled at this. "Who is Akbatatdia?" she asked.

"He's the Great Maker of Everything," White Moon replied, wondering what he'd gotten himself into. "He made everything that lives under Masaka, the sun. This is one of the legends of our people. But that's not the point here—"

She frowned and wrinkled her nose, interrupting him again. "I never heard about him, only God. God makes things, you know, takes them away, too, like that preacher was saying."

"Same Maker, only different names," Moon explained futilely. "No matter, just remember what I'm trying to tell you. Before you start rattling away from the top of your head, think of what you're going to say. Maybe by the time we get these stinking critters home, we'll see some improvement. It takes practice just like anything else. Those women you met at the ranch have been at it for a couple of years now. They're doing better every day. No more bad words, ei? Once you know the difference, it'll be easier. You just try it, see what happens."

Divinity Jones heaved a great sigh. "I'll try, Mr. Moon. I'd like to be a fancy lady. Sure don't want to talk shitty the rest of my life. Yes, sir, I'll sure try hard."

Later that night, Moon Tree prepared his bed-roll, tossing a protective tarp under the rear of the wagon. Divinity Jones already had disappeared inside, and the light of the lantern lit up the canvas covering with a dim orange glow. Moon grinned as he saw her lithe shadow doing dance steps up and down the floor of the small wagon. When the shadow faded, he went about fixing his pallet, but Divinity Jones heard his rustling about and demanded that he come inside. She had already prepared his bunk where her father had once slept. In no mood for further instruction or misunderstandings this night, Moon Tree reluctantly heaved up his bedroll and got into the wagon. Moon immediately discarded the old blankets of the late Burleigh Jones, threw them out for the dogs, and then spread his own suggins. He blew out the lantern and settled himself on the straw-covered bunk across from Divinity. He was one frazzled man. The last thing he heard was, "Mr. Moon, what's a thunder mug?"

At the Montana Billiard Arcade in Virginia City, there was a small enclosure near the back, and any night of the week a no-limit game of stud poker usually was underway here. When Moon Tree appeared at the entrance of the small cubicle, it was quite a while before anyone at the round table even recognized him. The first one was Jiggs Dulaney, a familiar face in the local saloons of the gold camp, a man who had contested

Moon more than once. Moon was dressed in his drover's clothes, not his usual evening card-playing attire, and this made him as inconspicuous as most of the other onlookers. Earlier, after securing the sheep in an isolated basin, and pacifying Divinity Jones, he had ridden over the hills five miles in the dark to visit one of his favorite haunts, the Arcade. When Jiggs Dulaney finally did speak up, he merely said with a casual nod, "You come to watch or to play, Moon? There's a seat open." At the mention of "Moon" several of the players curiously glanced around to get a look at the only man in the territory with a name like this, Moon Tree. Most of them knew the name, if not the man, particularly after the newsworthy incidents of the past week. Two horse thieves had been killed over on the Madison and another one, Gabe Arbuckle, was presently ensconced in the local jail, all because of some drovers led by Moon Tree.

Moon's eyes casually wandered around the table, searching out the prospects—several businessmen nattily dressed, undoubtedly men of means; two nondescript types, probably miners or drifters; and a fellow with a small mound of peanuts near his poker chips. Outside of Jiggs Dulaney and the house dealer, Hank Mosby, they were all strangers to White Moon. This appeared to be a well-mannered group of players. "Deal me in," he said, and he went back to the long bar where he bought one hundred dollars' worth of chips.

The open seat was in between the peanut man, who identified himself as Goober Atwell, and one of the businessmen, a prominent lawyer named Arthur Clawson. Atwell he had never met, but he knew him by reputation, another one of the gambling men who often made the territory circuit. Arthur Clawson, on the other hand, was a new name to Moon Tree, but not to the Tree family as it turned out. Clawson nodded politely to Moon as he sat down. He said quietly, "Your father and I are old friends." That was all, no further elaboration, and within moments, the cards were skidding across the green felt to each of the men. For the most part it was a silent game, broken only by the rake of the chips and the fluttering shuffle of Hank Mosby. And the ante was modest, usually a dollar chip, occasionally a five when someone felt lucky. Jiggs Dulaney, after several hands, looked across at Moon and asked, "Where's your friend old Sam these days?"

Moon Tree, intently watching the play, answered, "On the road somewhere, Helena, I think. Haven't seen him lately. I've been tied up with work, plenty busy."

Dulaney grinned. "So I've read in the newspaper." And several of the men chuckled. "Just passing through? Making a drive south?"

"Just passing through," Moon replied evasively. He wasn't about to admit that he was droving a band of sheep with a young woman and two dogs, even now wondered if the odor of the woolies had permeated his clothing enough to make him offensive. This would have been his undoing, a complete embarrassment, and without question, unexplainable to these men. Nothing more was said, thankfully, and he quietly played a dozen hands, carefully observing the other players, their mannerisms, facial expressions, how intelligently they played their hands, the consistency and amount of their wagers. Several were lucky, several cagey, several downright careless. But Goober Atwell and Jiggs Dulaney were professionals, only pushing the ante enough to keep a few of the other hands pat when they held a winner. No one was greedy, and the pots generally were modest, seldom over fifty dollars. After several hours, Moon Tree had won six hands, was almost sixty dollars ahead, but still waiting for one good kill. One of the drifters finally pulled stakes, and the lawyer, Arthur Clawson, checked the time on his watch, indicating that he, too, was about to call it a night. Moon Tree, feeling somewhat guilty about leaving Divinity Jones in the hills by herself, was also entertaining thoughts of hitting the trail. At this next turn of the cards, he came up with a deuce in the hole and one deuce up on the first go-around. Both Clawson and Goober Atwell had aces showing, and Clawson first away, contemplating this was his last hand, tossed out a five-dollar chip. Two of the other men promptly folded at the sight of the aces, but the rest of the table went along with the ante. Ultimately Atwell was dealt a second ace, and when Dulaney saw this, he drew in his horns.

Moon Tree quickly calculated that Dulaney had been holding on only because he himself had an ace buried, and up until this point had been top dog with ace-king high. Atwell's second ace killed him. Moon Tree's fourth card, however, was another deuce, and Clawson drew the last two-spot in the deck. He promptly folded, too.

When Goober Atwell saw this, he knew three of four deuces had left the deck, and his two aces up front had the board beaten. In addition, he held a queen in the hole, giving him two pair, a fine stud hand with seven men seated around the table. He wasn't too sure about the Red Man, though, the possibility that Moon had the fourth deuce buried, but the odds were against it.

Moon, on the other hand, deduced correctly that his friend, Jiggs Dulaney, had played along until the last because an ace in the hole had him hoping to catch another bullet. Unfortunately this ace, which Moon Tree believed to be the fourth, went to the peanut man, who with two aces up, was now in full command. As Moon expected, Goober Atwell looked directly at him. "Check to the Red Man," he said. If the Red Man had three deuces he was going to have to bet them, and Moon Tree did. He knew without a doubt that Goober Atwell's hole card was not an ace, because

Goober had checked instead of pushing chips. Without a smile, Moon bet fifty dollars—just enough to make Atwell curious and a cheap bluff. Atwell, trying to read something in Moon Tree's unblinking dark eyes, hesitated momentarily, then slowly edged out fifty, and inexplicably raised another fifty. The table fell dead quiet. White Moon then thought he may have misjudged Jiggs's play before he folded. But no, he knew him too well. The aces were all accounted for, two in the discards, one each from Dulaney and Clawson, and he was staring at the other two in front of Atwell. The best chance Goober Atwell had was two pair, and this wasn't going to beat Moon Tree's three deuces. He promptly called the fifty-dollar raise, thought about raising this again, but instead turned over his hole card.

A faint smile crossed the face of Goober Atwell. Pushing his cards away, he said, "Didn't want to let you buy it, Red Man." Scooping up his remaining peanuts and chips, he got up and walked toward the bar. "Good night, men," he called back.

Jiggs Dulaney looked over at Moon. "First time you played with him?"

"Ei," Moon replied, raking in the big pot. "First time I ever saw him."

"He'll know better next time, I reckon." Dulaney grinned.

"That's plenty good," answered Moon. "Maybe the next time I'll really buy one."

The bespectacled lawyer, Arthur Clawson, soon

joined White Moon at the bar and introduced himself properly. They walked across the street to a small cafe where they talked over coffee and pie. Clawson, who was in the process of moving his practice to Helena, had known Ben Tree for thirteen years. He was the attorney who had expedited the papers for the homesteads on Six Mile Creek and the first eight-thousand acres of deeded land of the Tree ranch.

"Your father had some powerful friends in those days," Clawson said. "One of them was the governor's son-in-law, and when he decided he wanted those lands, a few strings were pulled. Surprised me how quickly that transaction was completed." He politely wiped his mouth with a napkin and smiled at White Moon. "To my benefit, too. My first big commission. In fact, your father added a small bonus. I was no longer a poor solicitor. He's called on me twice since then, and of course I'm always at his service."

Later, as they prepared to leave, Moon asked, "Why are you moving to Helena?"

Arthur Clawson asked back, "Where are you selling most of your local beef these days?"

"The mining camps—Helena and over in the Butte country," said Moon.

"The power structure is moving that direction," Clawson said. "Toward Butte and Helena, territorial capital. Truth is, this place here will soon be a dead duck. The rails are all going the other way, across the territory, east to west. I hear talk of a line coming this way in a year or two, up from Utah, but it won't go through here. Over your way somewhere, I suspect. This is some indication of what happens to a gold camp once the glitter is gone. It gets bypassed. A few more years and this place is going to be history, Moon. I don't want to be part of it." After another pause at the steps, he asked, "Where are you stopping tonight? Hotel?"

White Moon shook his head. "No, I'm camped over the hill a few miles, just for the night. Leaving early, livestock, that sort of thing."

"Well, I was intending to have you over for breakfast," Arthur Clawson said. "This is the very least I can do for the son of a client. Once I'm in Helena, I'll probably go over to Bozeman City more often, at least anytime that Mr. Tree or Mr. Moore needs my counsel. Maybe I'll see you there one of these days."

Moon Tree tipped his fingers to his drover's hat, saying, "I'll tell this news to Mr. Clay. And maybe I might play a hand or two with you over in the Gulch sometime, get some more of my father's fees back."

"I'm certain you will," replied Clawson. "You missed your calling, Moon. You should be a gambling man, not a drover." With a return salute, he walked away, chuckling.

It was near midnight when White Moon rode up to the sheepherder's wagon. The two dogs, Salt and Pepper, their back ends wagging, were happy to see him. He slipped the cinch away from his pony, draped the saddle and blanket over the tongue of the wagon, and tossed the bit and reins upon the seat. His pony trotted away in the moonlight toward the hobbled mules and the two horses of Divinity Jones. Miss Jones was happy to see him, too. She wasn't in bed. She was sitting on the wagon step, huddled in a blanket, her shotgun beside her. When he mildly scolded her for not being in bed, she told him that she was afraid to sleep by herself. The road into town was too close, and she had heard several wagons, the creaking of their wheels, the voices of men. She imagined all sorts of bad things, like men sneaking up, maybe stealing her horses and mules, or attacking her, and she confused the word "rape" with "rope."

She went inside and lit the lantern. "You said you'd bring me something," she said. "What'd you bring me, anyways? I don't see no present."

Hopping in behind her, Moon Tree tossed his hat aside and began stripping off his denim shirt. "You don't have much patience, do you?"

Divinity Jones giggled and pushed a finger into his belly. "You sure got a pretty body, Mr. Moon, all slick and shiny. You ain't hairy a bit."

In the tiny passageway, he could do little more than back into the stove. "Get up there in your bunk, woman, and be patient," he ordered. "I'll show you what I brought." Divinity quickly obliged him. She threw her blanket on a little pallet, leaped up, and sat cross-legged, naked, grinning expectantly at him. "What'd you bring me, then?"

Moon Tree, snatching up the blanket, hastily covered her. He once again admonished Divinity Jones. "Young ladies never sit around without their clothes on, not in front of strangers. That's bad medicine, big trouble."

Her smile faded, and she pulled the cover around herself protectively. "You ain't a stranger, Mr. Moon. You're my buddy, only damned one I've got now. Sure didn't mean to rile you."

"You didn't rile me," he answered. He wasn't certain whether he should smile or run away into the darkness and scream. Her innocent abandonment of any kind of decorum, verbal or otherwise, completely perplexed him. "And watch your tongue. You just said a cuss word."

Pressing a finger to her lips, she grinned through it. "What'd you bring?" she mumbled through the compressed finger.

Moon Tree removed his money belt and carefully separated one of the flaps. He began pulling out folded bills, and when he had five of them, he carefully, very carefully, placed them in her lap. "There's one hundred dollars," he said. "This is your present, your wagering money."

Dumbfounded, she stared down incredulously at the riches. "Never had this much in my whole life," she finally whispered. Her eyes brimming, she glanced over at him. "Where'd you get it? You didn't go robbing the bank . . . something like that, did you?"

"Poker game," he said, nimbly exercising his fingers. "That's half, your share of the winnings, the present I promised. Plenty good, ei?"

"Plenty good, you bet," she replied, mimicking him. "But what you meaning by this wagering money? What's that?"

He sat on the adjacent bunk and quietly explained. "We're going to play a little game. That's your money, ei? I have mine in my belt. You hide that money—"

"I'm going to sleep on it," she interrupted. "Put it right here under my blanket. . . ."

"That's good." Moon nodded. He was as sure as where he was sitting that the animal spirit in this woman was the magpie, the constant flitting about, the incessant chatter, never ending, dawn till dusk.

"Or maybe I'll hide it in the box, put it right down under my fancy stuff from Miss Benjamin. . . ."

"Shush!" White Moon finally cried out. Divinity Jones shushed and thrust her shiny face out expectantly. "Now," White Moon continued, "starting tomorrow, when you say one of those cuss words, you pay me a dollar, only one each day. Each day you don't say a cuss word, I'll pay you two dollars. That's what they call two-to-one odds. You get the best deal, long odds. That's good medicine, *ei*? What do you think?"

She stared thoughtfully at him for a moment, trying to figure out the advantages of this strange game. Finally she shook her head disapprovingly. "This is my present. You gave it to me. Hell's bells, I don't want to give it back. I don't think I like this game at all. Why, I'll have to keep my little old mouth shut all day to win a damned thing, I will."

"Yes," he smiled, almost evilly. "But, by jingo, look at all the money I'll have to give you. Why, say in three weeks, that's another forty-two dollars you can put under those blankets . . . or box, or wherever you hide your money."

Divinity Jones eyed him skeptically. "What do I get when you cuss? Sometimes I hear you saying a bad word, too, you know. Don't I get nothing for that?"

White Moon, struck by her quick rationale, momentarily pondered this new twist. "All right, here's what I'll do. I'll give you an extra dollar when I cuss. How's that sound? Ei, and two dollars every day when you don't cuss. That's three dollars a day, plenty more than you get for herding these woolies."

She suddenly flew out of her bunk and planted a kiss on his lips, then darted back to her covers. "I bet you, then."

White Moon smiled inwardly. There was more than one way to skin a wildcat, and he thought that he had found it.

The next morning, White Moon Tree and Divinity Jones made a wide circuit around Virginia

City, and by late afternoon had the band of sheep grazing in the lower Ruby Valley. Wary of cattlemen, they set up camp near a spring several miles back from the main trail. Since Moon had seen signs of livestock along the bottom, he thought it safer to stay on the benchland, and Divinity, after her recent frightful escapade with the rustlers, agreed. While she set about washing some clothes, a task she had vowed to do each day, White Moon, armed with Burleigh's shotgun, sauntered down to the brushy flat, hunting for sage hens. Several flocks had winged away ahead of the sheep on the way up the valley, and both he and Divinity immediately began entertaining thoughts of fried chicken with biscuits and gravy for supper. About a mile from the wagon, White Moon at last spotted a few hens feeding on greens along the edge of the meadow bordering the creek. Slowly stalking and using the high sage for cover, Moon positioned himself about thirty yards from the big birds and waited patiently. When three or four finally lined up with his barrel, he touched off a round. He ground-sluiced three, then caught another one in mid-air, and it thudded to the ground, flipping and fluttering near the creek. In short order, he dumped the entrails and skinned the birds, then thoroughly washed them in the cold water. Satisfied, he put the birds in his bag and headed home. Everyone would get a plenty big meal this evening, including the two dogs. This was good, and White Moon was thankful for Mother Earth's bounty.

When he was nearing the camp, he noticed two strange ponies standing near the wagon. This unexpected and unwelcome sight brought him to an abrupt halt, because no one came around this time of the day to smoke a pipe. Undoubtedly, someone had trailed up behind them from the main valley. Always smelling trouble, Moon's dark eyes quickly frisked the area, sizing up the best cover to make an unseen approach to the camp. He had one problem: the dogs. Even if he managed to come in undetected by the two strangers, he realized that the dogs would sense his presence and come loping out to greet him. He saw no way to avoid this, so after some deliberation, he decided to walk in behind the wagon, take his chances, and hope for the best. He slipped two shells into the shotgun and took off. Circling the wagon from the back, he heard voices before he ever reached it, one a reedy, high-pitched screech. It was his magpie friend Divinity Jones, and it meant only one thing—trouble. When Moon came sneaking around the side, he saw the reason; Miss Jones, flanked by her two snarling sheepdogs, was backed up near the door of the wagon, a lanky cowhand poking at her with his finger; to the other side, another man, grinning, with his pistol drawn, was threatening the dogs. White Moon immediately touched off one barrel of the twelve-gauge. Its thunderous roar spun both of the men around, their eyes bulging, their jaws slack. White Moon, glaring at the man holding the revolver, said hotly, "Get rid of that thing before I take your arm off." Then he glanced at the taller man. "You get over there with your partner. Hurry up."

Divinity Jones, her arms waving wildly, screamed, "He was after my crotchie, the son of a bitch!" She rushed over beside Moon Tree and tried to wrest the shotgun away. "Was going to shoot my dogs . . . Let's kill the bastards!"

"Hold on," Moon said, fighting for control. "Now, hold on a minute." After he had partially calmed Divinity, who went stalking away to the wagon, sobbing, he addressed the two sullen drovers. "You fellows don't have good manners. If I gave this shotgun to her, she'd shoot your balls off, at least one of you. Plenty lucky I don't get so excited as she does, ei?"

Divinity Jones shouted from inside the wagon, "They says we can't stay here . . . have to get out!"

One of the men agreed, nodding at White Moon. "She's right. This is Tom Chambers' grazing country. You'll have to move up-country a notch or two. . . ."

"Have to?" Moon Tree asked coldly. "I don't 'have to' do anything on unceded land, brother. I'm not stupid. I know the law. I saw no markers here. If you have grazing rights, the law says you put out markers." He scowled at them. "What are you bothering this woman for? Where's your manners?"

"Just funnin' with her," the tallest one said with a shrug. "Hell, she's all ready to scratch me up. Didn't know she had a man."

"Shoot him, Mr. Moon!" Divinity called out. "He was gonna rope me, he was."

"She's plenty mad, ei?" White Moon said. "You don't know her like I do."

"Moon? She calling you Moon?" the smaller of the two asked.

"Hell, is your name Moon Tree?" And he gave his partner an apprehensive look.

"That's what the white people call me," Moon answered. He calmly set the shotgun against a wagon wheel. Then, facing the confused drovers, he nodded at the one with his revolver still holstered. "It takes plenty practice to use one of those," he said. "You practice, ei?"

"Not much, no, I reckon I don't," was the hesitant, uneasy answer.

Divinity Jones yelled out again, "Shoot 'em, Mr. Moon! Go ahead, do it!"

"Hmmmm," mused Moon, shaking his head sadly. "You shouldn't carry a weapon like that if you don't know how to use it. Bad medicine, I tell you. I see plenty of men shot because they don't know how to use one of those." Studying their drawn faces, he knew they were beaten men, eager to get back in their saddles and ride out. They had made a mistake, and were now afraid it might turn out to be a fatal one. He sensed that this was going through their minds. Fear had become their enemy, too. White Moon said, "My father was a good teacher. He taught me plenty things. You know my father?"

"Heard of him, for a fact," the shorter one replied edgily. "Just heard, that's all."

Contemplating them for a moment, Moon said, "Look here what he taught me," and in a sudden blur, the barrel of his Colt came whipping out like a streak of wildfire. It was aimed directly at the smaller man's belly. "That's a good trick, ei?" White Moon said, amusement twinkling in his eyes. Holstering the revolver, he motioned up the valley. "My brother, Benjamin, is up there, scouting ahead. You know, he'll be back soon. This is not so good for you. When he finds out you're with his woman, he'll be plenty mad. He's a different breed from me. He pulls the trigger. He does this all the time. That's how I know about all those men getting shot. He sure knows that trick plenty good. Maybe you'll want to ride out of here before he comes back, ei?"

The tall man shifted uneasily, stretched his neck out like a wary goose. "I think that's a good idea, for sure." Reaching down in the grass, he carefully retrieved his revolver. "Sorry we made a ruckus, but you still should get your sheep up above." He gave Moon an inquisitive stare. "What you doing with critters like that, anyhow? You ain't no sheepherder, none in your outfit over there, and your pa ain't no sheep man, either."

"Oh, those sheep?" Moon said, nodding. "Yes, you're right, they don't belong to our outfit. We're just helping move them down below, a favor to the governor. He has a little investment going—"

"The governor?"

"Governor Crosby," Moon said. "He owns them, the fellow up in Helena. Asked us to take good care of them. Wants to double his money down in the Lemhi. My father likes this fellow Crosby, does him a favor every once in a while. I think my father has too many friends, makes plenty work for me and my brother." Moon Tree leaned down and patted one of the dogs. "Good thing you didn't shoot these dogs. They belong to Benjamin, just like that white woman in there, only he likes these two old boys better. He'd kill you both if you hurt them. That's what happened to those rustlers up in the Crazies a few years back. Wasn't so much the cattle they stole, but they lamed one of this ponies. He was plenty mad about that. Pow!"

"Well," the shorter drover concluded, "we didn't mean no harm, Mr. Moon." He grinned weakly. "Sorry for the trouble, and if it's all right with you, we'll head on back now, let Mr. Chambers know you're just passing through. Reckon he won't mind a bit." He went hurriedly for his horse.

Divinity Jones, her tenacity unbridled, stuck her head out of the wagon again. "Don't you sons of bitches be coming back here, either. You leave us alone, go mind your manners."

"Good day, missus," the tall one called. "No, we ain't planning on coming back. Hope you have a good trip south. Yes, ma'am, good day to you."

The drovers mounted up, reined to the side, and set off at a hasty gallop. White Moon waved once and turned back to Divinity. "I shot four chickens up the flats. We can have a good supper, ei?"

Chickens, presently, weren't on Divinity's mind. Shaking a finger angrily at White Moon, she huffed, "Don't go talking to me about some shitty chickens! You told big lies to those men. I ain't got no man like Mr. Benjamin, and he ain't riding over the hill, either. How could he like my dogs better'n me, anyways, when he ain't even here? And who in the hell is this governor man, anyways? I never heard of him. You just made all this shit up, and that's bad. You're a goddamned liar, Mr. Moon, that's a fact. Bad, bad, bad."

"Ei, plenty bad, all right." He smiled. "You owe me one dollar, though. That's plenty good."

FOUR

It was near mid-August when Moon Tree and Divinity Jones headed down toward the wide, lonely country leading into the great Snake River basin. They had ranged the sheep back and forth across the Ruby River along the Gravelly Range and now were coming down to the little outpost of Dubois. They had no further problems with the cattlemen of the north. Down here, they were beginning to see bands of sheep every day or so, and sometimes in the distance, another herder, his hand raised in a friendly salute. Also by now, Divinity Jones was beginning to understand the little marks that Moon made each night on the piece of paper tacked on a board inside the wagon. Her name was on one side, his on the other. Below the names, Moon scratched these marks with his piece of charcoal. She was chagrined, because no matter how hard she tried, he seemed to catch her using a bad word almost every day, and she only had caught him three times, so she had way more marks than he did—in fact, fourteen of them.

Twice she went a whole day saying nothing more than "yes" or "no" in a desperate attempt to protect her money. But she gained nothing, because Moon Tree didn't talk much either, and she was unable to rack up any points against him. Though his game of cuss hadn't gone her way, she was making progress in other directions. She never squatted to pee where he could see her; she kept her blanket wrapped around her at night; she never wiped her mouth on her sleeve; and she chewed with her mouth closed. These were all ladylike refinements, Moon told her. He wanted to make another one of his wagers about the way she talked. It wasn't proper, he said, to use the word "ain't" all the time. She refused to bet with him about this, but she voluntarily tried to use the other words that he suggested, to little avail. She simply couldn't remember all of them. It was just too confusing. However, she was proud about one thing: she could now print her name, and because it was so beautiful, she scratched it out every day, over and over, in the trailside dust. DIVINITY JONES. It was truly grand, such a wonderfully pretty name.

They pulled the wagon over and made camp several miles from Dubois where a small creek ran toward the south. There were willow groves here, sage, juniper, and a few scrubby pines, little else, only those rolling hills and washed-out gullies as far as the eye could see. Somewhere down below, another week away, was Derby Flats, the end of the trail for Moon Tree. Fortunately, he was getting closer to freedom by the day, and after securing the sheep and mules, he decided to celebrate by taking Divinity Jones into Dubois. This was an old stage station for the Oliver lines that had mushroomed into a general store, two saloons, a livery, and a small hotel. A sign in the window of the hotel read "Good Eats," and Moon Tree explained this to Divinity. When he suggested that they find out how good the eats really were, she gleefully accepted, for she had never been in a hotel in her young life. Dismounting, they wrapped the reins of their horses around the long post in front, and entered Grant's Hotel, a one-story log and clapboard structure. Next to the dim lobby, there was a small dining room with two windows facing a side street. An elderly man with a full mustache was seated at one of the four tables. The only customer in the place, he paused to greet Divinity Jones and Moon Tree with a wave of his fork and kept right on eating. Presently, a large woman wearing an apron came in from the one long hallway, and it was very simple from this point on. She was Blanche Grant, sole owner of the hotel, chief cook and bottle washer. She had a menu of steak; liver and onions; fried eggs with calves' brains, or Mulligan stew. Additionally, she had made two apple pies this very day, and also had fresh cream and coffee. Divinity Jones, fearful of some outlandish breach of conduct, looked helplessly across the table at Moon Tree and whispered, "What?" He promptly ordered two steaks with all the trimmings, and Blanche Grant whisked herself away, disappearing in the darkness of the hall. Divinity, delighted to be in such a fine place, clasped her hands over her mouth and suppressed a giggle. When Blanche returned a second time she had two glasses of water, knives and forks, and two large orange-colored napkins.

Divinity stared curiously at her napkin, then glanced at Moon Tree again. "What?"

He said quietly, "To wipe up any food that misses your mouth."

She threw her hands back to her face and giggled again. "Lordy, ain't this—isn't this something!" she whispered excitedly.

Moon Tree nodded, but if the truth were known, Grant's Hotel was actually a rather shabby place compared to the fine new hotels in Helena, Butte, and Bozeman City, ones that he had visited during his trips with Sad Sam Courtland. They were built out of bricks, had two floors, and large dining rooms with white tablecloths. Some of the waiters were men who carried large trays uplifted on the palms of their hands. Of course, if he told any of this to Divinity Jones, she just might call him a goddamned liar and forfeit another dollar. So far this day, she was staying even in the cuss game, and Moon Tree didn't want to spoil her perfect record, or the afternoon. He smiled to himself as she sat expectantly, fidgeting nervously, her eyes wide and barely blinking. She was a pretty woman. Indeed, in three weeks' time, she seemed more attractive and fetching by the day, at least a far cry from his first encounter with her above the line cabin. Her blonde hair was full of luster instead of dust; she groomed herself meticulously; her shirts were clean and odorless; and Moon allowed that with another month or two of training, she just might turn into a lady, or a reasonable facsimile. By jingo, if she'd only keep her mouth shut.

The steaks soon were placed in front of them, also bowls of fried potatoes, beans, greens, and a plate of bread. Divinity anxiously began sampling everything. Moon quickly advised her to eat slowly. "When you eat slowly, you enjoy it more," he said. "The taste ends up in your mouth instead of your belly."

She heard him and promptly went into slow motion, but her pretty face never came up from the plate, not once.

Later, when Blanche Grant came back, Moon complimented her on the food. The sign in the window was right, the eats were good, he told her. She then inquired where Moon was headed, and how many days he had been on the trail. Moon explained the plight of Divinity Jones, and how he had come to her aid, but when he told her his name, she almost collapsed in a nearby chair.

"Good Lord, Henry," she called out to the man nearby, who had finished his meal and was now reading a newspaper by the window. "Do you know who this young fellow is? He's Ben Tree's boy!"

The man turned abruptly, put the paper aside, and asked "Which one? Ben has two boys. Went through here years back with one he called Little Benjamin, I recollect, his stepson. That'd be the blood boy of old Henri Bilodeau." He came over to the table and looked down at Moon Tree. "Which one might you be, son? Your pa's a friend of ours. Hell, I used to work for him!"

Moon identified himself and introduced Divinity Jones, who astonishingly, simply said, "Glad to meet you."

As it developed, Henry Billow was now a relief stage-line driver, but at one time rode the route to Virginia City regularly. Billow said, "Your pa and a fellow by the name of Digby down at Fort Hall used to own the whole shebang—freight, passengers, and all, had the whole territory, all the way over to Fort Boise. I knew your Nez Perce mother when she was Henri Bilodeau's woman, before she latched up with Ben. Ben and old Henri were great friends, traveled together. Reckon your half-brother, Benjamin, was nigh onto a year old when Henri died." Henry Billow's face saddened with melancholy and nostalgia. "Well, I helped bury Henri, me and ol' man Digby. Ben was over living with the Crow then, didn't even know about it. Your ma cut her hair off, all the way up to her ears, when Henri passed on. And by Gawd, she had the hair of an angel, that woman. Damnation, that was a sad time, boy, it sure was. Strange thing you know ... Ben lost his Crow wife just about the same time. Well, he came by Fort Hall, found out Henri had passed on. Him and your ma sorta fell in together, both bereaved and all. Went off by themselves, hitched up, and that was it."

Moon Tree and Henry Billow continued talking quietly, about the past and present, and directly Blanche returned with two pieces of pie, which she placed in front of Moon and Divinity. She said proudly, "Your dinner is on the house, Mr. Tree." When Moon politely protested, she adamantly waved him off and quickly explained her generosity. "If it wasn't for Ben Tree you wouldn't be eating here, young man. Didn't know that, did you? It'll be twenty years next spring when he loaned me the money to build this place." Placing her hands on the table, she looked Moon Tree squarely in the eyes. "There's people in these parts who remember your pa as a killer. That's hogwash! Let me tell you, he never killed anyone who didn't deserve it. Your pa was a gentleman, a fine young man who never turned his back or batted an eye when the traveling got tough. God bless that man, God bless him." She kissed Moon Tree on the forehead. And this much said for her benefactor, Blanche Grant turned to Divinity Jones, who was trying to listen and eat her pie at the same time. Divinity swallowed quickly and deftly caught a dribble of apple syrup with her big orange napkin.

Blanche Grant said to her, "You see, this boy

here is just like his father, going out of his way to help, answering the call. That's just the way Ben was, too, never made a big issue out of anything. Had a quiet way about him, he did. Asked a few questions and went right to work. This boy is just like him all right, straight as a shingle."

Moon Tree glanced glumly down at his piece of pie, suddenly feeling a twinge of guilt. What an underserved accolade. And this pie in front him! Molly Goodhart had bribed him with a pastry just like this to perk his interest in the deliverance of Divinity Jones. And he hadn't been too ecstatic about drawing those damned straws, either. Good Samaritan he was not.

Blanche Grant went on, "If you don't like it down there without your father all by yourself, you get on back up here. I can find some work for you, helping me with the rooms and the kitchen. That desert is no place for a young lady to be all by herself."

Of course, the mere mention of "young lady" almost caused Divinity to drop her fork. Her blue eyes lit up like two large discs of turquoise. She squirmed delightedly in her chair and said, "I'm obliged, Missus Grant. Leastways, next time I come this way, I'll sure to be stopping in to say howdy." Daintly patting her mouth with her napkin, she gave Moon Tree one of those little "I-told-you-so" smiles.

That night, White Moon returned and sat in on a poker game next door at Finney's Saloon. There were only six at the table, amateur gamblers all of them, and without ample funds. Moon played for practice, bet lightly, and feeling somewhat guilty about their inadequacies, only tapped them for thirty dollars. After about two hours of play, he bought everyone a round of drinks and left. When he reached the sheepherder's wagon around midnight, Divinity Jones, happily exhausted from the day's events, didn't even stir in her bedroll.

One week later, Divinity Jones pointed ahead to a distant conglomeration of sheds and corrals. Several canvas-topped wagons were pulled up around one large house, and beyond this there were hundreds of sheep dotting the range. This was the Coombes Livestock Company's headquarters. White Moon's eyes brightened, and a sudden feeling of euphoria swept through him. In another hour or so he would be free again, rid of the continual bleating of woolies, and free of one little blonde woman who often sounded like her two hundred friends.

The company manager, Owen Hoover, was shocked to hear about Burleigh Jones's death, also surprised that Moon Tree had helped Divinity bring the band home. In appreciation, he offered Moon a job next spring when the sheep were to be sent out again, a job Moon politely declined. Owen Hoover, as it turned out, was a generous, sympathetic man. After checking the sheep, he gave Divinity a twenty-dollar bonus for a job well done, and when she left with the promise of another ninety-day drive next season, she had two hundred twenty-two dollars. She owed Moon Tree twenty because of her losses in the cuss game, but with a kindly smile, he conceded the debt, allowing that she had improved enough to earn a bonus from him as well.

Divinity Jones was happy. In her meager, secluded world, she was now a rich woman, over two hundred dollars to tide her through the winter. As they prepared to trail over to Derby Flats with her two horses and the dogs, Owen Hoover came running out of the office and hailed them down. He was holding an envelope, waving it, and he explained that a man had delivered it two weeks past. It was addressed to Divinity's father. Luckily, her literate benefactor, Moon Tree, was by her side, and before they mounted up, he opened the letter and read it. It was from a man in Ogden, one J. A. Casper who dealt in real estate, and he was interested in buying Burleigh Jones's homestead at Derby Flats.

Divinity Jones, mystified as to why anyone would want to buy such a godforsaken place, nevertheless squealed with joy. She was ecstatic. The price of five hundred dollars was staggering to her, a fortune. A myriad of new and wonderful thoughts flooded her mind, and she excitedly began spilling them out to Moon Tree, who by now was accustomed to the frivolous outpourings. But in this case, there seemed to be some reality blossoming in her dream world; the terrible threat of her getting worms less serious. The reality was that she would now have enough money to relocate, possibly to some town in the territory, and this much of it from Moon's standpoint was plenty good. However, in his practical mind, five or six hundred dollars wasn't much of a grubstake for a young woman with no visible means of future support. This was bad medicine. Not to Divinity Jones, who optimistically told him that she knew how to cook and wash cloths, not to mention taking care of sheep. Moon Tree cringed inside. Ah, the naiveté of this engaging young woman whose heart was bigger than her mind.

Later that afternoon, they arrived at the little oasis of Derby Flats, one spot of greenery nestled into a wide, barren valley of sparse vegetation. Here and there a few scrawny, undernourished junipers dotted the landscape, along with ubiquitous sage and scattered clumps of bunch grass. Scrub pines fringed a distant ridge. It was a desolate land. The one exception was the bubbling spring. Around its source, to several hundred feet below, where a thin skim of water disappeared in the thirsty sand, the grass was lush and thick to either side. Divinity said that brush deer and antelope often came here to drink, consequently there was never a shortage of fresh meat in the larder. Above the spring, a long pole fence surrounded the ranch area, and within it sat a two-room house, one shed, and a weathered outhouse, all badly in need of repair.

Moon Tree, wiping the perspiration from his brow, said to Divinity, "You don't have a tree, not one, no place to sit in the shade and wonder why Akbatatdia made this place."

"When it's hot, I go sit in the spring," she said smartly, as if her educated friend had no common sense at all. "Water's cold in the middle, warm at the edges. You'll see." She reined up toward the small buildings. "Well, might as well see what the pack rats left me. They always come around when we're gone. Takes a couple days to let 'em know they ain't—they are—are not welcome."

"Aren't," said Moon Tree vainly. "Are not is two words. Run them together the way everyone does, and it's aren't."

"Ain't's easier, aren't it?"

He laughed. "Ei, every sodbuster I've ever met seems to think so. And look at us. It's plenty bad, Miss Divinity, when an Injun has to go teaching a white woman how to talk ladylike, and I'm probably the worst of the lot."

With great affection, she said, "You're the best teacher I ever had, buddy. Reckon I loves you a heap, I do. 'Cept for Paw getting killed, this has been the best damned summer I ever had." She suddenly clasped her mouth. "Didn't mean to say the bad word . . . "

"Cuss game's over, Miss Divinity. You're home."

It wasn't much of a home, though, and Divinity

Jones was right: the pack rats had been around, on the table, around the stove, in the wood bin, and had tried to gnaw their way into the cupboard. While White Moon took care of the horses and packs, and unloaded supplies, Divinity went to work cleaning out the house. Bringing up several buckets of water, she mopped the floors, cleared out the spiderwebs, washed the three windows and all of the furniture. Finally, she threw open the bedroom window and disappeared. White Moon searched around, saw her nowhere. He went into the bedroom, looked out the window just in time to see her naked body flying through the air into the big pool of water. There was a huge splash, and Divinity's head and shoulders presently appeared. Raising her arms to the sky, she cried out, "Hallelujah!"

Without the bleating of sheep and tinkle of bells, Moon had his best sleep since leaving the comfort of the Tree ranch. He was up shortly after dawn and coaxed a fire in the big iron range. When Divinity appeared, carefully wrapped like a tamale in her brown blanket, he already had the coffee boiling and was stirring up a batter for hotcakes. She reached up and kissed him on the nose, then went outside. By the time she returned, her hair damp and tiny grains of sand hugging her wet toes, Moon Tree was tossing four large strips of bacon in the big cast iron skillet. Divinity was delighted, for no one had cooked her a breakfast since her mother died almost five years ago. She ate in silence, her usual exuberance tempered. This was a farewell breakfast, and each mouthful became harder to swallow. Moon Tree unexpectedly discovered that he, too, felt somewhat disconsolate. It was like eating the last piece of sweet melon, nothing left but an empty plate and a memory of what had been. That she had found a small niche in his heart, there was no doubt—a paradox, since more than once he had relished the thought of paddling her ornery little butt. Truly, he had become her buddy, and he gladly accepted this simplistic but honored designation of deep friendship. Buddy.

Moon Tree, in departing, cautioned Divinity about making any hasty or foolish decisions, told her to keep her money well hidden, and last of all, to keep her mouth shut. He left his name neatly printed on a piece of newspaper in case she wanted to have someone write a letter or send a telegraph message. She knew that he was concerned about her welfare. Divinity Jones gave him a tremendous hug and an affectionate kiss, then watched him ride away. White Moon Tree felt relieved, but plenty sad.

FIVE

Across the Great Plains and mountains of the
West, the trails of men mysteriously cross in
strange and unpredictable ways, sometimes casually, sometimes violently, and often these chance
meetings direct destiny. It was hot, near midday.
About ten miles from where the main trail cut
back toward the hill country, Moon Tree saw two
wagons shimmering in the scorching blanket that
hung over the landscape. He took out his binoculars from the saddlebag and focused in, made out
the wavering figures of several men walking near
the stationary wagons. These people weren't immi-
grants or desperadoes, of this he was certain, but
he was puzzled by their unlikely appearance in an
area so seldom used by anything but jackrabbits
and rattlesnakes. He took another long look, wondering if they were making repairs on one of the
wagons. He saw nothing that would indicate this.
Curiosity piqued, he decided to saunter over and
investigate. Riding in easily and cautiously, Moon
was soon greeted by one of the men, a shirtless

one, wearing a broad-brimmed cavalry hat and khaki trousers. The man's spectacles were slipping down on his nose from sweat, but his lower lip was dry, a neat little crack right in the middle of it. Oddly, White Moon had seen this fellow before, and within a moment, knew who he was, Lieutenant Timothy Aubrey, a surveyor and the very same man who had stitched up Benjamin's badly slashed shoulder five years ago after a battle with two Sioux braves near the Yellowstone River. In those days, Benjamin One Feather and White Moon wore beaded headbands, eagle feathers in their braids, breechclouts; their legs were bare, their feet clad with beautiful tanned-hide moccasins. They mistrusted the troopers almost as much as they did the Sioux, Cheyenne, and Blackfeet. They also occasionally enjoyed playing jokes on the soldiers, and this fellow Aubrey had been the brunt of one of White Moon's pranks, not once, but twice. Even so, Timothy Aubrey didn't recognize White Moon on this hot afternoon in late August, not in Moon's white man's dress, his denim shirt, toed boots, and black drover's hat.

It was Aubrey who spoke first. Looking over his spectacles, he said, "Thought you might be one of our men riding out with some plats or a message from the office, but you're welcome to step down for a drink of water. She's a hot one, all right."

"Thanks, but I have my own here," Moon said, tapping the side of his canteen. He glanced around curiously. "What's this all about? What are you doing so far from the trail?" He dismounted and walked to the shade of one of the wagons where a small table and several chairs had been set up.

"A survey," Timothy Aubrey replied. Pausing, he wiped his brow. "Running a rail line up this way from Utah. Bit of a task in this kind of weather." He measured White Moon carefully, sensing some familiarity, but still not quite sure. "What brings you this way?"

Reflecting on another time long ago, White Moon once again was seized by temptation, couldn't resist the opportunity of making another joke, even a repetitive one. His face sober under his big hat, he answered "Hostiles. Ei, looking for hostiles. Scouting for a posse back over there a few miles. Damned hostiles are all over the place."

"Hostiles!" exclaimed Aubrey, pushing his glasses back up to the bridge of his nose. "Why, we've not heard about any hostiles around here!" Another one of the men came close. He and Aubrey exchanged anxious glances. "What kind of hostiles? Who are they?"

"Don't really know," replied White Moon innocently. "They come in raiding at night. Never see them, sort of like ghosts." Tilting back his hat, White Moon added somberly, "You know all about those ghosts, Mr. Aubrey, don't you, the ones that go 'ahooo' in the night? How could you forget? Scared the hell out of you, didn't they?"

Timothy Aubrey, suddenly amused and embarrassed, lowered his head and began chuckling, finally stared up into White Moon's smiling face. "I knew it, damn it! I knew there was something about your voice, something with a familiar ring . . . couldn't get the right picture in my mind, and then I had this faint recollection. But then I told myself, 'No, it can't be, not that crazy brother of Benjamin One Feather . . . impossible!'" He turned to his companion. "He's an old friend, army days. I sewed up a wound on his brother, and this one, well." And he placed his hands on Moon's shoulders. "This one went around scaring my men with stories about hostiles, ghosts, nonsense that some of us actually believed. He even had hair hanging on his horse's bridle, scalps, he said, only it turned out to be black tree lichen." Studying White Moon from head to toe, he said, "Good Lord, what are you doing way down here?"

They sat down at the cluttered table and talked, White Moon revealing that he and his family had left the Absaroke, were now living at the big ranch in the Gallatin.

In turn, Timothy Aubrey explained his presence in the outland bush country. He had served out his commission in the army and now was employed by the engineering division of the Union Pacific railroad. The rails, he said, were being extended north into the Montana Territory. White Moon reflected briefly on what the lawyer, Arthur Clawson, had told him almost a month ago, that the tracks would soon come up into the Butte and

Helena country, the demand was there, and obviously it was now being answered.

"How long have you been at this?" Moon Tree asked.

"Four months now," Aubrey answered. Placing a finger on the map, he said, "By next spring, maybe summer, we'll be way up here, the Montana Territory, almost due north, a zig here, a zag there." One of the engineers arrived with a platter of bread and cheese and two bottles of stout. Slabbing a piece of cheese between the bread, White Moon took a hefty bite and stared at the configurations on the map. The lines, as Aubrey had said, were essentially straight, sometimes bent slightly to right or left, generally they moved almost due north. Little squares occasionally appeared; and as his eyes followed a dark line, they suddenly stopped. The small, neat printing almost exploded in his dark face: Derby Flats! If his flinch showed, Timothy Aubrey hadn't noticed. He was casually downing several gulps of the stout. White Moon, likewise, sampled the malty brew, smacked his lips once and innocently asked, "What are these small squares? I notice one or two every so often here, and here, one way up here."

"Watering stations." Aubrey told him.

"Watering stations?"

Timothy Aubrey smiled patiently. "Steam engines, Mr. Tree," he said. "Your horse needs grass, hay. Steam engines need the water. So"—and his finger pointed for emphasis—"we have a station here . . . one here, every fifty to a hundred miles. Depends on the grade we're setting, how much power is being expended. The engine stops at one of the depots, takes on water for the boiler, sometimes fuel. Simple enough? We need the water."

"Very simple," White Moon smiled. "People at these stations?"

"Tenders," Aubrey replied. "Oh, sometimes a few shacks or a loading platform come along, depending upon the freight traffic."

"And what's the freight down around this country?" White Moon asked. "There's nothing down here except tumbleweed."

Timothy Aubrey set his stout aside and gave White Moon a hopeless look. "Look here, you just told me you helped some young sheepherder in distress, didn't you? Sheep, Mr. Tree, sheep. This translates into mutton and wool, and for the present, that's live freight. Who knows what this place will turn into when the railroad goes through? It's anyone's guess. The railroad doesn't change the land, but it sure changes the people, gives them new incentives."

White Moon agreed, and thought to himself that some of these incentives were already being pursued by certain real estate people, those who somehow knew where the rails were headed, insiders who wanted to profit on the land before the railroad right-of-way agents arrived with their purchase offers. After he finished his sandwich, White Moon shook hands with Aubrey, but had nothing more to offer him in the way of an Indian joke. The old days were gone, White Moon lamented. A pity, said Timothy Aubrey. White Moon agreed. Swinging around, he sidled off and tipped his hat in a friendly farewell.

Timothy Aubrey called out, "Hey, you're going back the way you came. Trail's over there."

"Have to find a hostile," yelled back White Moon. "Think I know just where to look, too."

When he came riding back into Derby Flats, Moon Tree was greeted first by two very happy dogs, then a little blonde lady who forgot her tongue again and cried out, "For crissakes, Mr. Moon, did you get yourself lost? 'Nother hour or so and the sun's down. What on earth are you doing back here?"

"Fix supper, woman," he said dismounting. "I'm going to teach you how to dance, and we have some unfinished business."

Her eyes widened, and a little smile of anticipation fanned across her pretty face. "Just what are you aiming to do, Mr. Moon?" Divinity Jones giggled. "This unfinished business. You talking about love business or something?"

"Shush that talk!" Moon said with a little scowl. "What I'm going to tell you will make you plenty more happy than any love business. And it will last a helluva lot longer, too."

It was a grand night in Derby Flats.

SIX

One sunny afternoon Dupee Clancy and Arvis James returned from the Idaho Territory, and Dupee was as mad as the day was hot. His partners, detailed to bring the stolen horses south, had failed to show within the designated time period, negating a transaction of nearly seven thousand dollars. Angry and looking for an answer to this inexcusable business failure, he and Arvis James rode into their Madison Valley hideaway only to discover another disaster—someone had looted their cabin, even caved in half of the roof. The door was smashed and varmints had devoured what was left of their larder and canned goods. The huge gnashes ripped right through the tins were an indication that a bear had been among the raiders. Worse yet, all of the horses were gone and half of the corral poles torn off. This was a matter for the law to investigate, the outright thievery and destruction of property, but there wasn't any way that Dupee Clancy could enlist the aid of the marshal in Virginia City, not when all of the horses had been rustled in the first place. Staring around at the destruction, he could only assume that after the gang's successful raid on the Stuart ranch, someone had picked up their trail. His men had been rousted and the stolen horses reclaimed.

Rummaging around inside the trashed cabin, Arvis James found an empty shell from a thirty-caliber rifle, and presenting this to Clancy, deduced that at least one shot had been fired. If there had been a fight, it must have been a brief one. Slamming his old hat against the broken door disgustedly, and wiping the sweat from his brow, Dupee Clancy decided that the best he could do now was head back into Virginia City and do some investigating on his own. Arvis James agreed. Besides, Arvis needed a few belts of rye, a change of clothes, and a good meal.

Arvis James got his rye, but little else. At the first saloon they hit, some casual conversation with the bartender soon revealed what had happened over on the Madison. Some cowboys from the Gallatin ranches, led by Moon Tree, had shot two rustlers and captured another, one Gabe Arbuckle, who was presently lodged in the local jail awaiting trial. The rumor was that Arbuckle had implicated several other men, too, but no one seemed to know anything definite about where they were. Probably went west over into the Beaverhead country was the best guess, the bartender opined. One of them was said to be a fellow by the name of Dupee Clancy, reputed to be the leader. Another drover called Arvis James was riding with him, and additionally, the marshal's office had put out a five-hundred-dollar reward on each of them, dead or alive. According to the bartender, there was some strange circumstances surrounding the incident. Seemed as though the rustlers had accidentally run into a sheepherder by the name of Jones. Jones was killed by the gang, but his daughter by the name of Divinity had been hiding by a creek and saw the shooting, had given descriptions of three of the men to the Bozeman sheriff. It was all in the newspaper, big headlines, most excitement the town had had in several years.

Dupee Clancy and Arvis James, their big hats pulled low, quietly left the bar, picked up a few supplies, and headed for the hills. Clancy, already nursing a festering boil over his losses, was now embittered further by the disclosure that Gabe Arbuckle had peached on him, and he erupted violently inside when he heard Moon Tree's name mentioned. The Tree family was the enemy. Young Benjamin was responsible for the death of his brother, Jim, a killing that he had been unable to avenge. Now Moon had suddenly appeared, shooting up two of Clancy's friends, along with destroying all of the summer's profit and the cabin as well. His gang had been done in by an Injun breed, a woman, and one of his own men. This was too much for one man to bear, not without re-taliation. An eye for an eye, Clancy bitterly vowed.

Arvis James, a stubby fellow who always wore his trousers tucked into his long boots to make himself appear taller, wasn't too happy about the five-hundred-dollar bounty hanging over his head or about hiding out in the mountains. In fact, he was downright afraid of what might happen if he continued to hang out with Dupee Clancy. Clancy was a dangerous man, one prone to taking too many chances, and any mistake now meant cur-tains for sure. Arvis didn't like the thought of end-ing up six feet deep on Boot Hill. In somewhat of a fret, he asked, "Just what you aiming to do about those Tree boys? You go stirring them up and they just might put a hole in your ornery gizzard. Those fellows got that Injun blood in 'em. Hell, no tell-ing what kinda tricks they might pull on us, sneak up and get us in the night just like they did your brother and those others fellows that time."

"Well, I don't plan on sleeping anywhere near them," Clancy replied. "Best thing we can do is keep on riding, head south, and hole up, let this damned thing blow over." With an air of confi-dence, he nodded back in the other direction. "I'm too smart for them. Go poking around over there now and you're likely right, they'd be all ready, stomp on us like a couple of piss ants. They got themselves five or six hands at that place, and they go around armed to the teeth. I saw 'em more'n once outriding, in town, too. No, Arvie, I ain't no damned fool. Have to bide our time, get our dues when they ain't expecting."

But Arvis didn't particularly care about collecting his dues from the Tree brothers. True, Moon Tree had robbed him of a big cut of the pie by raiding the camp on the Madison, but hell, anyone smart enough to follow a trail could have done the same. And that woman, Divinity, who saw them, that was just pure fate. Clancy's grudge wasn't his. Getting after those Tree boys would be like denning with a griz, most likely end up nothing more than a pile of bones and a hank of hair. He cast a wary eye over his partner. "Well, I think we oughtta keep right on riding, go on over to the Oregon country for the fall and winter. I don't cotton to the idea of some fellow bushwhacking me for five hundred bucks, and you damned well know there's a lotta bastards around these parts ornery enough to do something like that."

"Reckon I'd shoot someone for even a hundred bucks." Clancy grinned. "That is, if he was a bad one, understand." He cackled at that. "Naw, I figure there's a few of those old cabins down the line a piece. Scads all gone in those diggings, and the boys went over the hill looking for color somewheres else. Find us a place for a month or so, round up a couple drifters, and get ourselves some more horses. Be right back in business."

Skeptical, Arvis thought he'd rather put his faith in himself, hire out on some faraway ranch for the rest of the year where he could get a bed and three squares a day. Hanging around some abandoned miner's cabin with a hungry belly didn't appeal to him too much. Fact was, he didn't like anything Dupee Clancy was suggesting, particularly that last part about stealing more horses. People in this country were all riled up now, just itching to run down a few rustlers. "What are we gonna do for money?" Arvis asked. "I'm almost busted, no more'n a couple eagles to my name."

"Go down and play a few hands with those sheepherders," Clancy suggested. "I got forty or so left, enough to tide us over for a while, leastways till we get something going again."

Arvis shook his head doubtfully. He wasn't convinced, and poker wasn't his strong suit, either, even playing against sheepherders. Well, he'd go along with Dupee for a while, wait for the proper time, and then cut out for Oregon where it was safe, live with the sodbusters, do some of that plowing and planting. To Hell with Dupee Clancy and his big ideas.

One day later, the two outlaws rode to the south and found what Dupee Clancy had been searching for, an abandoned cabin in a timbered draw up above Ruby Creek. Not much chance of being discovered here, and it was only a short haul back down the canyon to Alder Gulch and Laurin, where Clancy thought he might be able to do some recruiting in a week or so. He also thought a raid or two over on the Beaverhead might provide them with enough horses to run south to his buyers in the Lemhi Valley. After making a few repairs on the cabin, Clancy decided to look for a suitable location for a corral, a well-hidden meadow with water, and within a night's ride over the ridge into the Beaverhead Valley. After a three-hour search, he was returning by way of a small pass when he heard the distant bleating of sheep from somewhere in the sage below. His last, unexpected confrontation with a sheepherder, a contributing factor to his present predicament with the law, made him wary. He pulled up, and sidled his horse into the pines. Far below he finally saw the band of sheep, a wagon trailing, and off to one side a rider, all moving up the side of the valley, south toward the grazing country. Let well enough alone, he decided, and when they had passed on safely out of sight, he rode back to the cabin. The sheepherders, unbeknownst to him, and had he known, it would have been unbelievable, were Moon Tree and Divinity Jones.

Later, when Dupee Clancy whistled a signal and came up to the hideout, he discovered that he was alone. His partner, Arvis James, had run out on him for parts unknown.

Arvis James in recent years had been a thief, and sometimes a drover, but he had learned to profit by taking advantage of others as miserable as himself. He often escorted them from the saloons and picked their pockets at the same time. Occasionally, he waylaid miners, sometimes sneaked in and stole their cache while they were at the diggings. He never worked the cattle unless he had to, not when he could find more lucrative and less arduous ways to eke out a living. Arvis James thought himself a clever man, and he now had outwitted Dupee Clancy, whom he considered a stupid man.

When Arvis came over the Snowcrest Mountains and dropped down into the Beaverhead, he entertained only one thought—getting the hell away from the Montana territory where a few people knew him—so he rode south toward the border, usually moving late at night, and holing up during the morning hours. Once he had cleared the stage station at Armstead, he thought he was in pretty fair shape. He was heading toward the summit, his destination Dubois in the Idaho Territory, a junction point for both sheep and cow men, a little town where people seemed to mind their own business and took a dollar or two without getting nosy. A short distance the other side of Armstead, he came around a wide bend and ran directly into a herd of cows and calves and three drovers. Luckily, the drovers were strangers to him and one of them, an older fellow who sat tall in the saddle, hailed him over. It was a stroke of luck. This man's name was Albert Whiteside, owner of the "W—slash" ranch, and he wanted to know if Arvis James was looking for work: cutting out calves and branding, maybe rounding up a few horses later. Arvis, who suddenly became Cletus, his dead brother's name, thought this was a good idea, at least something to tide him over for a month and take him out of circulation. He grudgingly accepted the labor and for almost three weeks, Cletus chased critters and took his three squares a day. No one paid him any mind. Cletus was one of those loners. Toward the end of August, he took leave of Whiteside's outfit with sixty dollars in his pocket, more than enough to get him over the hump into the Idaho Territory.

Arvis James's luck finally took a turn for the worse at the Mint Saloon in Dell. He ran into an old acquaintance from his Lemhi rustling days, a fellow thief by the name of Charlie Pollard, a drifter who worked off and on as a drover, and who was now living in a small cabin up in the Big Sheep Creek country, about a two-hour ride from the river bottom. Pollard said it was like old times running into his pal, Arvis James, and after several rounds of drinks, they hitched up together and rode off to the cabin where Pollard had invited James to spend the night. Much like Arvis, Pollard had been a little destitute during the summer, hadn't found any easy games to play, and working for two dollars a day wasn't the best way of making a living. He was out to get a stake, just waiting for the right opportunity, something that didn't require too much effort.

After a meager supper of fatback and beans, they were sitting at the table discussing a few possibilities when Arvis James suddenly thought of a clever scheme that fit right into their line of thinking. It involved some risk, but little work. Why not ride back over the Ruby and capture Dupee Clancy, turn him in to the sheriff in Virginia City, and split the reward of five hundred dollars? Arvis James said, "I can take you right to him. All we have to do is catch him coming out of that miner's shack. You can take him on down to town, get the bounty, and we can split it and ride on out."

Pollard thought this was a good idea but was a bit hesitant. "That ol' boy is a mean shooter, ain't he?" he asked. "What if he comes out all armed and ready?"

"Two of *us*, only one of *him*." James smiled, easing up close to the table. "Anyways, the posters say dead or alive. Don't make a whit one way or the other to me."

Pollard, thoughtfully staring into his tin cup, pondered the proposition. "That's sort of a mean trick to pull on your friend, ain't it? I mean, you done rode with him through hell and high water, and—"

"Friend!" scoffed Arvis James. "Why, hell, he ain't had a friend in his life. He'd take me down right now just for leaving him up there in that rat's nest, probably do the same to me if he could get someone to go in cahoots with him, turn me in and go halves just like I'm doing."

Charlie Pollard smiled coldly. "You know, Arvie, I was thinking. Maybe I got a better idea. Saw a poster on you, too, down at Dell. Now, you see if

I was to take both of you in, that'd be one thousand for me all by myself. Shit, man, that's a heap better than two-fifty, ain't it? Feller has to look out for himself these days, all the good games going to pot."

Arvis James grinned back at him. "Yep, I was sorta thinking you might figure something like this, maybe have a little fun with ol' Arvie."

"Well, I ain't joshing," Pollard said, standing and pulling out his pistol.

"No, I reckon you ain't, at that." From under the table Arvis James pulled the trigger of his forty-five once, twice, and blew the planking to smithereens, and Charlie Pollard along with it. And there went two hundred and fifty dollars.

Charlie Pollard didn't have but twenty dollars in his pocket, but one thing he did have was a fine gray horse and a good saddle. When Arvis James rode out, he trailed his horse with a few of Pollard's supplies packed on it. Once down below the border he could sell his own outfit, make another hundred, and he'd be well on his way. This was a helluva lot better than sitting around in a broken-down cabin in the Snowcrest Mountains with Dupee Clancy.

Arvis James reached Dubois the following night, rented a room at Grant's Hotel, cleaned himself up right and proper, and had a fine supper in the dining room. He had a few dollars to spare, so he went over to Finney's Saloon and played some stud poker, but without much success.

Some breed sheepherder seemed to have all the luck and took most of the pots, including ten dollars of Arvis James's money. He sold his horse at the livery, saddle and all, and picked up a hundred dollars.

The next morning, he saw the breed sheepherder again, accompanied now by a white woman, heading on down the valley. James was also riding south, after his talk with the late Charlie Pollard, he once again was struck with a brilliant idea. This time of the year the herders were moving to the home ranches, collecting their season's wages. Pollard had told him about the easy pickings down below in the flatlands, and what the hell, he was going that way, anyways. If he could make another couple hundred, he'd be all prepared when he rode over to the Snake and on to the Blue Mountains of Oregon. Why not? Light of heart, James clucked his new gray horse along, visions of more profit dancing on the fuzzy blue horizon.

A few days later, Arvis James holed up in the little rooming house at Yankee Flats, about three miles from the Coombes Livestock Company headquarters. Yankee Flats consisted of one store, one saloon, one rooming house, one livery, and three shade trees. The ground for miles around was fertilized with sheep manure, little round pebbles that rolled like marbles when the wind blew. From the porch of the boarding house, James watched a few people come and go, the arrival

and departure of the daily stage (no one ever
seemed to get off at Yankee Flats), and he shared
a drink or two with a few herders at the saloon.
One of the people he saw going several days after
his arrival was the Injun sheepherder with whom
he had played poker in Dubois. James wondered
what had happened to the woman wagon driver.
Somewhat curious about this young man who
hadn't said more than two or three words during
the card game, Arvis James inquired of one of the
men sitting in the shade of the porch. "Who's that
fellow? Know him?"

"Nope," was the indifferent answer. "Some
herder, I reckon. Never saw him till the other day.
Reckon he's heading back home."

"Stranger, eh?"

"Yep. Hear tell the Jones girl hired him to help
bring her sheep back home. Her pa got himself
killed up north past summer, left her high and dry,
all alone now she is." The man transferred his
toothpick to the other side of his mouth, and
stared away toward the western horizon. "Gonna
rain tonight," he said.

James barely heard the comment about the
weather. He felt as if someone had clubbed him
between the eyes. Jones! How could this be!
Scratching his jaw nervously, he asked, "Her name
wouldn't be Divinity, would it? Her pa was a
herder, I hear tell."

"Same one." He pointed a gnarled finger at the
lowering clouds. "See those thunderheads, the

black one? Coming right this way, they are. Good sign. We needs the rain. Puts down the dust."

"This Divinity Jones," Arvis James went on. "Where does she live?"

"Derby Flats, hellhole of creation, nigh on twenty miles or so out in the desert that'a way," and his finger came around from the storm clouds and pointed southeast.

SEVEN

Divinity Jones, buoyed by the promise of future riches, thought she would be relatively content at the homestead on Derby Flats. The weather had moderated from scorching heat to just plain warm, an occasional desert wind kicking up a few tumbleweeds and drifting small winnows of sand along the buildings. The first day she kept busy making several wood-gathering forays across the flats to the lone pine ridge, hauling back limbs and shattered pieces of trunk in a small, weather-beaten wagon. She also finished some minor repair work on the house, tacked up a few loose boards, reset the tin stack on the chimney, and made a new wooden latch for the inside of the door. Fixing the bolt was something that she had thought about continually since she found herself alone for the first time in her life. Although in the past it often had been weeks at a time before anyone passed by the isolated spring, news of the railroad surveyors working in the area had brought about a few alarming changes. She wasn't alone anymore and strangers frightened her. Twice in one day she saw riders, two men a mile or so from where she was getting her supply of winter wood. This very afternoon another solitary rider on a gray horse stopped some distance from the homestead and just watched for a short while before disappearing beyond the sandy hills. Divinity Jones propped the shotgun near the door and decided to keep the two dogs inside with her at night.

Two railroad agents also arrived in a buggy pulled by two handsome black horses. Divinity knew at first sight that these men weren't drifters, for they both were attired in fine suits under their dusters, and one of them wore a derby, which he politely doffed at her appearance near the gate. These men were gentlemen, and she invited them to the shade of the porch where the man in the derby presented her with a small card. Unable to read it, Divinity put it in her pocket, was relieved when he said his name was Vincent Poole. He had arrived to see Burleigh Jones, wanted to discuss matters concerning the homestead. Explaining that her father had been killed recently and that her mother also was dead, Divinity told Poole that she was now the sole owner of the homestead. After the two men had a drink of some cold spring water, they took out several papers. One was a map, which they spread out across the floor of the porch. Poole showed Divinity marks on the map, long lines, some of them in red, others in black, and small squares at various points. This, Poole told her, was the proposed route of the new rail-road northward into the Montana Territory. Divinity, of course, expressed surprise when they said that the route was planned to cross her property. Vincent Poole and his friend, an engineer named Timothy Aubrey, had come to see about purchasing the required land needed, particularly the acreage surrounding the great spring. They had the preliminary papers with them, Poole explained, and if the company's proposal met with her approval, the land would be surveyed and divided at a later date, probably later in the fall or early spring.

Divinity, after listening to Vincent Poole, said innocently, "Land sakes, I just can't imagine why this old place is so important. Nothing but weeds, snakes, and jacks around here. All the sage and rock. Grass ain't worth a whit. Why, I'm the only poor soul in these parts."

Timothy Aubrey pointed to the rolling hills in the north. "Our tracks will wind up that way, a grade of considerable length. We're going to need water for the engines. Don't you understand, the spring here is a necessity."

" 'Scuse me," Divinity said. She went into the house and directly returned with a piece of paper. Handing it to Poole, she said, "You'll have to talk to this man. He has the papers on my place, and whatever he wants to do is all right with me."

Vincent Poole and Timothy Aubrey quietly examined the paper, then exchanged surprised glances. Poole said, "This man is an attorney, so it says here . . . up in Helena. That's a far distance from here, Miss Jones. May I ask how this gentleman came into possession of your property deed? Have you hired him as your solicitor?"

"Don't know what a solicitor is, Mister," Divinity said, "but he's some fellow who knows his business about this railroad stuff. Mr. Moon told me to give his name to you people when you came knocking, so this is what I'm doing." She dabbed at the perspiration on her forehead with her bandanna, then smiled prettily. "You know, some fellow offered me five hundred dollars for this place and that made Mr. Moon mad, it did. Said people were gonna come along and cheat me if I didn't watch out. 'Spect he was right, too."

Adjusting his spectacles, Aubrey chuckled at this revelation. "This man, Mr. Moon, he wouldn't be a hostile, would he?"

"A hostile!" exclaimed Divinity, her blue eyes bulging.

"A nice-looking young man with a black hat, feather tucked in the band?"

Divinity Jones smiled. So many people knew Mr. Moon and all of his friends and family. She said proudly, "That's Mr. Moon, all right, but he ain't . . . isn't no hostile, only part Injun, I reckon. Talks better'n I do, for sure."

Vincent Poole, obviously perplexed and somewhat agitated, looked askance at Timothy Aubrey. "Moon? Hostile?"

"Used to go by the name of White Moon." Aubrey explained.

"That's him," Divinity declared. "He's my buddy. He's on his way home."

"I know the young man, met him when I was in the army. His father is Ben Tree, one of the biggest ranchers in the Montana Territory. Was a breed chief of the Crow Indians. This boy, Moon, is his second son, a great practical joker. But I'm afraid, Mr. Poole, this isn't a joke. He's wisely counseled this young lady, is probably delivering her deed to his father's attorney. Your people will have to move in that direction or we'll never get across this valley." With a weary sigh, Aubrey got up and took his glass. "I think I need another drink of that water."

"Thank you kindly, mister," Divinity called out.

"Thank you?"

"You bet," Divinity Jones replied emphatically. "For knowing a lady when you sees one."

With some consternation, Vincent Poole returned to the buggy, soon followed by Timothy Aubrey and Divinity. Aubrey, trying to suppress a smile, climbed in beside Poole and took up the reins. So this was the destitute sheepherder on whom White Moon had taken such pity. Little wonder that his young breed friend had ridden the wrong way yesterday back to search out "a hostile," a very pretty hostile at that. Aubrey, glancing around suspiciously, asked her, "Your friend isn't hiding around here somewhere, is he? He does things like this, you know. He's a bit of a rascal at times."

"Wish he was hiding here," Divinity replied. "Best buddy I ever had."

"No doubt," Aubrey said, giving the reins a flip.

Divinity happily whirled around several times, and with a wave, danced merrily back to the little house, her version of the two-step that Moon Tree had taught her.

A few clouds began to gather this same afternoon, and Divinity sniffed several times to the west, trying to pick up the scent of moisture in the dry, desert air. This is what Burleigh always did, tested the air with his big red nose. He had been an expert on scents, the smell of water usually displeasing him, but despite this, he always welcomed rain in the desert this time of the year. He had often reminded Divinity that water was meant for the thirsty land, not the stomach, and only a splash or two in the face was tolerable. Water made the old pipes rusty, he said. A good shot of rye cleaned them, and this had been his favorite remedy, curing everything from snake bite to the gout. Though she hadn't shared his outrageous beliefs, Divinity allowed that the homestead, as lonely as it was, was even more lonely without the old sot. True, he was cantankerous, and about as stubborn as a mule, but after all, he had been her paw, trying his best to make do. But it was like sawing wood with a toothless blade: he just got nowhere his whole shitty life, never got out of the groove. But talking to him once in a while was better than talking to the four walls and two grinning sheepdogs. She stared wistfully at the leaden sky, and out here, the sky was forever. Not much of a chance being a lady all fixed up nice and proper with no one to talk to and noplace to go. She missed her buddy, Mr. Moon, missed that small taste of life he had given her, even missed playing the damned cuss game. Fact was, she was damned lonely already. Well, she had the nose of her paw—it was starting to rain. Divinity hurried into the house and kindled up a cooking fire.

During the night, Divinity Jones thought she heard the sound of a horse, a distant whinny, but then it could have been Mariah, the wind. She sure knew that sound, had lived with it most of her life. Mariah came sometimes at night with a wailing cry, a moan, even a sorrowful whisper, like it was grieving, hurting inside, pleading to find a peaceful resting place. Divinity thought that Mariah was one of the loneliest sounds that she had ever heard. Later, when she heard one of the dogs growling low, she wondered if he was dreaming, maybe about that drover back in the mountains, the one who was teasing him when Mr. Moon fired off the shotgun. She listened. The rain had almost stopped, nothing more now than a faint puddling where the rain was dripping off the eaves alongside the house. She heard another noise, only the slightest sound of a step, then again, the growl of one of the dogs. Quickly throwing aside her blanket, Divinity tiptoed into the kitchen and grabbed her shotgun. At the door she listened again and heard nothing but the quickening beat of her heart and the growling dogs padding nervously around the wooden floor behind her. She shushed the dogs with several pats. Directly she saw the tin knob on the door twist slightly, realized then that someone was on the porch, and only the big wooden drop latch prevented his entry. Anticipating the intruder's next move, Divinity moved to the partially opened window, stood back from it four feet, and waited. When two hands suddenly appeared at the bottom of the window, Divinity thumbed back the hammer of the right chamber and pulled the trigger. After the resounding roar, both of the dogs, leaping frantically at the opening, finally wedged themselves through. Barking wildly, they disappeared into the damp night. Divinity pulled up a chair and placed herself squarely in front of the locked door, her thumb resting on the hammer of the left barrel. She sat there for five minutes, afraid to move, her ear cocked for the sound of a running horse, the dogs, anything. Finally, one of the dogs came up to the window and whined. Carefully peeking out, Divinity saw one dog below the shattered pane, the other one curled up on the porch. She unbolted the lock on the plank door and called them in.

Even though Salt and Pepper had returned, Divinity wasn't about to leave the house and investigate. That would have meant lighting one of the lanterns, and her hands, still shaking, couldn't possibly have struck a match. Instead, she rushed back into the bedroom, locked the window, and grabbing her blankets, she curled up under the kitchen table with the two dogs beside her.

When dawn finally came, Divinity Jones quickly dressed and went to each of the windows, carefully peered out and saw nothing but a thin mist rising from the warm, sodden countryside. Whoever her unwelcome nighttime guest had been, he apparently had escaped. It wasn't until she unbolted the door and looked down toward the bottom that she noticed the strange gray horse, fully saddled, grazing along the marshy meadow with her own two horses. Shouldering the shotgun, Divinity took off at a trot, but the two dogs bounded away, far ahead of her, toward the rocky outcropping of the spring. When she came up behind them, they were both standing to the side of a dead man, growling, hackles fluffed up along the back of their necks. This was the stranger that she had seen on the gray horse. His whiskered face was half turned, one hand stretched out toward the water, the other crumpled under his breast. A portion of his neck had been blown away. In this shocking moment of horror, Divinity Jones made a decision: she was leaving Derby Flats as fast as she could.

Later in the day, she came riding into the Coombes Livestock headquarters, trailing her pack and the stranger's gray horse. Owen Hoover, along with his wife, Maybelle, came out and greeted her. Sitting on the big porch, she told them that she had found the horse along the trail just a few miles back, didn't know the where-abouts of the owner, but allowed that someone might come along to claim it.

"I surely don't want to be accused of horse thieving, so I thought I'd better leave it here. Maybe the owner will come along."

Hoover laughed. "My goodness, Miss Divinity, no one's gonna accuse you of rustling a horse. That's ridiculous. If the fellow just went up and left it out there, serves him right if he has to hoof it in here to claim it."

Ultimately, one of Hoover's men came up and led the gray away to one of the sheds.

During the following conversation, Hoover con-gratulated Divinity on her impending fortune, told her that the Coombes people had wanted the rail-road to come through their way, but it was thirty miles in the wrong direction. He thought that one of the company owners might be contacting her one of these days about the possibility of putting in pens and loading chutes along with a ware-house and caretaker's home at Derby Flats. Divin-ity thought this was an excellent idea, promptly let Owen Hoover see the piece of paper that Moon Tree had left behind, and he, too, was surprised that Divinity Jones had retained a lawyer. "Well, looks like you've done gone and thought of everything, Divinity," he said. "I suppose there's not much reason for staying out there all by your lonesome, not now, anyhow. Yep, be a long winter at that place all by yourself, not safe if you was to come down ailing, broke a leg, or something worse, God forbid."

Divinity Jones readily agreed, particularly with the "something worse." Her stomach was still upside down from dragging the stranger with her horse up into the dry coulees where she covered his body with sand and rocks. She had removed his gunbelt and revolver, saw no reason for burying them, too, and after taking up the belt a half-dozen notches, she now wore it around her own waist. If she chanced to catch up with her buddy, Moon Tree, she was going to have him show her that fancy trick he had used on the drover who was after her crotchie.

Owen Hoover then asked, "Where are you planning on wintering? Down south a piece?"

Divinity, standing tall and tucking her hat down over her hair, pointed north. "Going up to Dubois, I reckon, get me a job there."

"Is that a fact?" said Hoover. "Tough country come winter, pretty cold to be riding around those hills tending cattle."

"No riding, Mr. Hoover," she said. "Gonna have me a room in the hotel, learn how to be a fancy lady, I am."

Both Hoover and his wife gave Divinity an incredulous stare. A fancy lady! Maybelle's face flushed in embarrassment, and Owen Hoover finally sputtered, "Why, you can't do something like that, Divinity! Good Lord, your paw will turn over in his grave, you taking on doing something like that. Why, you'll have some big money coming in one of these days from the railroad. You don't want to be working in some cat house, girl, for heaven's sake!"

"Owen!" Maybelle whispered harshly, "watch what you're saying." And in a firm but kindly tone she said to Divinity, "What he means, my dear, is that it's not proper for a nice young woman to be selling her body in a . . . a brothel, if you please. Do you understand?"

"Why, land o'Goshen!" Divinity exclaimed, her pretty face in a deep blush. "I ain't . . . amn't meaning nothing like that, no, ma'am. It's Missus Grant's hotel and good eats place. She says I can work there, learn to be real ladylike. I'm sure not aiming to sell my—sell nothing, no, ma'am. Mr. Moon says I have to keep that secret."

Maybelle Hoover's hand came up to her mouth in a titter. "Oh, my gracious, girl, then you shouldn't be using the word 'fancy'. Fancy women are . . . well, they just are. They do those things for money, and we thought—"

"Begging your pardon, Miss Divinity," Owen Hoover wheezed. "Looks like we all got off on the wrong foot there. Ha-ha."

This embarrassing incident was shortly interrupted by one of the hired hands who came back to report that the mysterious gray horse belonged to one Charlie Pollard. The initials C.P. were burned into the saddle. This news brought Hoover out of his chair, hotly exclaiming, "What's that scoundrel doing back in these parts? Thought he cleaned country after the last trouble we had. That fellow doesn't have a brain in his head, doesn't know when to leave well enough alone."

"Who's this Charlie Pollard?" Divinity asked uneasily, wondering now if she really wanted to know. Some desperado with a passel of friends? Someone who had a partner in on the deal to roust her from the homestead?

"He's a damned ring-tailed rounder, a robber and a thief," Hoover exploded. "Maybe a killer, too, for all we know. Bounty hunter sometimes, I hear, but he filched the wages out of two of our herders last year. Hear tell he used to run with a rustling gang over in the Lemhi country. Bad customer. Pulled a gun on me when I threatened to fetch the marshall's men in here last year. Lucky I didn't get myself shot." Scratching his chin whiskers, Owen Hoover pondered for a moment. "Wonder what he's up to this time? By Gawd, I sure don't want him hanging around here." He told the hired hand to take a few men and ride down the trail to where Divinity Jones had found the horse. "If he's afoot, just take him out a ways and leave him for the coyotes. Good riddance."

Divinity Jones knew the man called Charlie Pollard wasn't afoot—he was about two or three "afoots" under rock and sand. She left her two dogs with the Hoovers and rode north.

EIGHT

Blanche Grant, her usual jovial self, was delighted to have Divinity Jones at the hotel, not so much for the extra help, but to put a little youth back in the old place. The stage-coach driver, Henry Billow, was pleased, too, and began to look forward to his long layovers at Dubois, usually three days, just so he could enjoy the exuberant conversation of Miss Divinity and take a few years off his age. And Divinity Jones, it proved, (and Moon Tree would have attested to this) was a quick learner. Once she was exposed to the companionship of friendly people, her grammar and manners improved by the day. Blanche Grant, most helpful along these lines, was accommodating in other ways, too. She had a trunkful of clothes, some that she had outgrown, other dresses she had never worn. Some of these were taken in and hemmed in the proper places, and Divinity soon had a splendid wardrobe—dresses, petticoats, and a gown made of satin, blue like the color of her eyes. Though her speech was still a problem, Divinity only rarely reverted to her old invectives. When something struck her as shitty, it was difficult not to describe it in such a way, because it just seemed appropriate for the occasion, but she restrained herself.

Henry Billow, in a great display of generosity, rode in one day on the stage en route to Virginia City. While the team was being changed and the passengers fed, he sneaked into the kitchen and dropped off a package. Divinity didn't discover it until long after Billow had gone, but she knew it was for her. There on the neatly wrapped paper of the box was her name, just as she always printed it: DIVINITY JONES. When she opened it, she discovered two wonderful pairs of high-button shoes, one pair shiny black, the other light tan. They were beautiful, elegant in style, with high heels and pointed toes, and they fit perfectly. How could Henry Billow know such a precise thing about a woman as the size of her foot? Blanche Grant, smiling, happy for Divinity, said that Henry had been watching women's legs for almost twenty years; he was a master at judging women, not only their feet but most everything else from the ankles on up; there wasn't much that he missed. When it came to women, he was an appreciative man. Blanche Grant said that he was treating Divinity like the daughter he never had. Henry Billow's wife and newborn daughter had both died in childbirth twenty-five years ago.

Two weeks after her return to the hotel, Henry

escorted the new Divinity Jones next door to Finney's Saloon. It was a Friday night, and on Friday and Saturday nights Sean O'Grady always came down from Armstead to play the piano and sing. A dozen or so drovers, ranchers, and even a few wives usually showed up to listen to Sean O'Grady. Of course, a poker game was always in progress, and the bar was never closed. Even so, it was an orderly crowd, with someone being ushered out for boisterous conduct only occasionally.

Divinity Jones, shining like a new pearl, sat entranced and watched O'Grady's fingers fly up and down the keyboard of the great piano. His beautiful Irish voice trilled away like a meadow lark's. My, he was a fine singer! Her sarasparilla sat untouched, she was so entranced. Sean O'Grady sang songs that she had never heard before, sometimes with funny-sounding words too foreign to understand, but no matter, it was simply grand. When he played melodies familiar to the crowd, a few people sang along with him, and afterward, everyone clapped loudly, several even jumping to their feet and performing little jigs. Since the people enjoyed this so much, Sean O'Grady played a few of the old frontier tunes, and suddenly Divinity Jones was raising her voice high, inspired, just like her maw used to do in the little church back in Missouri, standing up and praising the Lord.

Henry Billow's face lit up like a parlor lantern. "Good Lord, Miss Divinity," he exclaimed, "where'd you learn to sing like that? Who taught you all those words, anyways?"

Divinity Jones, flushed with excitement, took a hefty gulp of her sarasparilla. "My maw used to sing in church, and my paw was always singing away, 'specially when he was all boozed up." She suddenly sighed and wrinkled her nose distastefully. "That was most of the time, you know, the old sot. But I never knew songs could sound so good till I heard that fellow at the piano. He's one of those experts, I reckon. Makes a heap of difference, don't it?" Smoothing down the ruffles in her dress, she leaned close to Henry Billow as though she were imparting a great secret. "I knows some of these songs by heart," she whispered. "Can't read a lick, you know, but once I gets them up here in my little old head, they just sticks like glue. Ain't ... isn't that the cat's meow?"

Billow, his judgment of women unfaltering, knew Divinity was one of those natural song birds who never had been heard before. He was now entertaining a small idea, one he thought would surely please Miss Divinity, and the assembled people as well. It would be a memorable first night for her, and there wasn't any doubt in Billow's mind that she could carry it off. After all, Divinity Jones was a rarity, an unbridled young woman of few restraints. When Sean O'Grady stopped for a ten-minute break, Billow called him over. They were friends, and Billow introduced Divinity, who in her mannerly way said, "I'm sure obliged to meet you, Mr. O'Grady. Never heard such a singer in my born days." They talked and laughed for a while until finally Henry Billow said to O'Grady, "You know, this little woman here ain't too bad a singer herself. Knows a lot of them good ol' tunes. Why, I'll bet you two could sing up a storm harmonizing away together, if you were so obliged." He glanced at Divinity. "What'd you say to that, anyways?"

"Me?" Divinity asked, her breath coming up short. "Why, land o' Goshen, I never did anything like singing with a regular piano man before, just sang a few tunes riding along on that old sheep wagon." But she stirred excitedly in her chair and looked expectantly at Sean O'Grady.

O'Grady, giving her a sly wink, asked, "Know a few songs, do you? Know some of the standards? The kind these prairie people sing?" His voice had a burr in it, and he rattled off his questions with crispness of a snare drum. "Want to give it a go with me next round, lassie? I'll be inviting you up to share the good times, eh?"

Taken aback by such an astonishing invitation, almost outlandish, Divinity Jones nevertheless collected herself in a ladylike fashion and replied saucily, "You bet, Mr. O'Grady, I'll give it a try, if you're asking me so politely."

Henry Billow gave her arm a friendly pat. But he already knew that Divinity wasn't in any need of encouragement, just a gentle push in the right direction. She was fearless.

And much to the great pleasure of everyone, Sean O'Grady and Divinity Jones sang melodiously, as though they had sung together many times before. O'Grady carefully blended his lilting voice with the unflinching lead of Divinity, whose throaty variations ranged from a husky alto to soprano, often stunning the Irishman with her clarity and tone. When he ran an introductory riffle to "Put My Little Shoes Away," Divinity picked up on it, and he let her sing the sadness in solo, playing softly behind her. The people sat in silence, even at the poker table and the bar. When she finished, a few of the women hastily dabbed at their eyes, yet applauded with the vigor of the men. When Divinity Jones concluded with a stomping, growling rendition of "Buffalo Gal," the men went wild, and O'Grady leaped up from the piano and embraced Divinity, gave her a tremendous kiss, and like a gentleman, escorted her back to her table, where Henry Billow sat with big tears streaming down his leathery cheeks. This woman was a winner. Billow knew it, felt it in his old bones. She was better than Lily Langtry. She was as slick as corn silk, and had the untainted beauty of Venus. To say the least, Henry Billow was one proud man.

That was Friday night. Saturday morning after breakfast, Sean O'Grady went to the desk in the lobby and talked quietly with Blanche Grant. Of course, Blanche already had heard from at least a dozen people about the amazing Miss Divinity, a young lady who had put on such a great performance in Finney's Saloon. O'Grady wanted to do a little practicing this morning with Divinity, thought perhaps they could work up a bit of a routine for the Saturday night customers. Undoubtedly, it would be a bigger crowd once the word about a new singer began circulating. Blanche thought this was a great idea, said she could spare Miss Divinity for a few hours, for after all, the hotel wasn't as busy as the saloon. When Divinity heard this proposal from O'Grady, she thought this was one of those times when she could actually squeeze her tits and squeal. With a great surge of happiness, she went rushing back into the secrecy of the kitchen. Henry Billow, sitting with two of his friends near the window, heard one loud shriek from the back of the hotel. One of the men looked up curiously over his paper. "What the hell was that?" Billow shrugged, his mouth drooped at the corners. "Probably saw a mouse in the pantry."

As many men before him, Sean O'Grady had come west seeking the riches of gold and had suffered the rigors of the trail, the heat of the desert, and the unforgiving coldness of mountains. He was in his early thirties when he came over from Ireland. He was a Dublin lad, his father a musician, and he had come by the piano and several other instruments through family tutoring and inherent talent. He played in the New York taverns and spent several years in Boston. Ultimately, lured west, he earned his way across the broad and inhospitable land playing and singing, sometimes by himself, sometimes with fiddlers and pickers. After several years of grubbing around Alder Gulch, he made enough money to homestead in the upper Beaverhead Valley. He was now in his forties, going bald, and was forever trying to protect his fingers. He had accumulated nearly a hundred head of cattle, a few sheep, and a dozen good horses. When he wasn't chasing critters, he was playing piano, keeping ahead of the cruel game of ranching by entertaining in the small towns dotting the western half of the Montana Territory.

O'Grady's accidental discovery of Divinity Jones gave him a new perspective on life, at least he was envisioning grand thoughts that had absolutely nothing to do with pitching hay, shoveling manure, or fighting the freakish, contrary elements of an onerous land. His salvation was going to be Divinity Jones, if he only could entice her away from the security of Dubois into the exciting field of entertainment. He was aware of her imminent change in status, the fact that she would soon be a moderately wealthy woman. This concerned him. One thing Sean O'Grady knew was talent, and once endowed with wealth from her homestead sale, there was always the possibility that Divinity Jones might lose her incentive to become a singer. The present task, as he saw it, was to take this spirited young woman, introduce her to the world of music, and transform her into an artist. She was that good, well worth the time and effort to groom. So, taking another great gamble in his life, O'Grady went to his neighbor, Albert Whiteside, and offered to sell his small spread that adjoined the Whiteside ranch. All he asked was twelve thousand dollars, lock, stock, and barrel. Whiteside bargained for ten thousand, and Sean O'Grady sealed the sale with a shake of hands. God knows, he wasn't cut out to be a rancher in the first place. Light of heart, he kept two horses and a mule, packed up and headed down the trail for Dubois to take a room at Blanche Grant's hotel. This was a start in what he thought to be the best direction, right next to the room of Divinity Jones.

O'Grady's new residency at Grant's Hotel brought about another rejuvenation; Blanche Grant was happy to have a permanent lodger, one so prestigious; and William Finney, the saloon owner next door, his eye to the future as well, ordered three new sets of tables and chairs. But the happiest soul of all was Divinity Jones who, after hearing Sean O'Grady's proposal to tutor her daily in musical presentation, once again retired to the kitchen and shrieked.

The duo of O'Grady and Jones began rehearsals this same night, next door in Finney's Saloon, and people from around the area gathered to watch, listen, and applaud. For several hours each afternoon, O'Grady and Divinity Jones sat together in the hotel lobby, where the Irishman, strumming on his guitar, taught her new songs, and polished up the old ones.

One day about three weeks after O'Grady's arrival in Dubois, two packages arrived on the stage, one addressed to Divinity Jones, the other to Sean O'Grady. Miss Divinity's package was rather large and cumbersome, heavily wrapped, and it had come from Salt Lake City. Sean O'Grady and Henry Billow joined her as she excitedly tore away the paper and opened the box. Inside was an angular case with bright metal fasteners, and when Divinity unsnapped these small locks and lifted the lid, her name leaped out in front of her in shining gold letters. Emblazoned on the new guitar were the words: DIVINITY JONES. She was speechless, her blue eyes wide and unblinking, her breath short. Henry Billow, one always appreciative of beauty, fleshly or otherwise, exclaimed, "Why, that's one of the prettiest gee-tars I've ever seen." He looked at Divinity, whose hands were folded prayerlike at her breast. "Miss Divinity, you think you can play that sucker?"

Sean O'Grady lifted the guitar from its case and placed it in Divinity's hands. "Aye, she'll be playing it in a fortnight, strumming away like it came in her cradle. The lass has good fingers and an ear for music. Don't worry, Henry, you just watch her."

Divinity gave O'Grady a kiss on the cheek. "It's

the best present I ever had, Mr. O'Grady." She started to kiss him again.

"Tut, tut," O'Grady cautioned, backing away. "Kissing's no part of the act, m'dearie. It's the playing of the instrument you be giving the affection, not me. We'll be starting on this in the morn, and I'll show you every step of the way."

He then tore away the covering on the second package, a flat, square box, about the width of a buckboard seat. Blanche Grant, hearing all the excitement, came out from the hall, gasping in surprise when she saw Miss Divinity caressing her new guitar.

O'Grady held up his hands, saying, "All right, now, turn around, all of you, and be looking the other way." With a flourish, he removed one of the large placards, whirled around gracefully, and ordered his friends to give him an opinion. They turned and faced him. And there it was, in bold letters surrounded by ornate scroll work: *For your pleasure, the music and songs of O'GRADY AND JONES. Appearing here nightly.*" "What do you think?" he asked proudly.

Blanche Grant and Henry Billow applauded. "An eye-catcher if ever I saw one," said Billow, throwing an arm around Divinity.

Even though she could not read it, Divinity thought it was a good sign, better-looking than "Good Eats" in the hotel window.

"A modest beginning," Sean O'Grady said with a smile, envisioning triumphs ahead.

NINE

Just the trace of a smile crossed Moon Tree's face. He was seated with his brother, Benjamin, at Claybourn Moore's big table reading a small clipping from the *Montana Post,* the weekly newspaper published in Virginia City. He had just returned from his journey south with Divinity Jones. The item Moore had snipped from the paper reported that Moon and Benjamin Tree, sons of the prominent rancher Ben Tree, had recently visited the area, herding a large band of sheep to the Idaho Territory. The sheep, it stated, belonged to Governor Crosby, and were being herded by Tree ranchhands, later to be sold to a large livestock company in Utah. Originating point of the sheep was unknown; however, everyone in Virginia City expressed surprise and some dismay that Governor Crosby had such a large investment in sheep. Was this a portent of the future for the territory?

Moon, his face masked in innocence, scratched his head and shoved the clipping away. He commented dryly, "Strange, isn't it, how people get things all twisted around this way."

"Not so strange to me," his brother quickly replied. "No, knowing the source, it's not so strange. But how did you get me mixed up in this? I haven't been ten miles from here in over two months—haying, branding, breaking ponies, putting up the new wire—while you're riding all over the country with some wild woman telling your tall tales again."

Claybourn Moore came over with a cup of coffee and sat down across from the two brothers. "Well," he said to Moon, "since you said nothing important happened on the trip, we were wondering if you might have missed something, maybe just forgot, like this little news item. How about Dupee Clancy? Any word down that way on him, where he can be holing up?"

Moon shook his head. "Nothing. I didn't hear a word about that bastard." Then he grinned a bit crookedly. "There was a little misunderstanding, come to think of it. These two drovers, fellows from Chambers' spread, ei, that probably explains this bad story. They came in one day on the Ruby and started acting up, wanting me to move the sheep out. Got Miss Divinity plenty riled." He stopped, idly traced the pattern on the oilcloth table cover. "Humph, they came in on Miss Divinity unexpected, and she thought they were after her 'crotchie,' as she calls it. Had me a real ruckus going, I tell you, before it was over."

Moore threw back his head and laughed heartily. "I'll be damned, that woman! It's a wonder she didn't scare the shit out of them, had them running the other way. Whatever gave her such a notion?"

"Well," asked Benjamin curiously, "were they?"

"Were they what?" Moon said somberly.

"Were they after her watchie?" Benjamin sputtered with exasperation.

"Crotchie," Moon corrected.

"Whatever, damn it," his brother said. "What happened?"

White Moon shrugged again, this time nonchalantly. "I told them to get out before I got plenty mad."

"Oh, hell," Moore moaned. "You didn't go bluffing them, did you? The last thing I told you was to be careful, watch what you were doing. That's a damned good way to get a hole in you, for sure, standing up to two drovers you didn't even know. Why didn't you just move the stinking sheep and get off their range?"

"No bluff," White Moon said. "Had some fresh chicken to eat, and I was plenty hungry. Too late in the day to be moving again, so I just showed them one of my father's tricks." He smiled at Benjamin. "You know"—and he snapped his hand up quickly from his hip—"pow! Sort of impressed them, anyway. I told them you were over the hill doing some scouting. They sure knew who you were. Well, one thing and another, the first thing

I know, the sheep belonged to old man Crosby. They left, rode off, plenty peaceful, too."

"And then they went back and told this to Tom Chambers," Claybourn Moore said, "and he—"

"Ei," interrupted Moon, "and he must have been talking to the fellow at the *Post*. Bad medicine, these rumors, wagging tongues."

"Bad medicine, all right," Moore said. "This gets back to Crosby, he'll roar like a banshee, him being the governor of the biggest cow territory in the West, catering to a band of sheep. Lord, Lord. Damn it, Moon, couldn't you come up with a better one than that?"

White Moon said, "Now, that's something I can see a little humor in, Mr. Clay. I thought it was a good joke, plenty good. Does Crosby know my father?"

"Everyone knows Mr. Tree."

In triumph, White Moon proudly stated, "Ah-hah, then that's one less lie. I told those two old boys he was a good friend of the governor."

Benjamin One Feather, with a consoling sigh, put his arm around White Moon. "Brother, we've traveled many trails together, from the Yellowstone to the Greasy Grass. All of our brothers know you. The troopers know you. One of these days everyone is going to know you. *Eeyah*, the biggest liar in the territory."

White Moon, in return, gave his brother an affectionate pat on the arm. "Something else I forgot. There was one other thing down there, plenty crazy, I tell you, hard to believe. I saw that soldier who put the stitches in your shoulder that time. Aubrey, ei? Very crazy meeting him way out in the desert. He's surveying for the railroad, making marks for the rails to come up this way. He asked about you, how you healed up, and I told him you went lame, only one good arm now. He didn't believe me."

"I can understand why." Benjamin smiled.

"Railroad?" Moore suddenly perked up, set his cup down and looked sharply at Moon Tree. This was some good news that he was finally hearing, and now for the first time more than just a rumor. "This surveyor," he anxiously asked, "did he say where the railroad was coming through? When's this supposed to happen?"

"It's coming over the hill," Moon answered. "The Beaverhead, and on to Butte, maybe Helena. Aubrey showed me his maps, plenty work left, maybe a year of making his marks, then laying tracks. A long time, ei?"

"That's good news, Moon, good news. They're finally starting to roll. By damn, we'll be able to get beef out of here in three directions in another year. Move to the south, east, and west, no more long drives. If your pa gets that yard and plant deal on the Yellowstone settled, we'll be riding high in the saddle around here." He suddenly stopped and frowned at Moon, and went off in another direction. "Why didn't you tell us this when you rode in? Damn it, this is going to change the whole cattle operation in these parts. It'll be big news. It's what everyone's been waiting for, and you just let it sit in your saddle?"

Lowering his voice to a whisper, Moon said, "Well, it's supposed to be kind of a secret. Aubrey says those maps aren't for the public to know yet. Some of those marks go through deeded land, plenty of problems, he says, maybe some changes, ei?"

"Legalities," said Moore sourly, facing reality. "Yep, I understand that much of it. We've had our share of them, too. Start pushing too hard and someone's likely to buck like a mule. Guess we'll have to take this as it comes, be a little patient, not expect too much too soon."

White Moon was thinking about Divinity Jones, the paper he had brought back from Derby Flats, the deed to the homestead. For safekeeping it was now in his hands, at least temporarily, until he could get up to Helena and turn it over to Arthur Clawson. He had stopped by Virginia City on his way home to see Clawson, but the lawyer had already moved his office to Helena. The stopover, however, hadn't been a lost cause. He had checked into a hotel, played poker until very late, and won almost two hundred dollars.

White Moon finally told Moore and Benjamin that Divinity Jones's broken-down homestead, in the middle of nowhere, was marked on one of Aubrey's maps, designated as a station stop. Apparently, she was going to be a wealthy young woman within a year. In fact, he had Burleigh Jones's deed tucked away in his pack over in the bunkhouse. Astounded, the two men both came up in their chairs, and Moore exclaimed, "She gave you her homestead paper? Good Lord, why did she go and do a thing like that? She's crazier than I thought she was, by damn. Does she know what she's done? If the railroad men come through there, she'll need that deed. She can't prove claim to that land without it. Why, they'll run her over like a grasshopper."

Moon's face wrinkled doubtfully. He folded his arms like a patriarch, and his heavy lids lazily fluttered once. "Maybe not so crazy as you think," he said calmly. "That spring she has is a regular gusher, almost as much water as up at the hot springs. It's the only water in that valley, ei? I checked on this. Plenty good, I say to myself. She knows this, too. She can't read or write, but she's plenty smart in her head. I told her I can take the deed and give it to Mr. Clawson, let the railroad deal with him on her behalf. She won't get cheated, maybe makes herself plenty of money. So, pow, just like that, she gave me the paper and one big kiss, too. She says she's going to be a lady, calls me her old buddy now."

Claybourn Moore took a deep breath, one of relief and gratification. A big smile slowly spread across his face, and he said, "Well, I'll be damned, if that's not taking the bull by the horns. Moon, you rascal, I shouldn't be surprised, but I have to hand it to you. Had old Lady Luck with you, for sure. You played a pat hand, by damn if you didn't, looking out for that girl the way you did. Congratulations."

"Ei," Moon smiled, a gleam in his dark eyes. "We have a stacked deck on this one, Mr. Clay, all the high cards and no joker, either." He stretched and flexed his fingers with great satisfaction.

Benjamin One Feather was proud of his brother, too, but a little less charitable. "Perhaps, my brother, there is a joker here, one you don't realize," he put in. "That woman is likely to be around your neck forever now. You just may have put your neck right into her noose. Ei, you're right, she's plenty smart. Esaccawata, the Trickster is holding your hand, Brother. If you smell his breath, you're a goner."

TEN

Sad Sam Courtland, a lanky, suave, and unsmiling gentlemen of white shirts and black string ties, learned his calling in Biloxi, Mississippi, later moved up and down the Big Muddy from St. Louis to New Orleans. After losing his credibility in a high-stakes game on the *Delta Queen* (he had leaped overboard to avoid being shot), he emmigrated to the gold fields of the West, where the pickings were less hazardous. He was forty years old, and he considered Moon Tree the Red Man, who was only twenty-six, his protégé. This relationship had its beginning at the Antler Saloon, a watering hole in Bozeman, where Moon first became fascinated, soon addicted, to the challenging game of stud poker. More often in those early days, Moon Tree went back to the ranch at night with empty pockets. He was a learner, and he banked his fortunes solely on luck. Nevertheless, Sad Sam, who frequently tapped Moon during these games, recognized the latent ability in Moon. Not only this, Sad Sam saw some

of himself in the younger breed son of Ben Tree.
Moon's calm, emotionless demeanor, win or lose,
his nonchalance and calculating style of play, were
a reflection of Sad Sam himself. So, ultimately,
they went off together on the stage to Helena for
a training session: Sad Sam Courtland played in a
few saloons along Last Chance Gulch, and Moon
Tree quietly observed. Another trip was made to
Butte, then on to Deer Lodge, same routine,
young Moon the observer, Sad Sam the player.
Each night back at the hotel, all of the evening's
play was recounted. What amazed Sad Sam was
Moon's uncanny perception and analysis of poker,
particularly when the young pupil had barely cut
his teeth on the game. Red Man had the makings
of a fine card player—he was disinclined to outright gamble—and this greatly pleased Sad Sam.
Together, they made a fine team, aware of each
other's abilities, helped on occasion by the blink
of an eye, a furrowed brow, or the casual rub of
the jaw. When the cards were coming their way, it
was usually a rough night for the rest of the table.
Theirs was a discreet relationship. While they occasionally appeared together in a high-stakes
game, they seldom associated with each other outside of the card room, usually stayed at different
hotels, only occasionally shared wine at the bar or
a meal in a cafe. Only a few of the professionals
knew they were friends, not that they were actually playing partners.

Several days after Moon's return to the ranch,

young Henry Blodgett, who spent three days a week on the property doing blacksmith work, came in with a note for Moon Tree. It was rather cryptic, simply stating that "something is on the fire in Helena. One week." That was the extent of it, but without too much imagination, Moon deduced that a stakes game was going down— something less than routine—and fortunately for him, at an opportune time. Claybourn Moore already had told him to get up to Helena with Divinity Jones's deed and put it in the capable hands of Arthur Clawson.

For the next few days little else but poker was on Moon's mind, but with Zachary Hockett and Willie Left Hand, he worked on the upper range, stringing the new barbed wire. Posts were brought up daily in one of the hay wagons, usually by James Goodhart and Little Blue Hoop, who most often stopped at the line cabin with Melody to visit Shell and Joseph. The wire now enclosed almost one-half of the deeded land, a great expanse of range and adjacent timber, including two creeks and several ponds. Two gates had been placed at the boundary of the unceded south range for use in the spring and summer when the drovers took the cows and calves up to the mountain meadows. Down below, Benjamin, Robert Peete, and Peter Marshall were finishing the new horse enclosure in back of the corrals, a hundred acres of bottom land, now fully fenced and much of it in view from Benjamin's new house. After the summer disaster with Dupee Clancy's gang, Clay Moore had decided on this preventitive measure. Good trail horses selling for up to a hundred dollars a head or more were too susceptible to depredations on unprotected range, a lesson already learned by Adam Stuart. Stuart had been one of the more fortunate ranchers: his colts and mares were recovered. However, Clancy and one of the other rustlers, Arvis James, had not been seen since the raid and subsequent fight over on the Madison. Wanted posters on the two men were now up throughout the western part of the territory, but Sheriff Bill Duggan, in a conversation with Clay Moore, said that the killers of Burleigh Jones probably were now lying low somewhere in the Idaho country. Gabe Arbuckle, the only man apprehended, already had been sent to the territorial prison at Deer Lodge for twenty years. His information on the other gang members spared him from the gallows.

Molly Goodhart, true to her promise, started baking the first of the pies for White Moon, his reward for escorting Divinity Jones back to Derby Flats. But to the chagrin of the bunkhouse crew, he didn't share his treat. He ate half of the first pie in their very presence, complimenting Molly several times on how tasty it was, and he took the remaining half over to James Goodhart's house for his niece, Melody, the other buddy of Divinity Jones. Later this same night, White Moon had his meeting in Bozeman with Sad Sam Courtland at the Antler Saloon. Two days later, with the homestead deed in his coat pocket, and five hundred dollars in his money belt, he boarded the stage for Helena. As his brother, Benjamin, had suggested, Moon Tree was not going to meet Governor Crosby.

White Moon arrived at Arthur Clawson's office shortly before the green shade was pulled, and of course the lawyer wasn't surprised to hear about the railroad's plans to move north into the territory. What did surprise him was Moon's knowledge of a future station at Derby Flats. Was this a certainty? Moon assured him that it was, but declined to go into details, simply handed over the deed and told Clawson that sooner or later the railroad agents would contact his law firm in Helena. He explained that he had left Arthur Clawson's name with Divinity Jones, whom he identified as a plenty poor white woman without a penny to her name. Clawson, an expert on land titles and water rights, scrawled out a voucher for the paper, dated it, and both he and White Moon signed it. This much done, Clawson said he would negotiate only on the water rights and a right-of-way, this entailing only a few acres of land. If Derby Flats suddenly mushroomed into a commercial enterprise or major freight depot, Divinity Jones would control all of the surrounding acreage, a real estate matter that he could deal with later, much to her profit, and his as well. When they had concluded the matter to Moon's satisfaction, Arthur Clawson suggested a drink and perhaps dinner at the New Placer Hotel. Moon had to decline this invitation, explaining that he already had a friend waiting, coincidentally, at the same hotel. His plans for the night, he was sorry to say, were made, and with a small smile, he flexed his fingers several times, this gesture understood by Arthur Clawson, who nodded knowingly when Moon added, "Room twelve, fresh deck every half hour." Clawson was welcome to watch the action if he wanted to drop by. They parted with a handshake.

After a two-hour nap, White Moon dressed in his dark suit and white shirt, dusted off his wide-brimmed hat, and went to the dining room for a light meal. At precisely eight o'clock, he entered room twelve to face the opposition. Several men were already seated at the table, and at least a dozen more were standing around talking, some holding glasses of liquor and smoking cigars. A waiter nearby promptly came to take Moon's order, but he gestured negatively. This was another Sad Sam Courtland rule: never drink anything but water or sarsaparilla when the cards are in front of you. Whiskey, Courtland said, affects the mind, makes a man careless, and boozers are foolish poker players, frequently obnoxious, too.

Until Sad Sam made his entrance, there wasn't a familiar face in the crowd, and when a few introductions were made, Moon Tree only recognized one of the names, that of Joseph Ellard, known around the circuit as Poker Joe. He was a rather stout fellow, probably in his fifties, who wore a brown suit, a gold chain across the front of his vest, and had a small goatee somewhat like Sad Sam's. His thinning hair was swept to one side in front and hung loosely over the side like a wind-blown pony tail. Rather jovial, he spoke excellent English, and for the most part, Moon Tree wisely listened and offered minimal comment in return. The rest of those assembled seemed to be business sorts, men whose soft hands and fingers adorned with gold bands marked them as escapees from the family parlor. Five of these fellows sat in the game, along with Ellard, Sad Sam, and Moon Tree, and they all knew Moon, not from his mild reputation as a poker player, but from the not-so-mild yarns about his family. The deal was rotation, the game, five-card stud, the sit-in, five hundred dollars, a gentleman's game, table stakes. The chips were distributed at values of twenty, ten and five, and one of the wealthy businessmen, Charles Wilder, was high man with a king on the draw, so he began the deal.

By ten o'clock, Wilder and a Mr. Finch, a hardware-store owner, had tapped out, and neither elected to buy in for another five hundred dollars. They took their drinks and joined the onlookers in the back of the room. Moon Tree, who had started slowly, drawing nothing but unplayable cards, improved steadily during the second hour. He never counted chips, another one of Sad Sam's rules, because it often indicated a sense of insecurity. But Moon figured he was ahead of the game by at least three hundred dollars. Sad Sam was holding his own, and Poker Joe had doubled his original stake. With only six playing, Moon Tree had to sharpen his wits and use a little intuition to keep track of the cards and changing percentages. He soon spotted a few idiosyncracies in several of the players, revealing expressions, nervousness, the constant examination of a hole card as though it might mysteriously change on a second or third peek, the occasional sigh, and the hurried raise. And Poker Joe Ellard, Moon discovered, had a bad habit. Without exception, every time his hand improved he compressed his lips and nodded his head like a stringed puppet. When he had doubts, either about his own strength or that of another hand on the table, his face revealed nothing. Moon wondered if Sad Sam had picked up on this. Probably not, or he would have mentioned it, as Sam had played with Poker Joe on several occasions.

Toward midnight, someone placed a glass of water to the side of Moon. He glanced up to thank the person and saw Arthur Clawson's face smiling at him through the thin haze of cigar smoke. Nodding, Moon took several sips, then turned back to the play. At least he had two friends in the room, one pseudo-competitor and one observer, a wise man who knew the law. Shortly, playing a buried ace with a king high,

Moon was dealt a heart flush on the fifth card. He immediately ran headlong into Poker Joe, who had a pair of tens showing, obviously backed with another buried one. Ellard, high with his tens, wisely checked to the possible flush, only to get a niggardly fifty-dollar bet from the Red Man. Poker Joe's lips compressed and his head bobbed slightly, indicating his confidence. The Red Man, he presumed, was trying to buy a five-hundred-dollar pot with fifty. Poker Joe knew he had a winner, so he met Moon's fifty, and jumped it another hundred. Moon, surprised that he had Ellard trapped, promptly called and raised back another hundred. Poker Joe's face went slack. He realized now that the Red Man wasn't bluffing, but he was in too far to back out, so rather than fold, he called the last one hundred dollars. With a tight smile, Poker Joe watched Moon Tree turn over his buried ace of hearts, heart flush. This wasn't science, simply the luck of the draw, and Moon knew it. So did Sad Sam, who gave White Moon a dark look and then stared at the ceiling in quiet dismay. If Sad Sam could have spoken to his young friend, he would have said in his slow southern drawl, "You lucky red scamp." And Moon wanted to say, "I never bluff." But this was a gentleman's game and he certainly wasn't lacking in knowing protocol. There was more than five hundred dollars in the pot, and after raking in the chips, Moon calmly took a sip of his water, then casually stacked them.

Three hands later, it was Sad Sam's turn to duel Poker Joe Ellard, but this time the quiet southerner had some unexpected help from his partner, the Red Man. Poker Joe was playing two kings up against two nines in front of Sad Sam. One of the other men folding had been dealt a king on the second go-around, the other remaining king had been White Moon's hole card, and he, too, had packed in when Poker Joe paired. Only Moon Tree knew that all of the kings were out of the deck, two of them in the discards. When Ellard finally shoved out three hundred on his two kings up to back off Sad Sam, Moon simply edged his chair back a notch and stared dead ahead. His lids closed lazily once, twice, but in that fraction of a second, Sad Sam's casual glance had caught the slow, fluttering signal. Poker Joe didn't have a third king, that was the subtle message; there were two of the big crowns in the discards, so Sad Sam, taking this visual cue, called and raised another three hundred. This time, however, Poker Joe wisely called and flipped over his cards. He knew Sam Courtland too well, and he wasn't about to lay out another three hundred dollars to see a lousy third nine spot in the hole.

The game finally broke up at one o'clock in the morning. Poker Joe Ellard wasn't a loser, but he wasn't much of a winner, either. The five businessmen, all enjoying themselves, were well on their way to getting drunk, and Sad Sam and the Red Man had a little over three thousand dollars to divide when they had a few minutes alone. Arthur Clawson, talking with Moon over a cup of coffee, had an observation. "That fellow Courtland over there plays a mean game of poker. For a while I was afraid you were going to bump heads with him, thought I might have to bail you out."

Moon Tree, with a small smile, thanked him for this kind consideration.

ELEVEN

In late September, the windmill and big wooden water tank went into operation, bringing fresh well water into the homes of James Goodhart and Claybourn Moore. This innovation was cause for celebration, and a small group of friends and neighbors came over to the Tree ranch to feast and dance. Owner Ben Tree and his Nez Perce wife, Rainbow, arrived from their Stillwater Mountain home to stay in the guest room at Young Benjamin and White Crane's home. However, Ben Tree was here for another reason besides the windmill inaugural; he was going to finalize plans for the stockyard and packing plant in the Yellowstone Valley to be built at a point adjacent to the Crow reservation. This location was upriver from the two old Goodhart homesteads, and the small town now springing up along the new train line there was being called Billings. It was in Ben Tree's mind to ask Claybourn Moore to supervise the construction of the yards the following spring, eventually to take over management of the entire shipping and packing operation, this a handsome promotion for the foreman who first appeared at the Tree Six Mile homestead twelve years ago looking for work. At that time, there was only a one-room cabin, a shed, and a small corral where an enterprising young breed woman by the name of Bird Rutledge had operated a horse business, breaking, selling, and trading stock for the gold miners. In those days, only several hundred head of cattle were on the open range, some of the original stock brought in by Nelson Story and a few owned by Adam Stuart, who was just beginning his operation. In the ensuing years, the Tree ranch branched out like its namesake, astutely managed by Clay Moore and backed by the money of Ben Tree. Moore now had excellent credentials, and he was the man Ben Tree wanted for his newest enterprise on the Yellowstone.

By late afternoon, about twenty people were on hand, among them the Stuart family from across the valley. Adam and Ellie Stuart were interested in the operation of the wind machine, since the well drillers from Denver had recently moved over to the Stuart property to put in two systems, one for the house, the other for a supplementary water supply for livestock. Ed Stuart was along to enjoy the festivities and companionship of the Tree ranch cowboys, and Jessie, of course, was in attendance primarily to see Moon Tree, part-time drover, card player, and of late, sheepherder, the latter occupation still being belabored in amusing conversations. New sheep jokes were invented daily by the men in retaliation for Moon's continuing refusal to let them share in his weekly fresh-baked pie from Molly Goodhart. Moon, the victimized cowboy, had converted the short straw of defeat into a minor victory. And the stories about Divinity Jones were constantly embellished, particularly after White Moon's revelations about the journey south and subsequent developments regarding the railroad station at Derby Flats. This past week Moon had received a post on the Oliver Stage Line from Blanche Grant at Dubois, a letter dictated by Divinity Jones, advising Moon of her new home, explaining that she was too frightened to stay at Derby Flats by herself, consequently had moved to the Grant Hotel. Would he kindly inform Mr. Clawson?

This was somewhat of a surprise to White Moon, how anyone could be frightened at Derby Flats, such a forlorn spot in the desert, a place only stumbled upon by sheer accident most of the time.

Moon was pleased that the little woman had found sanctuary with Blanche Grant. When Divinity mentioned in the letter that she was learning to play the guitar, and Moon related this to Willie Left Hand, suggesting maybe they could play at some dance in the future, the Salish breed fiddler grinned through his cracked teeth. This was an absurdity. The woman didn't even know how to talk straight, let alone take up a musical instrument.

The mere memory of Divinity Jones aroused something more than mundane interest in Jessie Stuart, especially when White Crane told her how pretty the woman was after they had attended to some of the necessities—a bath, new clothes, and a hair-do. And the fact that Moon had been on the trail with Divinity Jones for almost a *month* made Jessie jealous. For she would have run barefoot through an acre of hen hockey if she could have spent a month alone with Moon Tree.

Moon Tree had a peculiar habit, at least in the eyes of some of the neighbors, but after his many years in Absaroke villages, it came naturally. He enjoyed sitting cross-legged on a blanket, or in this instance, the great grizzly rug in James and Little Blue's home where dinner was underway. This was where Jessie Stuart and Melody Goodhart joined Moon, the three of them in a small circle, their plates in front of them. Moon said in his usual droll way, "Your mother might take exception to you sitting like an Injun when there's a chair around, ei?"

"Not at all," Jessie replied, forking up a bit of beef. "Mother will come around. I think she changed her mind about you a bit when you brought our horses back. You have some hot iron in you like your father." She gave him a pert smile, ate one bite, chewed quickly, and asked provocatively, "Do you?"

"We're all chips off the old block," White Moon answered matter-of-factly. "We just take different trails sometimes. Plenty hard to live in the shadow of a man like my father. I never had his visions, never had to suffer the injustices he did, either. Maybe my iron is cooler, ei. I don't have to prove anything to anyone, so I don't get too excited or much care what people think of me."

"I've never seen you excited, period," Jessie said, entertaining some devious thoughts of how she would like to excite him. "Tell me," she said, "how did you fare with the poor little sheepherder girl? Did she manage to excite you? Miss Benjamin says she was pretty darned cute when she left here. Now, don't tell me you didn't notice."

Moon shrugged casually. He had absolutely nothing to admit one way or another. Had he mentioned that Divinity Jones occasionally leaped around bare-ass naked at night, well, that wouldn't have come under the heading of indifference, only to someone like Miss Divinity. She certainly thought nothing of it. Moon effectively evaded Jessie's question with another casual reply. "The damned woolies kept me plenty busy. You call that excitement? Sheep? *Eeeyah,* that's about as exciting as playing a pair of dueces against aces. I got roped into that herding job. Bad luck on the draw, plenty bad luck." He deftly stole a piece of chicken from Melody's plate when she was looking the other way. "Do you know," he continued, "that little woman is going to have plenty of money one of these days, maybe a fine catch when she learns some manners. Right now, she's worse than an Injun." He grinned at Jessie teasingly and chomped down on the stolen chicken leg in mock savagery.

"And did you teach her anything, or was it the other way around?" asked Jessie, her brow arched inquisitively.

"Not much luck either way." White Moon smiled. "Maybe she'll have better luck in Dubois around more people. Some good friends there."

"Dubois?" asked Jessie, surprised. "What on earth is she doing there?"

"Learning to play the guitar. Plunk, plunk."

"Oh, good Lord, Moon, are you ever serious? What a joke."

Melody chimed in. "He plays jokes all the time, Miss Jessie. That's what Mama says. Uncle Moon is like Old Man Coyote. You better watch out or he'll play one on you one of these days."

"Tut, tut," Moon warned, waving his chicken bone. Turning back to Jessie, he went on, "Miss Divinity's working for the Grant woman, an old friend of my father's. She has a small hotel and dining room. Miss Divinity couldn't stand that Derby Flats, anymore, being all alone."

"Ah," surmised Jessie, "and you just helped her get a job, feeling all obligated and such. . . ."

"Nope, never gave it a thought," answered Moon nonchalantly. "People there seemed to take a shine to her. Her father getting killed, maybe they felt just downright sorry."

"Yes, I see," Jessie said with a small touch of sarcasm. And she believed that she was seeing some light in what had been a fuzzy, confusing picture. Knowing a little about the inclinations of men, she wasn't convinced that Moon was as innocent as he let on. If the truth were known, he probably rode her like a stud every night all the way to the Idaho Territory, and that brazenly bizarre thought sent a small rush of sensual anxiety through her. Men!

Directly, she got up and went to the kitchen, and when she returned with two cups of coffee, her father was hunkered down beside Moon discussing, of all things, a new Appaloosa horse he had just purchased for future stud use! More coincidental, the fine two-year-old prospect had come from the Nez Perce.

"Problem is," Adam Stuart was saying to Moon, "no one can get close to the infernal beast now. Like to break him to saddle, too, use him next year with my brood mares, build up the line a bit."

Moon Tree set aside his plate and thanked Jessie for the coffee she had handed him. Looking over at Adam Stuart, he said, "Well, if you can't get near him how'd you ever bring this Appaloosa in? How'd you manage the trick?"

"Had to buy his old lady," said Stuart. "Got me a seven-year-old mare I didn't even want. The horse follows her. Trailed all the way from the Bitterroot, he's right behind her all the way. Neither one of them understands a lick of English. Injun ponies true blue. Spent two days this week trying to keep a saddle on the critter, and now every time he sees one of the boys coming, he rears up like a goddamned lion and bares his teeth, takes right after them. Sure beats the hell out of me, it does. Hell, I don't want to hogtie him, break his spirit, or bust a leg. Get that devil gentled down and he's worth more than a thousand dollars."

"Good lines?" asked White Moon.

"Handsome horse every bit of the way," opined Stuart. "Paid eight hundred for him, two hundred for the mare. Fine stock, both of them. Yep, a handsome young stud he'll make, but we can't even get close to him."

Jessie, a sly smile on her pretty face, said, "Sort of like Mr. Moon, isn't he?"

Ben Tree, sitting on the fireplace hearth listening to Stuart's complaint, said to his son, "Why don't you go on over and look at the horse? Give Mr. Stuart some advice on this Nez Perce pony. Looks like he's bit off more than he can chew, and he's asking for some help."

"That's it," Stuart agreed quickly. "I need some help."

Ben Tree nodded approvingly at his son. "Well, I hear Moon is a fine poker player. That's his choosing, and I won't be interfering with any man's calling, but long before he ever saw a deck of cards, he was breaking ponies. He's the head

174

man in our family in that department. Only one person I ever knew was any better, and that was a young woman, Bird Rutledge, who used to break ponies right here where we're sitting."

Stuart said reminiscently. "The Bird woman. I remember. Bought three horses off her. She was a fair trader."

Jessie Stuart was looking at Moon Tree admiringly, expectantly, waiting for him to say yes or no. Ultimately, he gave Adam Stuart an affirmative nod, no more, and Jessie's hopes went soaring. Smiling happily, she said to Ben Tree, "Would you like for me to get you a cup of coffee, Mr. Tree? "

White Moon, his bedroll and a small sack of carrots behind his saddle, showed up at Stuart's ranch early the next afternoon. Ed Stuart greeted him, but Jessie was anxiously watching from the kitchen window. First business first, Moon dropped off his bedroll in the bunkhouse, unsaddled his pony, and returned to the house with Ed for a bite to eat. After some conversation with Ellie Stuart and a pensive Jessie, Moon and Ed went to one of the back sheds where the Appaloosa stud and the brood mare were corraled. Without equivocation Moon agreed with the elder Stuart's appraisal—this was a remarkably fine-looking horse, well-proportioned, sleek, good knees, and very alert. It was light gray with black spots on its rump, a few scattered across its flanks. "Mr. Stuart picked himself a good one," Moon said.

"A good mean one," Ed replied, shaking his head disgustedly. "Threw two of us the first go-around, rolled the saddle. All's left is that halter, and damned if anyone wants to take hold of it. Pa doesn't want him manhandled, no rope-and-post shit. He don't want him half-drowned in the river, either, breaking 'em like you boys used to do."

Moon Tree chuckled and carefully stepped inside the corral. "What you calling this boy?" he asked.

"Jediah," Ed said. "Leastways, that's what Pa calls him. Jediah."

"Jediah!" exclaimed White Moon with a scowl. "*Eeyah*, no wonder he's ornery. This is a Nez Perce pony, Ed, from the land of my mother. I fought for the Nez Perce in the Big Hole. Benjamin fought for them in the Bear Paws against the *piuap-siaunat*. This was an honor, but my life as I stand here, I can't work an Injun pony called Jediah."

"Well, call him any name you want. He's a son of a bitch. Call him that. He won't know the difference. Can't understand our lingo anyhow. Look at him watching you. He's ready to chase you outta there right now, Moon, so you better watch your ass."

"Ei, I see him," said Moon, checking the distance to the nearest poles. "He has the eyes of a hawk. Hawkeye, old Hawkeye, ei. That's your new name, you son of a bitch, and you better be plenty good or you get nothing to eat." Turning to Ed Stuart, Moon shouted, "We have to get that mare out of here, turn her out someplace far away from here. This is the first thing we do, Hawkeye, get rid of your mother. You can't be a big baby the rest of your damned life. No, sir, you have to grow up and you might as well start now."

When Ed Stuart ran to the other end of the corral and opened the gate, White Moon shagged the mare and quickly stepped in flagging his arms at the young horse. Hawkeye, nervously prancing, listed his upper lip and whinnied in disapproval. White Moon retaliated by saying a few words in Nez Perce and flipped a carrot near the pony's hooves. He walked calmly away, climbed atop the first pole and just sat. Ed finally came around and curiously stared up at him. "Is that all you're gonna do? Just sit and look at him?"

"That's all," Moon said flatly. "See you later, Ed. I'll let you know if I need anything." And as an afterthought, he called, "Keep your drovers away from this pony. He doesn't like white folks."

"You're full of sheep shit, Moon."

For the rest of the day, White Moon stayed at the corral, from time to time easing himself inside, walking to all sides of the young Appaloosa. Several of the drovers passed by, watched, then walked away, bewildered by Moon's strange behavior and the Indian words that he occasionally used.

Toward dusk, Adam Stuart arrived, followed by Jessie, who told Moon that his supper was waiting. Truthfully, so was she.

"What the hell are you doing?" Adam Stuart asked, "Ed says you been out here all afternoon just ogling my horse. Said you didn't like his name, either. What's wrong with Jediah?"

"He didn't like the name," White Moon said. "He was plenty mad about that crazy name. He likes Hawkeye. Suits him better, ei?"

Jessie giggled, turned quickly away, and headed back for the kitchen. Adam glowered at Moon for a moment, searching for an adequate reply, but unable to find one, gave up, turned on his heel, and followed his daughter.

"I'm coming, I'm coming," White Moon called after them. Then, talking to the young stallion, he said soothingly, "Nothing to eat for you, *palojami*, my fair one. Later I give you another carrot and a drink of water. *Sepekuse*. So be it."

After supper, eaten in the presence of an attentive Jessie Stuart, White Moon went to the bunkhouse, exchanged a few words with the two drovers, thought about a game of poker but gave up the idea. No challenge here, no money, and besides, it was now business before pleasure. Snatching up his bedroll, he took a tarp from the rafter, and disappeared in the dusk. "*Kaiziyeuyeu*," Moon called out, approaching the corral. "Greetings." Hawkeye, sniffing the air cautiously, gave him a snort of recognition but was reluctant to come up and drink from the pail of water Moon had placed below the poles. However, the tasty offering of another one of Molly Goodhart's carrots did interest him. He plucked it from the ground, and with two or three lusty crunches, downed it and curiously sniffed the surrounding area to see if he had missed anything. He was a hungry horse, and when feed was forthcoming, it would be White Moon who supplied it.

"What on earth are you doing?" came Jessie's hushed voice. She had sneaked up behind Moon Tree, who was huddled up against a post inside the corral. His hat was low on his forehead, his coat collar pulled up close to his ears. The fall evening was cool, a hint of the first frosts in the air.

Moon whispered back, "Watching my *tekash*."

"Your what?"

"*Tekash*, my cradle-board baby," Moon replied. "I took away his mother today, so I'll keep him company tonight. By tomorrow, this pony will know I'm here to take her place. Plenty hungry, happy to see me bring him hay, fresh water. Then we'll talk some more, get to know each other."

"Good Lord!" Jessie exclaimed. "Why, you'll be here for weeks if you keep this up." She nudged him through the poles. "Not that I'd mind it, if you want to know." Presumptuously, she climbed through the corral and sat next to him. Moon Tree said nothing, but cautioned her to be quiet by pressing a finger to his lips. They sat for awhile watching the young stud, and Jessie moved closer to Moon Tree. She whispered, "Does he know I'm here?"

"He's dozing," Moon whispered back. "He knows I'm here, though. Maybe he gets plenty jealous if he wakes up and sees you, ei? I don't know. Your brother says he likes to bite. Tomorrow, I'll find out." He looked across his shoulder at Jessie. "Your mother know you're out here with a gambling man?"

"She's already in bed," Jessie said softly. "See." And she pointed back toward the house. Moon peered through the poles, saw nothing but a few shadows from the cottonwoods tracing black patterns on the big clapboard house, not the slightest glimmer of a lamp. Jessie talked close to his ear. "For once in my life, I wanted to be alone with you without all of your relatives around to protect you. Impropriety be damned. Does this make me a hussy . . . a jezebel?"

Moon chuckled at this. Hunching his shoulders, he whispered straight ahead. "I don't think you could be one of those if you tried, Miss Jessie. I've seen a few along the towns I play, and you just don't fit the description. Have to get yourself a few of those lacy dresses, some long black stockings, and a pink garter or two. They don't go around at night wearing boots and dusters. Fact is, they don't go around wearing much of anything some of the places I've been."

With a huffy sigh, she said, "Hah, you don't

think I'm pretty enough to be dressing myself up like that?"

"Tut, tut," he protested quietly. "No, not at all. Why, you're pretty as a picture, a plenty good woman. What I'm saying is it takes a special kind of woman to put on a show like they do. It's a job, one I don't think you'll ever be needing."

"Do you like to look at them all fancied up that way?" she whispered. "Are they beautiful? Do they excite you?"

"Never pay them much mind," he said, amused by her little fishing game. "My business is poker, Miss Jessie. About the only time I get excited is when I have four ladies lying on the table in front of me just waiting for me to run my fingers over them."

"Four!" Jessie gasped. "Moon, you're a devil behind that mask you're always wearing. Four, I do believe!"

"Queens, that is, ladies with crowns," he continued. "Cards."

"Oh, damn you, Moon, no wonder I'm getting no place," she said huffily. Crawling to the side, she nestled in between his knees and boldly kissed him. Once wasn't enough. The second kiss smothered Moon Tree, was hard and passionate, and before he could react in some manner of his own, she pecked him a final time on the tip of his nose and said good night. He didn't know whether he was excited or not, but Hawkeye, his ears pricked, was standing there watching this strange moonlight interlude. Moon clucked at the young stud once and said, "Yes, I know what you would have done, boy. Go on, quit staring at me that way and go back to sleep."

The next morning, Moon Tree ate at the long table in the kitchen, contributed very little to the talk, and shortly was back at the corral with the maverick Hawkeye. Greeting the horse in Nez Perce, Moon produced another carrot, but instead of tossing it to the ground, he held it out temptingly and slowly walked up to the young stallion. There was a moment of hesitation before Hawkeye extended his long neck and lipped the morsel away. When Moon turned to leave, the horse followed, his muzzle lifted curiously to Moon's back. Moon Tree then fed his young charge three or four forks of green hay, brought back the water pail, and retired to his observation perch. Several hours later, he moved Hawkeye into a chute and tied a lead rope to the halter. At this point, Jessie Stuart arrived on the scene. "Need some help?" she called cheerily.

"Matter of fact, I do," answered White Moon. "Need a couple of blankets and a saddle for this *palojami*."

"You going to ride him?" she asked in quiet amazement.

Moon Tree gave her a sour look. "You think I'm crazy? *Eeyah*, why should I get him mad at me now after I take a day and a half just making him my friend? Mr. Stuart says take it easy, so I take it easy, ei? No rough stuff with this little man, treat him like a gentleman, and this takes some time." He pointed a finger at Jessie. "My time is plenty valuable, you know. Hah, fifty dollars for this? This is a poor pot, I tell you."

Jessie left, and when she returned with the blankets and saddle, White Moon had disappeared. The stud was standing in the chute placidly munching on a pile of hay. Moon came riding up mounted on his own pony, a brown and white mare of Crow origin, and after some maneuvering, edged her next to Hawkeye's chute. "You see," he said to Hawkeye, "I bring you a friend. She has good manners. You watch, maybe you can learn something good this morning." Moon took one of the blankets and draped it over Hawkeye's back. The horse promptly managed to flip it to the ground. "*Taz, taz,*" whispered Moon, replacing the blanket and patting the side of Hawkeye's jaw. "Take it easy, take it easy." This was repeated several times before Moon motioned to Jessie to bring the other blanket and the saddle. After sticking another carrot in Hawkeye's mouth, Moon had Jessie cover the horse's head, and simultaneously, he gently eased on the saddle, and in between a few protesting bucks, deftly pulled the cinch and secured it. "Now we'll get a cup of coffee," he said to Jessie. Let these two become friends for a while." Taking Jessie by her hand and giving it a squeeze, he walked back with her to the kitchen, Jessie measuring him stride for stride and enjoying the feel of his flesh, his firm grip.

By late afternoon, the Appaloosa was trotting around the ring alongside Moon Tree's mare, Moon with a firm grip on the lead rope, continually talking to the horse, coaxing, soothing, until a frothy lather showed up on Hawkeye's neck. At this point, Moon leaped off at the chute and rubbed the stud down, patted it affectionately several times, and stuffed another carrot in its mouth. He said to Jessie, "Tomorrow, you can ride this pony. Green-broke, teach him a few manners, when to go, when to stop."

Jessie, her hands in motion, waved him off. "Oh, no, Moon, not me. Is this another one of your jokes?"

"No joke." Moon Tree grinned. "Now we'll see how much this *palojami* has left in him." And with that, he eased into the saddle, coiled the rope several times around his fist, and ordered Jessie to pull the gate. She did. The Appaloosa took several great leaps, threw his back legs high, bowed his head, and went snorting around the corral like a smoking dragon. Jessie Stuart was squealing. Moon Tree, his legs locked in, doggedly held on until abruptly the young horse eased off, went into a trot, and with several great wheezes, came to a stop. Moon immediately leaped off, stripped the saddle, and jumped back on bareback. Hawkeye bolted twice this time, quickly settled down again, and trotted aimlessly around the circle with Moon leaning close to his neck, patting him gently. "You see," Moon shouted to Jessie, "he's my friend. Just had to find out I meant him no harm. Those other boys scared the hell out of him. You get down now, bring him a good drink, talk to him. He's good medicine, this one. Tomorrow, let him taste the bit, easy." And he slid off, slipped the lead rope, and watched admiringly as Hawkeye walked away. "*Hiyah!*" he called. "*Hiyah,* Hawkeye. *Tasnig.*" It is done.

Jessie, smiling happily, said, "Papa will be delighted." Moon shouldered the saddle and blankets. "Ei, and you tell him that horse doesn't have a mean streak in him, never did, just a little disappointed with getting roughed up too much. You treat him good and he'll be following you around like a big puppy. Keep him away from the mare, ei?"

"Are you going to spend the night with him again?" she asked jokingly. "Bed down by the corral?"

Moon Tree grinned. He had just partially gentled a fine young stud prospect and now he was dealing with a devious filly. "Why?" he asked. "You want to sneak out again, maybe get your little butt paddled when your mother catches you? Or get me shot?"

"Unfinished business, Moon." And she pointed a finger at him, leveling it like a pistol. "Aren't you just a little bit interested? Do I have to use a carrot on you?"

White Moon stopped and looked back over his shoulder. He thought he should be heading for the tack shed about now and keep right on moving. "I'm not ready for a halter," he said as tactfully as he could. "Not just yet, Jessie. Interested, yes, but there's no profit in disappointing a fine young lady like you. Bad medicine. Wouldn't be fair, understand? I think I'd feel miserable, you too. No, I better be getting along."

She pulled the trigger. "Who said anything about a halter? And disappoint me? Oh, come now, Moon, I don't think you're capable of disappointing any woman." Jessie blew him a kiss. "See you at supper . . . maybe later, too."

White Moon trudged away to the tack shed, the saddle on his shoulder suddenly multiplied in weight by a hundred pounds. Unfinished business, indeed!

Later that night, when the big house was dark, Jessie Stuart, carried away by the romance of the moment, and disregarding all convention, appeared once more at the corral. The bedroll was there as usual, the canvas tarp over it, and Moon's drover hat neatly perched at the head of it. At first Jessie was tempted to slip in beside him, quietly awake him with a kiss or two. But this was perhaps too unconventional, too bold even for Jessie Stuart, so she hunkered down and whispered, "Moon. Moon, wake up, it's me." Nothing. Reaching out, she shook his shoulder, a shoulder that wasn't there. The tarp collapsed around Moon

Tree's balled-up coat where his head was supposed to be. All that she saw was a carrot, a goddamned carrot! Jessie jerked upright and stared around into the darkness. "Moon, you bastard, I'll get even with you if it's the last thing I ever do." Kicking the bedroll, she stomped angrily away to the house. Tossing her coat aside and shucking her boots, she fell into bed and started to laugh, but that was short-lived, for a hand suddenly came over her mouth, and she heard a whisper in her ear. "I hope you had mind enough to give that carrot to Hawkeye."

TWELVE

As Sean O'Grady had carefully planned, by early November he and Divinity Jones were on the stage heading south to make train connections in Utah. Their inaugural tour up through the mining towns of the Montana Territory, heralded by O'Grady as a smashing success, convinced the Irishman that it was time to move on to more lucrative surrounds for the winter. His destination was San Francisco, with stops in Carson City and in Reno, where he planned to polish the act and hire a bass player. Divinity Jones, as O'Grady had predicted, picked up on the guitar frets without any trouble, and was already strumming an accompaniment to his piano. Her ear for the music never faltered. Sean O'Grady, of course, had his problems with Miss Divinity—diction and phrasing—but even these were improving daily. Her inability to read anything but her name made his work more difficult; however, the end result was well worth the effort—the talented, tenacious Divinity came through with gratifying perfection.

O'Grady was a happy man and considered himself most fortunate to have such a delightful, persevering partner. And beautiful, too. Her most ardent fans had been the men—hardy miners, mutton-chopped businessmen, and raucous cowboys who clamored for just the touch of her hand. To the fortunate and not-so-fortunate, Divinity Jones was a joyous person, the singing young lady who brought light into their lives, and when she and Sean O'Grady made their exit from the Montana Territory, every saloon or entertainment hall where they played was waiting for a return engagement.

At Carson City, O'Grady recruited the mulatto Beauregard Lincoln to play bass. Actually Mr. Beau, as everyone called him, was an outright fiddler, but he was versatile on the strings, and could also play the harmonica. The problem was that no bass fiddle was available when Beau Lincoln was hired, and O'Grady had to wait ten days before the big gut box arrived from San Francisco. This made no difference at all to Beauregard. He played along with O'Grady and Jones with his regular fiddle, occasionally plunked on an old banjo, and sometimes, in an impromptu moment of exuberance, wildly mouthed his harmonica. Often when Beauregard finished one of these rollicking riffs, he would grin broadly, make a sweeping gesture to the stage floor, and shout out, *"Merci, merci beaucoup!"* Of course Beauregard, being light in color, considered himself Acadian, or French, not Negro. This distinction was much to his advantage when O'Grady, Jones and M. L. Beauregard checked into hotels, his surname Lincoln converted into a first initial. And he never said "yes." It was always "*oui*." Divinity Jones quickly picked up on this. She thought Mr. Beau, who always wore a derby and a long black cloak, to be an extremely fascinating person, not only as a musician and a gentleman, but as one who could also teach her a few linguistic refinements. Mr. Beau knew French, even a Cajun variety, and he was happy to teach Divinity Jones, who just happened to be quick at learning most anything that promoted her goal of becoming a lady. She practiced religiously, and soon surprised everyone, including Mr. Beau.

After working up a few new routines in Carson City, they played Virginia City, Reno, where they performed for two weeks at the New Frontier Saloon and Showhouse, and finally on to San Francisco's bustling waterfront, where O'Grady, by grace of his origin, signed on for a week at O'Dell's Palace. Their success at the casino and restaurant lengthened the engagement to a month. During this time, Sean O'Grady met the nattily dressed F. Bret Harte, a writer of gold-mining-camp stories who was acting in an Irish play downtown. Actually, it was the delectable Divinity Jones who caught F. Bret Harte's attention, and he was so amused and delightfully impressed by the versatility of this little blonde sprite that he came back a second night, ultimately introduced himself to O'Grady, and from this acquaintance, a few brief conversations with Miss Divinity developed. Bret Harte, a dashing, mustached dandy with dark, wavy hair, was intrigued by Divinity Jones, particularly her background and unique mannerisms. Her adventure with Moon Tree, plus a few tales about Derby Flats, prompted him to scribble notes on one of the little pads that he carried in his coat pocket.

On another night, Bret Harte arrived to see the O'Grady and Jones show accompanied by a man he introduced as Dion Boucicault, a producer-actor whose latest Irish play, *The Shaughraun,* currently was showing at the California Theater. Insisting that Boucicault see for himself what Harte described as "unbridled talent and showmanship," he came early with Boucicault and left very late. Boucicault was impressed, and he and O'Grady had such a grand time they ended up drunk, and the great leader of the Eastern Dramatic Company spent the night in O'Grady's hotel room, where he awoke the next morning with a terrible aching head.

In the hotel dining room, Dion Boucicault, somewhat bedraggled, sat with O'Grady and Divinity Jones, watching Miss Divinity devour a hearty breakfast of biscuits and bacon, and eggs. Nursing along a cup of coffee and commiserating with O'Grady about the aftereffects of fine Irish whiskey, he complimented Divinity Jones on her voice. "For someone without training, you have exceptional tonal qualities." he said. "Your phrasing is also quite good. I can't believe that you've been performing this way for such a short time. You and Mr. O'Grady will have to move on to better things. Certainly you have the talent, young lady. I have an idea or two that you people might be interested in hearing."

Divinity, daintily probing a slippery piece of egg, paused long enough to say, "*Merci*, Mr. Boucicault. I think Mr. O'Grady has plans. Whatever he decides is all right with me." She touched her napkin to her lips once and went right on eating. One thing Divinity had learned in her exciting new life was that hotel dining was an experience she thoroughly enjoyed. Her sourdough and mutton days were over.

Dion Boucicault asked O'Grady, "Just what are your plans? From here, where?

Sean O'Grady, a man who promoted as well as he performed, said, "I have three more rooms to play here. We'll be holding on until springtime, we will. The lass wants to go back to the Montana country when the grass is green, and I'll oblige her in that. She has business, and we'll be taking a bit of a break. I do have plans for a tour to Denver. That's about it for the near future."

"My business is railroad," Divinity chimed in. "I have a solicitor in Helena taking care of it. A solicitor is an attorney, you know."

"Yes." Boucicault smiled understandingly. "I

think Bret mentioned something about a railroad running through your property. . . ."

"At Derby Flats." Delicately breaking a biscuit in half, she went on. "I have good water there, *beaucoup* water, a big spring, flowers all about, a fine garden it is. My father called it an oasis in the desert, his beautiful estate. He was a wise man, my father, God bless his soul."

"Well," Boucicault said, "your father had a good ear for music. A singer, was he?'"

"Sort of," Divinity Jones replied. "When he was feeling good . . . happy, he sang a song or two." She offered Boucicault a half of a honey-covered biscuit. "Would you like a bite? You should eat something, you know, feed the little green man with the big red nose."

Amused by her quaintness, Dion Boucicault politely refused. He mused, "The little green man with the big red nose, is it? Sounds like some kind of an Irish tune, very appropriate this morning, eh, Mr. O'Grady?"

O'Grady nodded glumly. "It has an Irish ring to it. I suppose I could put some music and lyrics to it, but I'm not doing it this morning, lad."

Boucicault set aside his coffee and said seriously, "You mentioned a tour to Denver, Mr. O'Grady, a fine idea, in the late spring, perhaps, or early summer. Is this a proper assumption?"

"Yes, it is," answered O'Grady. "Denver will be a fine city for us—our repertoire, understand, will be varied. Perhaps, Cheyenne, too."

Boucicault, contemplating O'Grady, then watching the food in Divinity Jones's plate shrink dramatically, said, "Well, I have a tour of my own planned next fall and winter. It wouldn't interfere with your plans, and I thought you two, along with that Mr. Beauregard, might consider joining the tour. It will be a variety, musical, a play or two, good theater entertainment. Get you out of the saloon-and-dance-hall circuit for a while. You'd be a great addition to my company. I'd be pleased to have you." He glanced over at Divinity, who hastily put her fork aside, abandoning what was left of her breakfast. Watching her clutch her napkin to her bosom, her mouth agape, Dion Boucicault momentarily thought she was going to make some sort of outcry. Only surprised, thoroughly taken aback by his sudden proposal, he assumed. He knew that she was a very animated, expressive young lady. He said to her, "I assume you would agree to this, Miss Divinity? You have that certain look on your face."

Properly recovering, Divinity said melodiously, "*Oui, oui,* Mr. Boucicault, it would be a pleasure." And she looked expectantly at Sean O'Grady, who was already searching through one of the pockets of his vest for his small calling card, the one that said: *O'Grady and Jones, Music for Your Pleasure.* He slid it across the white tablecloth. "You can be reaching us here, Mr. Boucicault. The message will get through. You'll be stating your terms in the contract, and we'll be getting back to you in plenty of time for rehearsals."

With an Irish twist of his own, Dion Boucicault said, "That I'll be doing, Mr. O'Grady, and thanking ye, too."

Later that afternoon, F. Bret Harte arrived at the hotel in a fine black carriage, handles and trim of shiny brass, driven by a man wearing a fancy suit and a large black hat. The writer-actor escorted Divinity Jones, dressed in one of her fine new gowns, a luxurious cloak and plumed hat, to the California Theater, and ushered her to a private box where she enjoyed the matinée performance of *The Saughraun*. It was an amazing play, she thought, because everyone in it talked exactly like Sean O'Grady. She enjoyed herself immensely, laughing and applauding when other people did so, but the intermission was the most delightful experience of all. She had tea and small biscuits with Mr. Boucicault and Bret Harte. There were many other finely dressed women present, none of whom had a dress as pretty as the one she was wearing. Several men came up and politely introduced themselves, expressing pleasure at meeting her. They knew who she was, had enjoyed her performances at O'Dell's Palace, such an attractive, talented young lady.

Never in her life had Divinity Jones used the word "*merci*" so many times. This was Miss Divinity's introduction to society, and Mr. Harte told her that she passed with flying colors on refinement and culture. She winked at Harte, saying that Moon Tree once told her to keep her mouth shut, that this was the best way to learn. Divinity emitted a little snicker, reminded of the story that Moon had told her at the time, and with a small lapse of decorum, she told it to F. Bret Harte.

"There were these two crows," she said. "They were getting ready to fly south, you know, like they always do in the winter. Well, there's this big mound of cow manure, so they stop to feed. They figure they're going to need all the strength they can get—"

Bret Harte asked, "You mean they eat this . . . this substance?"

Divinity grinned. "They surely do eat it. I've seen them."

Bret Harte smiled, too. "Excuse me, Miss Divinity. Please continue."

"This was a good pile, too," she went on. "You see, there's a pitchfork sticking right in the middle of it, and it's aimed right up at the sky. They're going to use this for their perch to take off. Well, this one crow flapped his wings a couple of times and he took right off. The other one, he was a greedy bird, all right. You see, he ate too much, so when he flapped off of that pitchfork, he didn't get far. He crashed and broke his neck, that's what."

"Greed, the curse of humanity," Bret Harte commented.

"Well, that's not the moral of the story," Divinity replied. "That's not what Mr. Moon told me."

"Ah, yes, Mr. Moon. And what did he tell you?"

Whispering close to his ear, Divinity said, "Never fly off the handle when you're full of shit."

F. Bret Harte laughed heartily. "A moral worth remembering. You think a great deal of this fellow, Moon Tree, don't you?"

"Best buddy I ever had." She smiled wistfully.

Before winter was over, O'Grady and Jones made appearances in a half dozen of San Francisco's best night spots, always drawing large, enthusiastic crowds. Sacramento was their last stop in California, and it was a memorable one for Divinity Jones. One night after a performance at the New Palace Casino, a young man, Jay C. Redmond, appeared backstage asking to see O'Grady and Jones. He was an ardent fan who had seen their act for two consecutive nights. He was also an aide to Governor George C. Perkins, and since the governor was hosting a small party at the mansion on Friday night, he wondered if O'Grady and Jones might spare an hour to entertain Governor Perkins's guests. Of course, a liberal stipend of three hundred dollars would be paid for their work, if they could find the time to get away. Because of such a benevolent request from Governor Perkins, O'Grady quickly assured Redmond that there would be no problem with the Palace management. After all, it would be an honor to perform for Governor Perkins.

So at precisely nine o'clock on this Friday night, Sean O'Grady, Divinity Jones, and Mr. Beau came out from behind a velvet curtain to the applause of some fifty ladies and gentlemen. They took their positions and began their act, playing and singing a few contemporary numbers, some nostalgic frontier and Irish melodies, and they finished with several original scores, interspersed with comedy between Mr. Beau and Divinity Jones.

Afterward, Jay C. Redmond introduced everyone to the governor and Mrs. Perkins and several other dignitaries. Divinity, stunning in a white gown and a jeweled tiara, became the center of attention. Governor Perkins was anxious to know all about her. Was she a Californian? Where did she receive her voice training? Had she appeared in New York? And what profession did her father follow?

Divinity, her elegant chin held high, enlightened Governor Perkins and his friends.

"My late father was a sheep rancher," she said. "But most of my property has been sold to the railroad. My solicitor is in charge of these affairs, a gentleman up in the Montana Territory. After this is settled, Mr. O'Grady, Mr. Beauregard, well, we're all going on tour next year with the Eastern Dramatic Company." She smiled as a waiter presented her with a tray of cocktails. *"Merci,"* she said daintily. *"Oui,* maybe our tour will end in New York, but California, oh, I like it so much, *oui, le California me plaît beaucoup."*

"Well, this is great," Governor Perkins told her.

"We're all happy to hear that you like our great state. And when your tour comes this way, we'll be delighted to see you again. I hope it's not too long, Miss Jones, don't keep us waiting." He bowed graciously and moved away, Mrs. Perkins hanging on his arm.

After a lengthy stay in Sacramento, O'Grady and Divinity, along with their companion Mr. Beau, returned to Blanche Grant's little hotel in early April for a well-earned rest. There were letters awaiting, several requesting the act to reappear in Virginia City and Butte, another from the big Placer Hotel in Helena urging O'Grady to take a three-week engagement in June. Another post for Divinity Jones from Arthur Clawson was read to her by Blanche Grant. Clawson expected the final papers and payment of seventy-eight thousand dollars for the railroad right-of-way and use of water sometime in May. Additionally, the Coombes Livestock Company had agreed to purchase forty acres of the homestead for thirty thousand dollars. If it was convenient, Clawson wanted Divinity to come to his office within the next several months and receive her money.

All of this was great news, and in appreciative celebration and thanksgiving, O'Grady and Jones, with Mr. L. Beauregard, went next door to Finney's Saloon the following night, a Saturday, to put on a free show.

THIRTEEN

Dupee Clancy wasn't used to being alone. Not that he couldn't fend for himself—it just made the work double, and he had never cared much for hard labor. Making a pole fence was labor. Despite Arvis James's desertion, and that was sorely stuck in his craw, he went about his business, grudgingly, cutting lodgepoles, erecting his hidden corral up in the Ruby Mountains. Wearing his hat low, he occasionally sneaked down to Alder Gulch to ferret out the latest news and buy or steal a few staples. He had one thing going for him—his beard. By the day it grew longer and bushier, and after a month it fully covered his face. No one, not even the men in his old gang, would have recognized Dupee Clancy, unless he opened his mouth. His gravelly voice was beyond disguise. Even though beset with misfortune, Clancy still entertained thoughts of rich rewards in his favorite profession—theft—rationalizing that it was only the accidental blunder of the sheepherder, Burleigh Jones, that had cached him in the first place. After that one accident, that unfortunate meeting above the Stuart property, a whole pack of dogs had been sicced on him, and of course, leading the hounds was one of those breed Tree boys. All of this was one big mistake that could never happen again in a million years. This haunting belief spurred him on to new endeavors, this and the deplorable fact that he hated working alone.

He had adjustments to make in his present miserable life, and his first priority was to recruit some help, convince others of his kind that he had a prosperous business venture in the bag. Rounding up a few wild mustangs on the open range came under the heading of free enterprise. If an occasional foreigner got mixed up in the process, that was only accidental. Those wild stallions were always luring away a few mares from the ranches, and it was the ranchers' own damned fault for not keeping their stock closer to home, fenced in properly. Clancy figured this was bad luck on the part of the owners, and his good luck to capture the wandering critters.

One night in Nevada City, he met his first recruit in between the Nugget Saloon and the Hunter Boarding House, a dark passageway where he had just knocked out a drunken miner and was searching his pockets for a few dollars. A voice behind him said, "You're onto my game, buster. I had this fellow all set up for myself." When Clancy glanced up in the darkness, it was light enough to see the barrel of a pistol pointed at his head. There wasn't much profit in squabbling over ten dollars, so Clancy threw a bone out for the man to chew on.

"I say we split this money, mister, move on to better things. You seem to be a fair-minded ol' boy, and I have a place up in the Ruby. Together, we could make these coins look like chicken feed. Now, what you say to this?"

This was precisely how Clancy met Bowie Turnbow, a first-class thief and killer like himself, a man who would shoot anyone in the back for bar change, or steal every chicken from a coop while the old lady was in the milk house churning butter. Turnbow, as he related to Dupee in the security of the hideout, had wandered up from the Beaverhead country where he had last worked at Albert Whiteside's ranch. He wasn't much for hard labor, either. He loved to play poker—gamble really—and this recreation usually kept him broke. Actually, he envisioned himself as a great poker player, only there always seemed to be one or two lucky fellows at the table, or else his own luck was running poorly, the cards just weren't coming his way. Because he was always in hock, and seldom paid his debts, Bowie Turnbow had become somewhat of a loner. Everyone seemed to be down on him. Dupee, of course, knew just how he felt—he had the same problem. Clancy had met a true-blue new partner.

Since Dupee Clancy had such an isolated corral

tucked away in the mountain meadows, the two partners saw little reason not to use it. There was a spring at the head of the draw, and the grass below was knee-deep where the water coursed. In three nights, they had six pilfered horses in the enclosure, a modest start, but one purposely undertaken with great caution. It was Clancy's idea to nab only a few horses at a time, making their nighttime excursions in remote range areas where the theft of one or two horses might not be discovered immediately. Once Clancy and Bowie Turnbow had a good accumulation, they could do some brand blotting and move out for the Idaho border. It was a very simple job that paid handsomely, provided one made no mistakes.

Thomas Chambers' spread wasn't more than twenty miles from Clancy's cabin, a little close for rustling but very tempting. Chambers had about forty head of horses on a range in full view of the stage road east to Virginia City. Clancy and Turnbow had spotted these horses several times, and they agreed that Chambers probably wouldn't miss two or three, especially since none of his drovers ever seemed to be around this particular section of land. They were always working on the other side of the valley where most of the cattle were being herded down from the high country. This was early October, a time when everyone was preparing for winter, laying in wood, repairing sheds, mending fence, and doing an assortment of other related ranch chores that no one wanted to do in inclement weather. So it stood to reason that this was also a good time for stealing a few horses, which Dupee Clancy and Bowie Turnbow did without a hitch. They cut out three mares, hoping to double their take, ran them up the road at midnight, and were back at their camp before dawn.

Elated with their progress, the two men decided to take a ride over the ridge and case the Whiteside ranch range the next day. Bowie Turnbow, being a former employee, knew the Whiteside operation—where the horses usually were and the drovers' routine—which made for easy pickings. After scrutinizing the horse herd along the creek bottom, the two men rode on into Armstead to while away the time until dark. They reined up at Fat Hoag's saloon. No one called Hoag "fat," not to his face, anyhow. Actually, his name was Fred, but few people called him that, either. For some reason, probably caution, he was known as Tiny Hoag, this quite incongruous since Fred weighed well over two hundred pounds and had a paunch on him like a pregnant buffalo. Most often, he wore huge blue denims held up with red suspenders. He never paid much attention who his customers were, either, as long as they had money. This particular late afternoon, Fat Hoag was haggling with two muleskinners who had their freight wagons pulled up in front of the saloon. There was a misunderstanding on the delivery of cases of whiskey. Hoag, by some quirk in shipping, received only two cases when he had ordered four, and despite his girth and domineering posture (one ponderous foot on the two stacked cases and shaking a very big fist), there wasn't anything he could do but swear. The two muleskinners, doffing their big hats, climbed back upon their perches, yelled, "Geedap," and went lumbering on down the road toward the distant camps of Laurin, Alder Gulch, and Nevada City.

Dupee Clancy, his eye always out for business, thought he could help Fat Hoag do something about his shortage of whiskey. For instance, he knew that the freighters would stop down the line ten miles or so for the night, probably in the flats near the riverbank. So once inside, and with whiskey in front of him and his partner, he made Hoag a proposition. Staring through the stains of his glass, Clancy asked, "Say, if we was to come up with those two lost cases, Tiny, what would they be worth, you reckon? You know, if we just happened to put 'em right down here kerplunk on the bar, no questions asked."

Fat Hoag, making a small mental calculation and figuring in some profit for himself, replied, "I'd have sixty dollars for you boys if I had that whiskey." His yellow teeth appeared through the whiskers. "Thirty each, that is."

Dupee Clancy was an illiterate man, but not entirely stupid. He grinned back, tossed his shot down, and said huskily, "Make it forty each and you got a deal."

Refilling Dupee's glass, Fat Hoag said, "This

one's on the house." Winking at Dupee Clancy, he added, "Forty each, no questions asked."

That same night at about ten o'clock, Dupee Clancy and Bowie Turnbow returned to Fat Hoag's, carried in two cases of whiskey, and set them on the bar. This caused hardly a stir in the saloon. Several men at the poker table took a casual look, but soon went back to their cards. Hoag toted the two cases to the back room, shortly returned and counted out eighty dollars. He had saved himself twenty dollars by dealing with these new whiskey salesmen, men he didn't know, or wouldn't admit to knowing if someone just happened to ask.

One of the poker players who saw the transaction was a little more than casually interested. His name was Harley Frame, a young cowboy of twenty-five years. He had drifted the entire Montana Territory since he was seventeen. A drover to Albert Whitside, he knew Bowie Turnbow, not as a friend but as a debtor. Bowie, the luckless poker player, owed him ten dollars, and the opportunity to collect his money had now arrived. Folding his cards, young Harley Frame sidled up to the bar next to Bowie and said calmly, "Bowie, I see you hit paydirt, and I reckon you can spare me a ten, seeing that's how much you owe me."

Bowie Turnbow edged around to the side, smiled faintly, and replied, "Well, hello there, Harley. By Gawd, you're right as rain. I sure do owe you ten, but I was figuring on building a stake with this here money. Me and my partner here, we're taking a room upstairs for the night, maybe playing a couple hands in your game over there. Seeing there's two of us and only one of you, I was wondering if you wanted to hold off until the morning. I'm feeling pretty lucky tonight."

Harley Frame nodded understandingly. He appreciated an honest answer, but he didn't think he wanted to wait until morning to get his ten dollars. Actually, knowing Bowie Turnbow, he didn't think Bowie would even be around in the morning. Harley Frame, despite his young age, sparse mustache, and cherubic face, was a man of considerable experience. While not exactly a marksman with a pistol, he knew how to draw one from his holster. He did so now, quite quickly, and he said evenly to Bowie Turnbow, "Your odds ain't good enough, old friend. I have six to one that says you lay ten on the bar. You see, I know how you play poker, and I'd rather have my ten than see it wind up in someone else's pocket. So you just fork it up nice and easy like."

This, of course, brought a hasty nod of approval. Bowie, in fact, looked a little sick, and his mouth drooped right along with the contour of his mustache. No one had ever poked a revolver in his ear before. Likewise, Harley Frame's pistol trick brought the rest of the customers to a hushed silence. Fat Hoag started to intervene with a curse, only to be cut off by Bowie's nervous, high-pitched laugh. Bowie went digging into his pocket for his wad of bills, finally fished out a ten-spot, and slapped it on the counter. With affected nonchalance, he said, "Hell, boy, you don't take to a joke much, do you? Didn't realize you was so damned persnickety. Now, put that thing away. . . ."

Fat Hoag slid a bottle down the bar, saying, "Have a drink, boys, and stop the tomfoolery before I have to start bustin' heads. Go on now, take a drink and forget it."

"Much obliged, Tiny," Bowie Turnbow sighed in relief. He poured himself a shot and threw it down, clearing the cotton from his throat, then dabbed a few pebbles of sweat from his brow with his bandanna.

Dupee Clancy eased his tension by letting out a harsh cackle. Duly impressed with young Harley Frame, he slapped the drover on the shoulder once and poured him a drink. "You got some spunk in you, boy. Understand, now, we ain't looking for trouble. Makes no sense to argue over ten bucks, anyways. Downright crazy. That's chicken feed. What's your name?"

A subdued Bowie Turnbow, amicably waved a hand, said, "Hell, I wasn't going to hold out on him, Dupee, just joshing a bit, that's all."

"Yes, sir," Clancy said, "I reckon he was just making a little fun."

"Name is Harley Frame, and ten dollars is a week's wages, mister," was the sharp retort. "Makes sense to me."

"Yes, maybe it does," Clancy agreed. But this set his mind off in another direction. Ten dollars was a lot of money if one had no money at all, and obviously Harley Frame didn't have much of a grubstake. Anyone who would pull his pistol for a measly ten dollars was his kind of man. Here was another likely prospect for the art of rustling. Dupee took a drink of his whiskey, smacked his lips, and whispered to Harley Frame, "If you've a mind to make a hundred a week the rest of the season, come on up to our room later for a little parley. If you ain't, no harm done, and everything is square."

Harley Frame wasn't too enthusiastic about Dupee Clancy's proposal. He was not above rustling a few horses. He just didn't particularly trust lowlifes like Clancy and Turnbow. They weren't too dependable when the chips were down. He did, however, like the thought of gold jingling in his pockets, and running a couple dozen head of horses down to the Lemhi wasn't much of a chore. But what really persuaded him to throw in with Dupee Clancy was the surprising disclosure that Clancy held a deep hatred for the Tree family, a conglomeration of breeds who owned half of the Gallatin Valley, one of whom had killed Clancy's brother, Jim. Clancy, on the other hand, was equally surprised to learn that young Harley Frame had been rousted five years ago on the Yellowstone buffalo grounds by Young Benjamin, set afoot in the middle of nowhere with three other hide hunters. Harley Frame was the only one who survived, the others perishing from starvation and exposure. The Crow Indians didn't appreciate hide hunters on their land, and Harley and his trespassing friends had paid the price. The fact that both Frame and Clancy were still nursing old wounds inflicted by Benjamin One Feather and Moon Tree sealed the partnership, for they were haunted by the desire for revenge, and each had waited years to get it.

Amazed that Frame wasn't aware that these were the same brothers who had once lived with the Crow, Clancy warned him that it was foolhardy even to consider riding around the Tree ranch at the present time. "They's watching the place like hawks these days" he said. "We stirred up the whole shebang over that way shooting that old sheepherder. Just have to wait our time, and it'll come one of these days."

Harley Frame still couldn't believe that Young Benjamin was none other than Benjamin One Feather, the English-speaking Crow brave who had led the raid on the buffalo camp. "Soldiers at Fort Keogh who found me just said it must have been the one called Benjamin One Feather. Said he was an ornery devil always chasing white folks off the land. Why, that Injun killed some trappers, too, friends of ol' Ulis Birdwell. Fact is, one of 'em was Birdwell's brother, Amos. Trapping wolves, they was. Never did find their bodies, either. Couldn't prove a thing on those sneaky Injuns."

"Probably 'et those two trappers." Clancy grinned.

"Naw," Frame replied. "No such thing. Ulis, he came back the first time and found 'em dead, scalped, too. Says he buried 'em, but when he brought the troopers back with that Benjamin One Feather along, well, the bodies were plumb gone. No graves, either. Made a liar out of Ulis, and he never did get over it." Frame clucked his tongue and shook his head sadly. "Last time I saw Ulis, he was crawling on his hands and knees behind me, right down a gully filled with prickly pear. Tried to eat some of that shit. Nothing worked. I looked around later, and hell, I was the only one left. Rest of 'em just gave up and went belly up."

"Well, you had some luck, anyways," Bowie Turnbow said. "Way my luck runs, I'd be no more'n a pile of prairie bones just like your partners. Boogers always seem to be after me, for a fact."

With a deep sigh of resignation, Harley Frame said, "Figger the Lord spared me for one reason—to get that Injun someday. By all rights, I should be dead. No way I was going back into the Crow country looking to take on a whole goddamned tribe of 'em, but shoot fire, if I knew that fellow was all by hisself over in the Bozeman country, why, hell, I'd been there a long time ago."

He shook his head again disbelievingly. "Sure beats all. Injuns ain't supposed to be rich like that, either."

Dupee Clancy, frowning in disapproval, wagged a finger at young Frame. He didn't want to be losing a new recruit before his business venture even got underway. He wanted some long-term use out of Harley Frame, not some gun-happy maverick who overnight would sour the cream. His whiskered jaw was long and heavy, and he warned, "Now look, boy, don't be pushing your luck too much. From what I hear, those Tree boys know how to use a pistol—their old man taught them, and nobody ever beat him, nobody. Didn't notch his handle, they say, but if he had, it probably woulda' looked like a chopping block."

"Makes no difference to me," Harley Frame said with a scowl of his own. One way or another, the job'll get done. Dues have to be paid, always have, always will. I've been wasting a lot of time not knowing that Benjamin was the same rascal that damned near got me dead." With this, he left and went back to Whiteside's to get his gear.

The next night the three cowboys cut out four of Whiteside's horses, took them up a small valley, and dropped over the other side of the Ruby Mountains to the hideout. After several more forays in the Beaverhead, Dupee Clancy thought it was time to move the stock south for sale. The first snows weren't too far away, time to reap the reward for their endeavors, find a warmer place to winter. They boarded up the cabin until spring, and one frosty night, moved their band of stolen horses up the Ruby Valley toward the divide. Traveling southwest to Blue Dome, they sold the stock, taking nine hundred dollars each for their shares of the pot. It was getting cold on the prairie. They rode on to Nevada and ultimately found another shack outside of Reno where they decided to stay until spring.

Clancy, satisfied that the world was finally treating him a little better, decided it was time to celebrate, to buy some new clothes, get a good bath, a shave, and have a night on the town. He was a moderately wealthy man, had lived frugally for the past six months, so he reasoned that he had a good time coming. Turnbow and Frame went along with this. Neither had ever accumulated more than fifty dollars in his life, and nine-hundred put both high on the hog. They all headed for town, and by sundown they were new men, at least in appearance. After a big steak and potato dinner, they wandered along the boardwalk, had a drink here and there, finally moved on to the New Frontier Saloon and Showhouse to take in the entertainment, a great show, they heard— O'Grady and Jones and a Cajun man called Mr. Beau.

What the three men had heard was true— they stood at the long bar with their drinks, found themselves, as others did, tapping out the rhythm with their boots, and applauding enthusiastically after each number. Harley Frame, fascinated, could have stayed the night, especially watching the beautiful blonde lady whose voice was as fresh as high mountain air, but suddenly in the middle of a song, she stopped and stared directly at him. At least, that's what Harley Frame thought she did. She cried out, "*Sacre bleu,* that's him!" and everyone turned and looked his way. Leaping down to a nearby table, the lady picked up a whiskey bottle and hurled it right at his head, screaming, "The son of a bitch killed my paw! Get him, get the bastard!" Harley Frame ducked. So did everyone else in his vicinity, but Dupee Clancy ran, hurdled several chairs, knocked over a table, and in all the confusion, bolted out the side door. A huge man next to Harley Frame grabbed him by the shoulder, and sticking out his angry face, thundered, "All right, mister, who was that man? A friend of yours?"

Frame, shrinking away to the size of a bar stool, searched futilely around for Bowie Turnbow, his other partner, but Bowie had mysteriously disappeared. Frame, his face a mask of innocence, cried out, "I never saw that feller before in my life, so help me God!"

Later that night back at the shack, Harley and Bowie Turnbow looked down at a dejected, dumbfounded Dupee Clancy. How could this be? How could that sheepherder's daughter and this Divinity Jones be the same person? His coffeecup turned cold in his hands. His newly found world of enjoyment and freedom was dissolving right in front of him like a piece of ice in the desert sun.

Harley Frame spoke up, saying, "She told everybody there's a five-hundred-dollar reward on your head. Every damned man in the place wearing a gun left, all out looking for you, you big jackass. That's what you get for shaving your fucking beard!"

"It ain't possible," Dupee mumbled.

"It's possible, all right," Frame replied. "You better get your ass outta here tonight, head a bit further south. Me and Bowie hang out with you, and likely they'll get after us, too. Fact is, I don't even think I want to spend the winter here at all, 'specially with Bowie. You bastards left me hanging high and dry in that goddamned dance hall. Big feller was gonna throttle me right there out on the spot for spoiling that woman's song that way."

Clancy moaned, "How's I to know thing like that? For crissakes, I still can't believe it."

"I'm leaving," Harley Frame announced emphatically. "See you next spring in the Ruby, boys. That's business, but you ain't making my stay here much pleasure, that's for sure."

"Where you headin', Harley?" Turnbow asked plaintively, watching him grab his bedroll and clothes.

"Far away from you as I can get," Frame replied. "You're a Judas. Hell, you both are."

Dupee Clancy and Bowie Turnbow also separated the next morning, and Clancy once again found himself alone.

FOURTEEN

White Moon was a busy man, and as Young Benjamin warned, he was burning the wick at both ends. Along with the routine chores, Moon had helped Willie Left Hand and Robert Peete take fifty head of horses over to Butte for sale; he had been on a short cattle drive to the stockyards in Helena; and he was managing to get in a few hands of poker every other night while he was on the road. Additionally, Moon wedged in frequent visits to Stuart's place, ostensibly to check on the progress of Adam's Appaloosa, Hawkeye. The fact that he often rode along with Jessie Stuart didn't seem to stir much curiosity or suspicion. No one seemed to be aware of the discreet relationship developing between Jessie and Moon. Jessie, presently content to let nature take its course, actually did harbor some secret thoughts about a permanent future with Moon, but at the same time she was a practical woman—a half loaf was better than none. And luckily, there were no other women with whom to contend. She thought it better to compete with a deck of cards than another woman, heaven forbid. So for the present, at least, she felt happily secure in this fervor of love, if that's what it was.

Early in December, Moon received a letter at the post office, brought home by Claybourn Moore. Clay was as curious as Moon about the postmark on the envelope—Reno, Nevada. They shared mutual surprise when they found out it was from Divinity Jones, written for her by one Sean O'Grady, who identified himself as her partner. Partner? Partner in what? White Moon read on, astounded, pausing occasionally to stare at Clay Moore in utter disbelief. Divinity Jones was singing and playing a guitar, and doing quite well, according to O'Grady. They were headed for San Francisco to spend the winter but would be back in Dubois come spring. More important, however, she had recognized Dupee Clancy in a showhouse in Reno, but unfortunately, the killer of her father had escaped. Divinity said that she would like to receive a letter from her *mon chéri*, Moon Tree, but she didn't know where she would be staying in San Francisco.

Ruth Moore came in, followed by young Joshua, who set about stomping the snow from his boots. Ruth stared at her husband and White Moon, both bent over the letter, reading it a second time in stunned silence. "Who is it from, Moon? Who do you know in the Nevada country?" she asked.

Moon almost whispered, "Divinity Jones . . . in Reno, of all places. Ei, plenty strange. She has a song partner."

Clay Moore, his brow arched, looked up at his wife. "That's only the half of it," he said. "She's going to San Francisco."

"Oh, lordy," Ruth Moore scoffed. "Moon, is this another one of your pranks? San Francisco, indeed! Let me see that letter."

"She calls me '*mon chéri*,' whatever that means." Searching the faces of Clay and Ruth, Moon asked, "What the hell does *mon chéri* mean? Sounds French. How would Miss Divinity know something like that? That woman can't even speak English."

"Ask your brother," Ruth said. "Benjamin's half French."

Moon Tree grunted. "He never knew his father, never spoke a word of French in his life."

Ruth Moore pointed at the letter. "May I?"

Moon handed it to the foreman's wife, saying, "Yes, you may, but you won't believe it." Mystified, scratching his head, he got up and put on his heavy coat. "*Mon chéri*, ei? Probably some cuss word she's using on me. She's plenty good at that, you know, some word I don't know, pulling a little joke on me."

Clay Moore said, "Well, we know one thing. Dupee Clancy isn't around these parts, anymore. We can stop looking for him, tell the hanging man

219

he's cleaned country. One less bad apple in the valley."

Moon Tree paused at the door, shot Moore a negative look. "Ei, but he won't stay down there. He'll be back with the geese. His roots are up here. He knows this country. When the snow is gone, he'll be back. Maybe we won't see him, but he'll be somewhere in the territory up to his old tricks, thieving livestock, looking for his chance to get even. Old dogs, new tricks, something like that white folks' saying."

"Can't teach an old dog new tricks," Clay Moore said with a smile.

"Ei, and Clancy is an old dog," said White Moon. "When one of the ranchers starts missing some of his horses, we'll know he's around. I'll tell you one thing, next time I get on his trail, I won't be stopping to wipe the soot off my face. I promised Miss Divinity we'd catch up to him, and that's one promise I want to keep. That horse thief caused the whole mess, almost got me killed falling through that damned roof, and made a sheepherder out of me most of the summer. I'd go back to my people on the reservation before taking on something like that again. *Eeyah!*"

Ruth, holding up the letter, smiled happily. "Why, this is something, Moon, it sure is, and I think you better be showing this to your brother and White Crane. They'll be happy to know their sad little tree is starting to bear fruit. This is a revelation."

White Moon put on his hat and pulled his collar high. "Ei," he agreed. "I think I'll read it to Willie, too. He's the one who said she couldn't tell the neck of a guitar from the box. I'll forget that *'mon chéri'* part, though. He's likely to start calling me that just for the hell of it, and once something like this gets started, it might become a habit. Willie went on with that bleating stuff for two months." He took a final puzzled look at Ruth and Clay Moore. "Can't imagine Miss Divinity taking up singing, can you? All that woman could do was swear and push sheep. And San Francisco? *Mon chéri? Eeyah,* I think she met up with Old Man Coyote somewhere along the trail."

Of course, Benjamin and White Crane were delighted about the letter; Benjamin read it aloud with some minor translation to his wife.

Back in the bunkhouse, Willie Left Hand was a trifle skeptical until the name of Sean O'Grady was mentioned. Sean O'Grady, he knew, had played fiddle with him in Virginia City two years ago at a jamboree. He vouched for the Irishman, a great piano player and singer, undoubtedly the best musician in the territory.

Moon Tree said with a trace of annoyance, "Just what kind of man is this Sean fellow? You don't suppose he's struck up with her because of the money she has coming, just joking her along?"

"Now, how'd I know such a thing?" Willie Left Hand grinned. "Hell, Moon, O'Grady is a music man. I don't reckon he's no fancy gentleman slicker. If that little hellion is a singer like he says, well, then she is, that's all I knows, but it beats me how he ever found out. Never heard any music come outta her when she was here at the spread. Sounded more like a chicken to me. Now, as for O'Grady, well, he had a little spread over next to old man Whiteside's place on the Beaverhead. That's the last I heard. He sure is something special, though, for a fact."

"A rounder?"

Willie Left Hand, a twinkle in his eye, gave Moon a suspicious stare. "Taken a shine to that Miss Divinity, have you? All that time with her and those woolies done got to you? Just what are you getting at, like if he's gonna get in her bloomers, something like that?"

Moon Tree, feeling somewhat like a turtle pulling in its neck, shrugged lackadaisically. "Wouldn't like to see someone take advantage of that little wench. She's likely to make a gelding outta any darned fool who tried tickling her. 'Sides, O'Grady's old enough to be her pa. Reckon he'd rather keep his voice than end up sounding like a field sparrow."

Willie Left Hand eyed Moon again and grinned. "Make you feel a bit more easylike, eh? I'd say she's in good hands with O'Grady, might make a lady outta her. Who knows?"

White Moon responded dryly, "Ei, and the river might freeze over next July, too."

* * *

Several days later, Molly Goodhart came into the bunkhouse to prepare supper, a worried look on her face. A nervous fluster was about her as she shoved around the pots and pans. The signs were bad. The Crow blood in her was telling her this. For the second consecutive day, she had seen many snowy owls in the gaunt cottonwoods, and at night, she had heard their ominous calls. Only once in her life had she seen this phenomenon, years ago on the Yellowstone at Manuel's Fort just after she and her late husband, John, had been married. At that time, the river had frozen, bank to bank, and below the trading post she saw the buffalo crossing the ice, making their way into the shelter of the timbered bottoms, and all of the animals that weren't already sleeping for the winter went into hibernation, dug deep holes and hid. An eerie silence came over the land. Cold Maker soon came bringing the dreaded white-out of the *kissineyooway'o*, icy gales and glassy particles of snow as fine as flecks of mica.

This night, after the drovers had eaten, she bundled up and went back to James and Little Blue's home where she slept, talked with her son about what she had seen, and what she believed—*kissineyooway'o* was coming. James, placing credence in his mother's words, went over to Claybourn Moore's house and related the story. The foreman listened understandingly, and after James left, checked the thermometer on the porch. It read twenty-eight degrees above zero, not too bad for a mid-December evening. The skies were sprinkled with stars and not a trace of a wind touched the valley. But, he, too, heard the owls this night.

The next morning, the skies had turned ugly gray and a sharp wind was coming in from the north. When Moore glanced at the thermometer, it was hovering around ten degrees above zero but dropping. He knew in an instant that Molly Goodhart's forecast was more than Indian myth, and he took off in a trot for the bunkhouse. At the best, Moore figured he had five or six hours to bring the herds down into the covered shelters of the Six Mile bottom, the long sheds that he and some of the men had built several years back at the insistence of Ben Tree His first order to the men was to bring in all of the cattle as quickly as possible, and once secured, get a good supply of hay banked around the enclosures. Hitching up a wagon, he went up the snowy ruts toward the hot-springs home of Zachary Hockett and Two Shell Woman to bring them and little Joseph down to the main ranch. If a severe storm and cold front set in for any length of time, he didn't want them snowbound in subzero weather. Moore saw no sign of the snowy owls along the way this morning, for the messengers of the *kissineyooway'o* had already flown south.

Benjamin and James Goodhart quickly set about using another wagon, taking extra wood to the houses, building up the stacks by the doorways. By the time they had finished, the porch thermometer at Moore's house read exactly zero. They were drinking hot coffee in James's home when Moore returned from the line cabin with the Hockett family, their horses trailing behind. Late in the afternoon, the horse herd was milling about in the big corrals and doors to the sheds and main barns were opened. Then the first winds came with blowing snow, and a few hours later, in the middle of the blizzard, Willie Left Hand, Robert Peete, Peter Marshall, and Moon Tree returned by the creek trail, took their horses into the nearest shed, and went running for the bunkhouse. Peter Marshall's long, drooping mustache was frozen to his face, a froth of ice circling it from his moist breath. Later, Clay Moore arrived to tell the men it was now twenty below zero; there was only one chore until further notice—see that there was adequate hay along the shelters for the cattle to keep up their energy. He, James, and Benjamin would take care of the horses and the wood supply. Zachary Hockett would supervise the livestock feeding. No other work would be attempted until the weather broke, and no one was to venture out alone.

The next morning the ranch was locked by frigid, arctic air, and a ten-inch blanket of powder snow covered the range. The men, faces wrapped with woolen scarves, jumped aboard the hay wagons, and the horses, spewing steam like miniature dragons, trundled away up the creek bottom. Pulling away the poles from the stacks, the men hurriedly loaded several days' supply of feed for the hundreds of cattle that were sandwiched like cordwood in the shelters. The old cows knew feed was coming. They bawled. Sharing body heat, the milling cattle sent clouds of steam filtering up from the protection of the long sheds. Because of Clay Moore's swift action, the herd was now secure, protected from the brunt of the storm, and he figured that losses, if any, would be minimal. The temperature had bottomed out at forty-eight below, and it was to stay in that general area for the next five days. For the men in the bunkhouse, it was a time of short work, hot coffee spiked with brandy, and games of nickel and dime poker, while in the homes of James Goodhart, Young Benjamin, and Clay Moore, fireplaces blazed during the day and were banked heavily at night. Everyone was now captive to the *kissineyooway'o*.

Zachary Hockett, Two Shell Woman, and little Joseph were staying with Benjamin and White Crane. Their friendship went back seven years to the Indian wars and a time when Lieutenant Hockett had lived for a month in Man Called Tree's village on the Yellowstone. Two Shell wasn't any stranger to the Tree ranch. During her return to the Nez Perce in seventy-six and before her marriage to Hockett she had been brought to the ranch by Benjamin One Feather and his bride, White Crane. Two Shell Woman and Benjamin had delivered Ruth Moore's child, Joshua, who was now a little more than seven years old.

Shell was a healer. She had also removed a bullet from Hockett's leg when he had been shot by hostiles on the raid at Goodhart's old trading post.

Early in the afternoon on the fifth day of the *kissineyooway'o,* Shell was called into the side bedroom by White Crane, who was sitting on the bed with her son, Thad. White Crane had a big, satisfied smile on her face, and her hands were clasped around her rotund belly. Since neither woman spoke the other's native tongue, Shell being Nez Perce and White Crane Absaroke, they made do with sign and the English they were always learning. In between a few meaningful gestures and a few words of English, White Crane announced that she thought her baby was coming. With a gleeful shout, Shell rushed away to the front room and began giving orders to an astonished Zachary Hockett and to Young Benjamin.

Benjamin, of course, had been through this experience, though Hockett had not. Hockett, alarmed, immediately threw on his heavy coat and twirled a scarf around his head, and went up the snowy lane to Goodhart's house to fetch Molly and Little Blue. Women, he allowed, were always better at these things, and any thought of bringing old Doc Tudor out to the ranch was a hopeless case in forty-below weather.

The men, along with young Thad and Joseph, sat around the fireplace in the big front room while the women busied themselves between the kitchen and side bedroom, flitting back and forth making all the necessary preparations. Several of the minor chores went begging, for within two hours a small cry was heard, and Benjamin's sister, Little Blue Goodhart, stuck her head out of the open door to announce the newest member of the Tree family, a baby girl. Benjamin One Feather proudly accepted congratulations from Hockett, and a short time later went into the bedroom to see his new daughter.

After five days of bitter cold and icy mist, the first rays of sun were touching the frosty window-pane, projecting a myriad of sparkling patterns across the glass. It was a mystic moment for White Crane, with ancient tribal significance. "Sunshine," she said with a tired but happy smile. "Sunshine will be her name."

"Ei." Benjamin One Feather smiled. "The gift of Masaka."

The night after the birth of Sunshine Tree, a chinook from the southwest rippled over the frozen slopes of the Gallatin, and by dawn, the temperature had climbed dramatically to thirty degrees above zero. By midday, a thaw set in, and the men were all out opening gates to the lower range and bottom land hay fields. Most of the cattle spilled out from the enclosures, threading out in long strings through the drifts of melting snow; others were content to stay near the creek-bottom sheds where they munched the last gleanings of hay. Moore and Hockett, scouting together up the creek trail and nearby slopes, found only two dead heifers and one old cow, luckless animals that had strayed too far from the hay and warmth of the herds. Moore considered this a miracle, the loss of only three head out of over three thousand. The horse herd, numbering almost one hundred, came through the siege in excellent shape. Moore, indeed, was gratified and thankful, and he let this be known to Molly Goodhart.

It wasn't until later that afternoon that Moore realized how fortunate the Tree ranch had been. Jessie Stuart came riding up the main ranch road on the Appaloosa, Hawkeye, and reined up at Moore's house with a dark, troubled look on her pretty face. The Lazy Bar S ranch hadn't fared well over the past week—losses were going to run into the thousands. The upper Stuart lands were dotted with frozen stock, some animals still standing like stone statues, their jaws locked, flecks of ice in their nostrils. Adam Stuart estimated the cost of the *kissineyooway'o* to his outfit alone at close to forty thousand dollars, and he feared when the reports came down from the Judith Basin country, some ranches would be bankrupt.

Jessie visited with White Crane and held the new baby. Sighing, she said to Benjamin and White Crane, "I'd love to have a little one like this."

Benjamin quickly replied, "I'll tell this to my brother, see what's holding him up."

Jessie blushed, offered no immediate reply to this, but she certainly knew what the delay was all about, namely marriage, and her own precautions that she had rigorously practiced. Her trysts with Moon were joyous, but often followed by small frets. "My time will come," she finally said.

White Moon, saddened by the news, saddled up his brown and white mare and rode back to the Stuart ranch with Jessie, not for romantic reasons but to express his condolences to Adam Stuart and to see if he could be of any help in a disastrous situation. There really wasn't much he could say, and he thought that when Stuart learned the Tree ranch had only lost three critters, it would probably put the old man right under the table. There never was much that an Indian could teach a white man, a gambling Indian at that, except maybe how to break Nez Perce ponies. Adam Stuart never did understand all of those expensive wintering shelters, for instance. He thought Ben Tree had built them to shade the cattle in the heat of the summer. Moon knew that white men always had to learn things the hard way. Plenty ranchers had the notion that if the buffalo could freely roam the plains and fend for themselves, so could a herd of tough, old Texas-strain steers. All that grass, all that water, all that free land, all plenty good. Truth was, and it was taking a long time to sink in, a cow wasn't a buffalo; a cow was a downright stupid critter, no sense of direction, dumb enough to stand out in the middle of a snowstorm and freeze to death. Moon wondered how he could explain this to an old cowboy like Adam Stuart. Well, he wouldn't. He would just sit and commiserate with the old codger, maybe offer to bring over a few drovers to help haul away all the carcasses cluttering up his range.

Moon heard Jessie talking, felt her leg brushing his as they rode up to the gate.

"You'll stay for supper?" she asked. "Papa is distressed. Some conversation might help."

White Moon protested, but kindly. "No, I don't think he'd be much in the mood for my kind of conversation, not tonight, anyhow. I'll just pay my respects, Jessie, get on back before dark if I can. If I told him he should have moved his stock to the bottom to his stacks, he'd probably get sore. Pouring salt into the wounds."

"We did get some down," Jessie said. "Too late on the others. Did what we could, Moon. We never had a week like this before, never." She sighed forlornly. "Poor Papa. If not rustlers and killers, it's a freak winter. He's had a bad year."

"Won't have to worry about that Dupee Clancy and his boys for a while." Moon said, dismounting in front of the house. "He's down in Nevada somewhere."

She gave him a curious look. "Where did you hear that? Did they catch him?"

"Nope," replied Moon. "Received a post from

that Miss Divinity. She saw him in Reno, in some big saloon. She recognized him and he ran out plenty fast. That's the last I've heard."

Both surprised and suddenly suspicious, Jessie said, "She wrote you a letter? Really! What's that woman doing all the way down there? And in a saloon!"

Moon grabbed her under the shoulders, swung her gracefully up to the top of the stairs, and laughed, saying, "You wouldn't believe me if I told you. Ei, a crazy story."

"What about that woman?" she demanded, pushing a fingertip against his cold nose.

"She's making music, singing. She and some fellow, O'Grady's the name," Moon Tree said. "Willie knows O'Grady, says he's a good one. He's the man who sent the letter. She's coming back this way in the spring to get her money and such."

Jessie Stuart stared incredulously as Moon opened the front door. Why was he so indifferent, so blasé about all of this? Or was he? She wasn't concerned about the singing, the making music part of what he was telling her, but she didn't like the idea of Divinity Jones returning to the Gallatin, particularly the "and such" part.

FIFTEEN

Everyone in the high country welcomed spring, the early rains that melted the snow, the warming sun that nurtured the tender grass, the celebration of rebirth. Everyone except Dupee Clancy. It was early April, a rainy day, low clouds hugging the ridges. He was sloshing along the road north to his secret cabin in the Ruby Mountains. His poncho draped over his shoulders, his canvas duster hugging his legs, and raindrops dripping from the brim of his hat, Clancy was a lonely, disconsolate man. Luckily, he wasn't broke. He still had a hundred dollars left after his long winter in Nevada. But he was riding alone, and to Dupee Clancy, there wasn't much comfort in this, even on a sunny, warm day, which it *wasn't*. He was truly lonely. He hadn't seen hide nor hair of Harley Frame or Bowie Turnbow since they had hauled freight on him down in Reno. Hell, he couldn't blame them. After all, it was a move for their own safety. Why be seen consorting with a man who had a price on his head? Well, he thought, maybe this was going to change for the better once they were together again back at the old cabin. He reckoned he'd let his beard grow back, sniff the air to see if the hound dogs were still about or whether they had forgotten him over the long, hard winter. And he'd heard that it had been a bad one, lots of cattle lost in the territory. Not much profit in rustling cows anyway, too tough to move quickly, not to mention sell, and a good horse was worth more. Yep, he figured everything would fall neatly into place once he and the boys were back on the track and running again.

By nightfall Clancy, hungry and thirsty, came up over the rise toward the divide and saw a few welcome lights up ahead. The spring drizzle had stopped, but he was a tad chilled. Clancy needed a bed for the night and a good meal in his belly. He knew this place, Dubois. He'd played a few hands of poker at one of the saloons in the past years. They had a small hotel too, he remembered, and not too steep for what little wad he had left. Besides, it was just too far down the line to Hoag's Saloon at Armstead, and Hoag's cooking wasn't much to brag about, either. So Dupee Clancy, tired in the butt and with a big gnaw in his gut, reined up in front of Blanche Grant's hotel.

After paying for his room, he satisfied his first need, a hot bath in the big tub at the end of the hall. He paid a dollar extra for this, but it was well worth it. He jumped in feeling like a bone and came out feeling like a rag. He had a good steak in the dining room too, where he was the only one seated. There was some excitement in the little town, the big, jolly woman called Blanche said. Two of her old friends had come in from the big city of San Francisco, and were next door at Finney's Saloon putting on a show. She was in a hurry to get over and see what was going on.

Clancy didn't want to hold her up, so he just paid his fare for the meal and continued eating. Later, when he walked outside to put his horse in the livery for the night, he noticed all of the wagons and horses lined up along the boardwalk, a good crowd on hand, he reckoned, to see the show at Finney's place. Even the livery man was gone, only a boy there tending the barn, so Clancy flipped him a coin and told him to give the horse hay, water, and a stall for the night. Curious about all the ruckus, and allowing that he could use a drink or two before bed, he sauntered on up the street. At the big doors of Finney's, he tucked up his coat collar, set his hat straight, and walked on into the big crowd. He couldn't see a thing from the doorway, only heard the music and the people keeping time with their stomping feet. He thought most everyone from the countryside was here, a regular Saturday night hoedown. No one paid him any mind. Of course, that wasn't anything to jaw about, because he didn't have a friend in the place. He did manage to get a drink of whiskey, but still couldn't see the entertainment. In fact, he couldn't even understand the words the performers were singing.

"What the hell is that lingo?" he asked the bartender.

"A French song," was the reply. "That dark fellow is French. That's our Divinity singing with him. She's sure something, that little lady, a real looker, too. Get on up there close, take a look, mister, give your eyes a treat. Sweet Divinity from Grant's Hotel."

"Divinity?" Dupee Clancy asked hoarsely. "Did you say her name's Divinity?"

"Yes, sir, Divinity Jones," the bartender replied proudly. Got her start right here." But when the barkeep glanced back to the side, the stranger was gone. Half of his whiskey was still in the glass, though, and it still had a little ripple in it.

Clancy didn't bother to go back to the hotel, no need to, he was wearing his traveling clothes and was ready to make long tracks, even in the blackness of the night. The boy at the stable was surprised to see his customer of a half hour ago come back and claim his horse. "Ain't no one leaving 'cept you, mister," he said to Clancy. "Everybody's seeing the show at Finney's. Thought that's what you came for."

"I seen it," Clancy mumbled, throwing on his saddle. "Once was enough."

Dupee Clancy wasn't angry, just defeated and demoralized by circumstances beyond his comprehension. Was this woman, Divinity Jones, out to haunt him? All the way down to Nevada and now back, of all places, to Dubois? For crissakes, what was she up to? Maybe the ghost of her old man was putting her up to these shenanigans. Damned if he'd ever had such an experience in his life, two of them, in fact. But Clancy considered himself lucky this time—she hadn't seen his face and sicced the house down to him like a pack of wolves. Well, maybe if he rode far enough this night, he could make it to Fat Hoag's place, catch a few hours of shut-eye in peace, far away from all the goddamned stomping sheepherders. One thing for certain—he wasn't about to sleep under the same roof with Divinity Jones and have it cave in on him.

Divinity Jones wasn't content to rest on her laurels. She felt indebted to Blanche Grant, and though she was now a lady of means, having saved almost two-thousand dollars from the winter tour, she didn't forget where it all had begun. When she wasn't practicing her guitar or improving her French, she helped Blanche, sometimes in the dining room or in the hotel. And in the evening she always sang a few songs. As they did in the beginning, O'Grady and Jones entertained at Finney's Saloon on Friday and Saturday nights, as a favor to Finney as well as for a practice session, because Amos Finney could not afford what was now the standard fee for their performances. The paltry fifty dollars a weekend that he paid took care of their weekly hotel bill and a few meals, so their respite in Dubois wasn't totally a lost cause. They enjoyed what they were doing, and Sean O'Grady never stopped promoting their act. He had new posters made in Salt Lake City, ordered fashionable clothes from San Francisco, and continually worked on new routines that the trio would try out at Finney's. O'Grady planned only one appearance in the Montana Territory before taking the act to Denver, where he had also arranged to meet Dion Boucicault and sign on for the Eastern Dramatic Company revue. O'Grady had agreed to play two weeks in Helena at the New Placer Hotel before heading south for Denver. Divinity Jones had a legal matter to settle in the territorial capital, so O'Grady scheduled their opening there at the end of the first week in May.

After several days of final preparation, the trio boarded the north-bound stage. Divinity's close friend and fatherly adviser, Henry Billow, was one of the two men driving the stage.

During the change of teams at the stage station, Dell, Billow escorted Divinity to the Mint Cafe, while the two men and a fourth passenger, William Gladstone, a salesman for Colt Arms, went into the adjacent saloon. It was late in the day, another three or four hours before a night stop at the hotel in Dillon. Billow thought it only proper that his Miss Divinity have some coffee and a snack to tide her over until they reached the hotel at Dillon. The three men passengers would sustain themselves, as they usually did, on a bottle of beer, a shot of rye, and a hard pretzel or two. There were five small tables in the cafe, one of them occupied by two men dressed in khaki, wearing long brown lace-up boots. It was a few minutes before Divinity's sharp blue eyes, always roving excitedly, fell on one of the men at the nearby table. After she was quite certain, she said, "Why, I declare, is that you, Mr. Aubrey?"

Indeed, the man was Timothy Aubrey, the railroad surveyor, but when he turned to the young lady addressing him, his face went blank, for he couldn't remember ever seeing this woman before. Nevertheless, he got to his feet and nodded politely. "Yes, my name is Aubrey," he said, somewhat embarrassed. "I don't recall—"

"Quelle surprise!" Divinity exclaimed, offering her hand. "But you don't remember me, do you? *Comment allez-vous?*" And she removed her velvet hat and shook out her long, blonde hair.

Aubrey, with a dazed expression, came closer, adjusted his spectacles, and whispered, "Is that you, Miss Jones? Divinity Jones? What on earth happened to you?"

She laughed lightly and turned to introduce Henry Billow. "This is a friend of mine, Mr. Billow. Mr. Billow drives the stage. And this man is Mr. Aubrey. He works for the railroad."

The two men shook hands, but Timothy Aubrey's eyes never left Divinity. Yes, this was Divinity Jones, but not the wild young daisy he remembered, nor the "hostile" that White Moon Tree had taken under his wing. A smile finally crept across his face. "You must have received your money for the water at Derby Flats. You look very nice, Miss Jones. Why, the last time we talked, you were chasing those two dogs and kicking the dust off of your boots on the porch steps."

"She's a singer now," Henry Billow put in proudly. "Been down in San Francisco, all over, playing and singing. That's something, ain't it? Going up to get her property money now, all the way to Helena."

"Please sit down," Divinity said to Aubrey. "We have a short time to talk."

Timothy Aubrey did so. He was flabbergasted. "A singer?" he gasped. "Really? I didn't know you sang, Miss Jones. Sheep . . . I thought . . ."

Her coffee and biscuit came, and with a little wave, Divinity Jones said, "No more sheep, *mon ami*," and in a rush, she told Aubrey most everything that had happened to her since they last talked at Derby Flats.

Aubrey was happily astounded. In turn, he informed Divinity and Billow that the railroad survey was continuing on down the Beaverhead Valley. That's why he was here. It was going all the way to a junction point near Butte, then on to Helena. Tracks were already laid through Derby Flats, a station house built, and the train was bringing supplies for the rail workers to a point thirty miles north of her property. By the following year, he said, service would be beyond Dillon. Ultimately, Aubrey asked her whether she had heard from White Moon.

"One letter, *oui*, that's all," she said. "He told me about the terrible winter. It was so cold! And the stories he tells, *mon Dieu!*"

Aubrey grinned, nodded affirmatively. "I know. Yes, I know all about his stories."

"Why, he said this man, a town drunk, fell one night," she hurriedly went on. "*Oui*, they found him the next morning frozen to death, his hand reaching out for one last drink. Mr. Moon said the man was so stiff they couldn't get him in the coffin. And do you know what those people did? They just stood him up on the corner, *oui*, hung a lantern on his arm and used him for a lamppost the rest of the winter. This is what Mr. Moon told me." She gave Timothy Aubrey a funny look. "You don't believe this, do you?"

Grinning, Aubrey said, "Your Mr. Moon has a reputation."

"Yes," Divinity continued, "And Miss Benjamin had her baby, too. A little girl. She named her Sunshine." She paused to sip her coffee. "You remember Benjamin. Mr. Moon said he was your friend a long time ago."

"I remember." Aubrey smiled, reflecting momentarily on their two meetings on the Yellowstone near the Goodhart homesteads. The little conversation abruptly came to an end when Henry

Billow's partner stuck his head in the door announcing that the stage was ready to leave.

Divinity took Aubrey's extended hand and gave it a pat. "When I write to Mr. Moon, I'll tell him I saw you, and sometime I hope you can come to hear me sing, see our act."

Aubrey replied graciously, "Maybe in New York or Boston, who knows? I'll watch for you, I promise."

"*Au revoir,* Mr. Aubrey."

"Yes, *au revoir,* Miss Jones."

When the stage rattled away from the station, Divinity Jones was waving out the window with her handkerchief to a smiling, thoroughly amazed Timothy Aubrey.

A short drive down the valley, Billow swung by Armstead to throw off several packages and some mail. It was near dusk, about a twenty-mile ride to the hotel in Dillon, and except for a few men standing along the porch at Hoag's Saloon, the lone street was empty.

After her chance meeting with Timothy Aubrey in Dell, it never occurred to Divinity Jones that she would see another old acquaintance. Yet among the three drovers watching the stage from the Hoag's porch, she saw a face from out of the past. Just as the coach pulled away, Divinity Jones, the elegant lady, stuck her head out of the window, pointed across the dusty street, and screamed, "You son of a bitch, I'll have the law on your ass when I get to Dillon!"

The three observers, Dupee Clancy, Bowie Turnbow, and Harley Frame, back together again, didn't pause to give Divinity Jones a parting wave. Before the stage was even out of sight, they were mounted and riding back up the canyon toward a distant ridge of the Ruby Mountains.

The billing outside the hotel in Helena read "Direct from San Francisco, O'Grady and Jones," and even though the trio had spent the greater part of a month in little Dubois, no one quibbled with this splendid introduction. With Sean O'Grady's penchant for promotion and publicity, he had also let it be known to the newspaper people that he and his two partners (Mr. L. Beauregard was now receiving one-third of the take) had made a personal appearance at Governor Perkins's mansion in Sacramento. Music lovers in Helena had been adequately prepared for this great musical engagement at the Placer. So had the hotel management. Miss Divinity Jones was ensconced in a two-room suite on the upper floor, and O'Grady and Mr. Beau had two large connecting rooms resplendent with ornate wall mirrors and Victorian furniture.

Each night, they performed before large crowds in the big lounge and taproom on the main floor. There were no vacant seats—many people were forced to stand along the back wall or at the long bar—but no one complained, particularly when the exuberant Divinity Jones frequently danced right out into the crowd, in between the tables, along the bar, presenting her charms to everyone.

"What a delight," the weekly newspaper, *The Independent,* reported. "This winsome young songstress captured the hearts of all the ladies and gentlemen who were fortunate enough to see the first night of the performance."

On the following Friday night, Sad Sam Courtland arrived in town for a weekend poker game in the back room of the Silver Slipper Saloon. Fresh from a winning streak in Dillon and Butte, he had written Moon Tree the previous week, advising him of the no-limit game, and Moon, who hadn't been tested too much lately in Bozeman, readily accepted the opportunity to combine talents with Sad Sam.

Moon came in on the stage from Bozeman late Saturday afternoon, checked in at the Broadway Rooms, and went off searching for his partner. He located him at Barney's Billiard Parlor engaged in a pool shoot-out with three other men. Pool wasn't Sad Sam's strong suit, but he managed to leave with twenty-five dollars, enough to invite Moon to dinner at the New Placer Hotel. They always had a few subtle signs to rehearse before the night's action began.

At the hotel entrance, a large placard in bold black letters suddenly jumped out at Moon Tree. His jaw dropped a notch, and he stood staring up at the sign: "O'Grady and Jones, Direct from San Francisco, Appearing Nightly." Divinity Jones! She was here! But why hadn't she told him? But then again, she had said she was coming to Helena in May to meet with Arthur Clawson. More than meet, she was going to collect her fortune from the Derby Flats' transactions. But she hadn't mentioned anything in her letter about performing at the New Placer Hotel, and this, while happily surprising Moon, also mildly upset him. If he were her buddy, her *mon chéri*, the least she could have done was invite him to the opening.

"Signs fascinate you?" he heard Sad Sam saying.

"This one does, ei," Moon replied. "I know this woman, the Jones part of it. Hard to believe."

Sad Sam's brows arched. He was used to Moon Tree's tall stories, his frequent exaggeration of the facts. "She's from San Francisco, friend. When have you been that far west?" Pushing the door open, he said, "Come on, we came for dinner, not a dish of bull."

"No bull," Moon Tree told him. "Divinity Jones."

"Yes, I know, saw the show last night," Courtland said dryly. "She's a classy entertainer, not exactly your type."

"I know her." Moon said adamantly. "Know her plenty well, maybe more than most of the folks around here do."

"Well, well." Sad Sam grinned. "You been holding out on me? Keeping something stashed under the table? Enlighten me, Mr. Tree, enlighten me."

And as they passed on into the dining room,

Moon Tree quietly said, "Remember the old sheepherder Dupee Clancy did in up above Stuart's place? Burleigh Jones? That fracas I got myself in last summer? Well, by jingo, this is his daughter, the one I had to play shepherd to all the way down to that damned sheep country. Divinity Jones."

Sad Sam merely edged his lanky frame into his seat, stared at the white table cloth, and drawled skeptically, "If she's a sheepherder's daughter, then I'm a military mule. We've been talking about different women, son. She sang a couple of songs with a Cajun boy, sang 'em in French. Now, there's a few of those herders around that are Basque, but no Frenchman that I know about."

But Sad Sam, sipping on white wine, a captive at the dinner table, had to listen as White Moon told the tale of Divinity Jones. When the meal arrived, Sad Sam ate, and listened no more. Moon Tree told good stories, unbelievable and entertaining, but a steak, well, this was something he could really swallow.

The two men played well at the Silver Slipper that evening, even contesting each other for big pots several times just to make the opposition more gullible. Toward eleven o'clock, Moon made a graceful exit. The action had dwindled down to five players, anyhow, too many cards left in the deck to do anything but guesswork. The Red Man, nearly eight hundred dollars ahead, figured Sad Sam had a thousand or more, and this would make a tidy split for a short night's work. Paying his respects, and buying a round of drinks for the men at the bar, Moon Tree deserted the Silver Slipper and headed up the street for the New Placer, allowing that he had time to catch most of Divinity Jones's late performance.

O'Grady and Jones were singing together when he entered the packed lounge. There were no seats, but he managed to wedge himself into the line at the bar, ordered a glass of wine, and finally found a vacant niche near the corner of the small stage. What he then heard and saw was more than he had ever expected, and he realized that Sad Sam Courtland had every reason to doubt his veracity about knowing Divinity Jones. This wasn't the Miss Divinity he knew, or for that matter, had ever known. Before his eyes, sometimes quietly swaying, other times stalking the stage like a hungry panther, here was a creature that only Akbatatdia could have made. She was gorgeous. She presented herself as though she had been born to entertain, and she was more than good, she was great.

Moon Tree felt a lump in his throat, tried to squelch it with a swallow of wine, only to discover that his whole body felt funny, little goosebumps chasing each other up and down his spine. His wine disappeared like a vaporous mist, inhaled, and he ordered another one.

Divinity and the man she called Mr. Beau came forward and sang together—one of those French songs that Sad Sam had mentioned. Mr. Beau, his white teeth flashing, thumped on his big bass, and Divinity played a guitar with her name written across the face of the box.

Seeing this, Moon smiled reflectively. He remembered how she had printed her name in the dirt over and over, remembered some of the other things he had tried to teach her.

Moon Tree, thoroughly enjoying himself and the wondrous transformation before his eyes, was well into his third glass of wine when Miss Divinity finally saw him. She was in the middle of a song, but quietly set her guitar aside, and with O'Grady and Mr. Beau not missing a beat, she stepped from the stage and began moving through the crowd, singing and smiling, touching the extended hands, until she came directly in front of Moon. Grasping his arm, Divinity pulled him from his little niche, gently led him into the glare of the lights at the front of the stage. She ended the song joyously, then amid all the applause, reached up and kissed her *mon chéri*.

"This is my buddy, ladies and gentlemen!" she cried out. "This is Mr. Moon Tree from the great Tree ranch in the Gallatin Valley."

For some strange reason, many people applauded again, a mystery to White Moon. But then Divinity Jones said loudly, "The story is too long to tell you, but he's the reason I'm here tonight." To Moon's embarrassment, she hugged and kissed him again, shouted to the crowd, "*Mon chéri, Monsieur Tree, quel homme!*" What a man!

Everything after this was somewhat confusing. A small table and two chairs materialized from out of the darkness, and a bottle of wine and several glasses came with them. After every two or three numbers, Divinity appeared for a short break and sat beside Moon. Occasionally, some stranger would come up, shake his hand, and tell him that his father was an old friend, a statement Moon thought might be a bit farfetched, somewhat like many of his own stories. Under the circumstances, he took what came as graciously as he could, but all the time wished he somehow could crawl back into the seclusion of his corner niche. He was uncomfortable and also a little light in the head. Sad Sam would have been disappointed to see a half-empty wine bottle on the table.

Fortunately, the finale came. Much applause again, good nights from Sean O'Grady, Divinity Jones, and Mr. L. Beauregard. Few of the people wandered away. Not Divinity Jones. She came to the table and whispered in Moon Tree's ear, smiled, patted him on the cheek, then disappeared.

White Moon, his head whirling like a desert devil, retrieved his fancy hat, went out the front door of the hotel and deeply inhaled the midnight air. He walked down one side of Last Chance Gulch, then back up the other, and after stopping in the men's room by the bar, he climbed the flight of stairs to the upper floor, went to suite twenty where he quietly tapped on the door.

The voice from within was melodiously inviting. Wide blue eyes appeared in the crack of the door, it opened, closed softly behind him, and Moon Tree knew that he was a long way from Derby Flats. Divinity Jones, her golden hair streaming down both sides of her shoulders, was dressed in a white, silk robe, so silky that Moon wondered what it was supposed to cover. Or hide? Practically nothing, in fact. Taking his hat and gambling coat, Divinity placed them on a rack, then ushered him to a small table. There was coffee in a silver pot, cakes and small biscuits, all on little silver plates, china cups and saucers, a service for two. Divinity poured coffee, then settled herself across from him.

Moon casually took a sip of the hot coffee, then asked, "Why didn't you tell me you were going to play here? Maybe I could have come up the first night, brought along some of the family."

"Because I knew you were coming, anyways," Divinity Jones said. "This was all arranged, *tout suite.*"

Moon Tree gave her a puzzle look. "You knew? And how'd you know a thing like that? Only the people at the ranch know I'm up here."

Divinity smiled saucily, reached over and tweaked the end of his nose. "I have friends, *mon chéri*, your friends. A Mr. Courtland. Do you know him?"

"Know him!" Moon exclaimed. "Hell, I spent half of the night playing poker with him." He gave her a curious stare. "Where did you meet Sad Sam?"

"On the stage down at Dillon," she replied almost casually. "Two weeks ago. He was going to Butte, on business, he said. We talked for a long time. He was surprised when I mentioned your name. He said you were going to be in Helena on this Saturday night. Business. And *voilà*, here you are!" She laughed merrily, then whispered, "Did you win tonight? Did you bring me some money for the damned cuss game?"

Moon Tree chuckled. "He suckered me in, that man, played a crooked deck on me. Let me go on and on at dinner tonight, knew all the time about you."

And Divinity Jones laughed again, promptly got up and placed herself on Moon Tree's lap. "Did you like me tonight? Did I please you like a lady? Am I a quick learner?"

"You were plenty good, little sheepherder," he said with a slow grin. "Ei, you've learned well."

"I owe it to you," she said, kissing him. She ran her hands over her silk robe, traced the contours of her body. "This is better than that old blanket you always made me cover myself with, don't you think?"

How in the name of Bakukure, the Great One Above, could he deny this? The brittle shell of indifference wrapped around him crumbled like a withered leaf. "I agree, Miss Divinity, it sure is."

Divinity Jones proudly marched herself to the big bed with the beautiful canopy. "*Va!*" she commanded, letting the robe slip away. "No more blankets, no more waiting."

And Moon followed. She ran her hands up under his shirt, felt the smooth body that she had once tickled in the sheepherder wagon. "*Comme vous êtes gentil.*" She whispered.

"What does that mean?" Moon asked with a slight tremble.

"How nice you are."

The first thing Moon Tree did when he returned to the ranch late Sunday was inform his brother and Claybourn Moore that Dupee Clancy was back in the territory. The rustler had been seen in the Beaverhead by none other than Divinity Jones. This revelation had two barrels: the men were curious about the circumstances of the sighting of Clancy as well as about the financial outcome of Divinity's negotiations with the railroad.

As to the first, obviously Clancy had returned from Nevada where he had been seen by Divinity Jones during the winter, but whether he would resurface in the Gallatin was anyone's guess. Clay Moore could only assume that it was going to turn into a "wait and see" game. However, he didn't think Clancy was foolish enough to make the same rustling mistake twice, not with a price on his head, and certainly not on the Tree property.

As for the appearance of Divinity Jones, everyone had been expecting this, knew she was destined to become a wealthy young woman, so they weren't too surprised to learn that she had a little over one hundred thousand dollars after Arthur Clawson had taken out a modest legal fee. At Clawson's advice, she had deposited the drafts from the railroad and livestock company with the intention of accumulating another fortune in interest. But when Moon said that Divinity Jones really didn't need any of the money because of her new career, this astounded everyone. Was Divinity Jones actually going to make a career out of singing? More than a singer. The trip to Nevada and California was more than a lark, too. She and her friends, Sean O'Grady and Beauregard Lincoln, were now booked to go on a big eastern tour with a New York dramatic company, beginning in the summer. And after this, of all things, Sean O'Grady was making plans to take the act to Ireland, England, and France. What need did Divinity Jones have for money? Presently, none. She was not only a singer, she also played the guitar and banjo, and had the unique ability to wrap an audience right around her little finger. Moon Tree told them that he'd never seen such an astonishing performance in his life.

As for the performance of Divinity Jones in the bedroom, he made no mention, but it had been equally astonishing. So the second thing Moon did upon his return to the ranch was to go to bed to recuperate.

The next afternoon, Ben Tree and Rainbow arrived to visit their family, especially their three grandchildren—Melody Goodhart and Thad and Sunshine Tree. There were other matters, too. Ben Tree, Sr., as he had promised, was going to help Ruth and Clay Moore with the move to the new property on the Yellowstone. Construction of stockyards and packing plant was to begin within a month, hopefully completed by fall in time for winter shipments of beef to the Midwest and East Coast markets. He had already hired a man to travel east and establish contracts, one Elbert Craig, an old friend of the horsebreaker Bird Rutledge and T. B. Garth, the man Bird married. Craig, a former supply officer in the army, had been in charge of shipping for a packing company in Omaha, and now had sought out Ben Tree in Billings to be a part of the new venture.

Moore's promotion left a void at the ranch— who was to be the new foreman? Ben Tree settled this matter to everyone's satisfaction. Young Benjamin didn't feel he had the experience, and White Moon, living in a world all of his own, likewise had no immediate aspirations for ramrodding such a large outfit. So since Moore's house and headquarters were available, Ben Tree told Zachary Hockett to bring his small family down from the line cabin and take over. Robert Peete got the job of foreman of the upper range to replace Hockett. A farewell party was arranged for the Moore family the following week.

Hearing this, Moon Tree, with a gleam in his dark eyes, rode into Bozeman later that day and sent a telegram to Divinity Jones.

SIXTEEN

It was just plain old bad luck, Dupee Clancy believed, the way this woman, Divinity Jones, kept popping up like stinkweed. He tried to explain to his two partners that everyone had a run of bad luck once in a while. Bowie Turnbow and Harley Frame weren't entirely convinced.

Bowie, for instance, was a believer in signs, a superstitious sort of a man. It was his opinion that these peculiar appearances were more than coincidence or bad luck. Perhaps they had some hidden meaning, a foreboding of unpredictable events to come. And anything Bowie couldn't actually see, he deeply mistrusted, such as the buzz of rattles in tall grass, the throaty rumble of a bear in deep timber, or a mysterious hoot from dark woods. These were ominous warnings, too. He also was highly skeptical about this Divinity Jones. How could a lowly sheepherder's daughter materialize into a creature of song almost overnight?

Maybe not so farfetched, thought Bowie Turnbow, who had sucked sugar-tit in his cradle in the Great Smoky Mountains. He knew all about boogers and haints from his childhood. If this Divinity Jones didn't have a booger working with her, well, she had a witch, because she certainly had everyone on the run-and-hide. It wasn't too pleasant to be around a man like Dupee Clancy, who had a woman's curse on him.

Harley Frame, on the other hand, was quite practical for a man who had already experienced considerable misfortune in his young life, most often because of others' mistakes. Harley said, "You can't take chances, Dupee. You oughtta know that by now. Like that beard. You were a damned fool for ever shaving it. Likely if anyone recognizes you it's because of your own stupidity, not the ghost of some fool woman."

Clancy glowered. "I ain't stupid, boy. Bad luck gets on every man's back once in a while."

"And another thing," Harley Frame added. "That woman seen us at Armstead. I'm not hanging 'round Fat Hoag's no more, not on your life . . . my life. There's some sayings, you know, 'bout one bad apple, birds of a feather, so I don't see profit in bucking the odds, getting all wrangled because you boys make mistakes." He gave Dupee a hard look. "You better let your goddamned beard get nice and long, pal."

Harley Frame had the stage. He ranted on. Since Divinity Jones was headed for Dillon, he believed the Beaverhead was a poor bet as a place to be rustling livestock. She would tell the law, and the law would tell the ranchers. That's how it always worked. It wasn't much of a trick dealing with one or two inept marshalls in such a big country, but when all of the ranchers got angry and joined forces, well, that was damned scary, for a fact, that vigilance committee stuff. Frame didn't like the idea of getting a hornet's nest stirred up, so it was his contention that the three of them confine their work to the other side of the Ruby Mountains, over in the Madison, maybe even the Gallatin. No one was going to be looking for them over in that country now. No one would even expect Clancy to return after the incident a year ago. The dust had settled enough to consider evening old scores with the Tree brothers. Only one thing: Clancy would have to let his beard grow back. If it set him to scratching all the time, tough luck. Better to be scratching chin than hauling ass all the time because of some little sheepherding wench who seemed to be lurking around every corner.

So Bowie Turnbow and Harley Frame went out scouting by themselves for the first several days. They left Dupee alone at the cabin, told him to fix up the place, ride up and repair the secret corral, and forget his razor. Dupee Clancy did all this, but he didn't like being alone. This seemed to be his biggest misfortune since the killing of Burleigh Jones—he was becoming more and more of a loner. As Harley said, a Judas.

Turnbow and Frame, on the other hand, were

free as birds and had little to hide. So as the days went by, they often spent a night in Virginia City and rode down the gulch casing prospective horse herds along the Chambers and O'Keefe spreads, taking mental notes for future use. At night in town, when they chanced upon some unfortunate drunk or disoriented businessman, they relieved him of his change, watch, and weapon, and through this activity managed to keep their own pockets jingling. Clancy was always happy when they returned with news and grub after these short trips, figured that within another week or two his beard would be full enough to allow him to get back into civilization again and join the fun.

One spring afternoon toward mid-May, Turnbow and Frame, having inspected most everything in their immediate vicinity, rode on down the Madison, crossed over a few hills, and came out near the open range above the Tree and Stuart ranches. Several thousand cattle, mostly cows and calves, were spread out below them almost as far as they could see. Turnbow pointed to a far ridge where a straight line appeared to slice across the grassland. New fence, he informed Frame, barbed wire, an innovation of the Tree ranch, and everything on the far side of the line to the distant, dark blue eastern ridges belonged to the Tree outfit. Down below to the left was Adam Stuart's spread, running west toward the three forks of the Missouri River.

Frame wasn't interested in the Stuart property.

His eyes were still scanning the country beyond the wire—thousands of acres—and it made him angry. How on earth could a bunch of breed Indians own so much land? What right did they have to come over here and live like white people when they had all that reservation land over on the Yellowstone—the very same land that almost had cost him his life. Harley Frame was a bitter, unforgiving young man, and he thought that one of these dark nights he could do some wire cutting, raise a real ruckus, let some of those cattle wander from hell to breakfast. He'd catch a few strays up in the hills later. Just an idea, one of the many ill thoughts he harbored ever since he discovered Benjamin Tree was in the valley and living among the privileged.

The two men moved on toward the bottom, finally hit the road into Bozeman and arrived at the Antler Saloon where they hitched their horses and went inside for a drink. They were more than seventy miles from their cabin in the Ruby, a long way from their bunks. So after a brief discussion, they elected to stay the night in a hotel room upstairs. Neither man was too familiar with the town of Bozeman, had no idea that the Antler Saloon was Moon Tree's favorite gambling parlor, nor did they know the Red Man had a permanent room on the second floor, a place to sack out when it was too late to ride back to the ranch.

The Antler Saloon, in truth, had a silent partner, a fact of which only three people were aware:

the registered owner, Lacey Tubbs; the silent partner himself, one Sad Sam Courtland; and
Courtland's frequent poker cohort, Moon Tree. It
was a cozy arrangement, and of course, on this
late afternoon when Moon Tree arrived with a
wagon to borrow the saloon piano for a couple of
days, Lacey Tubbs had no objection. Besides,
hardly anyone came in to play and sing
anymore—it was too distracting to the poker players.

It so happened that Bowie Turnbow and Harley
Frame were the only two men at the bar. A small
game was underway near the back table, not
much use of interrupting it, so Lacey Tubbs asked
his two customers if they would mind lending a
hand at moving the piano onto the wagon. It was
a heavy beast and would take at least four men to
hoist it aboard. Bowie Turnbow and Harley Frame
were obliging and they promptly put their muscle
into the task. Along with Lacey and Moon, they
hustled the piano out the door to the boardwalk.

A small crack in the walk proved to be the undoing of Bowie Turnbow—the piano's back left
wheel momentarily hung up, and he made the
mistake of getting his foot a tad too close to the
roller. When the men heaved to clear the obstacle,
the piano wheel moved right over Bowie's toes,
abruptly ending his moving adventure. Howling in
pain, he hopped away like a one-legged turkey,
and this outcry brought a few of the men running
from the poker table with the notion that the pi-

ano had fallen on someone. There were a few hoots when they saw Bowie Turnbow doing his dance down the boardwalk, so they all pitched in and hoisted the piano onto the wagon. Moon Tree thanked everyone and ordered a round of drinks. He told Lacey Tubbs to set up extra rounds for Bowie Turnbow and Harley Frame. Moon Tree, as everyone knew, was a generous man. With a final call of thanks, he drove away.

Back inside, Bowie Turnbow, grimacing with pain, quickly shucked his boot and a badly worn sock, and inspected his damaged toes. The big one was flaming red, almost purple, around the nail.

After a dark, foreboding look, Lacey Tubbs said, "You better put that boot back on, mister, else you'll never be able to get it on in the morning. That toe's gonna be bigger than a tomato if you don't."

"Bad luck," said Frame, taking a peek. "Reckon it's broken? See if you can move it . . . back and forth like."

Turnbow did so, and the toe moved. "Ain't broke," he growled, his face clouded with agony.

"Have a shot," Lacey Tubbs said, handing Bowie a glass of whiskey, which he immediately chucked down. "Get that boot back on like I said, keep the swelling down."

"Fucking pianer," Bowie moaned. Hobbling up to the bar on the heel of his boot, he seized the whiskey bottle and poured another one. Miserable luck, all right, just trying to do some fellow a small favor. He fished out a coin and slid it along the bar.

"Keep your money, mister," Tubbs said. "The drinks are on Moon. Have another if you want. Moon's family here."

"Moon!" Bowie Turnbow exclaimed, giving Harley Frame a shocked look.

Equally surprised, Harley Frame repeated, "Moon?"

"Moon Tree," Tubbs said. "That feller who just took the piano away. Thought everyone around these parts knew Moon. Hell, boys, his old man owns half of this town."

"Never met him before," Bowie Turnbow grumbled. "Mos' likely won't forget him, either." His toe throbbed painfully, and he suddenly had a few horrible thoughts. Was this just one of those freak accidents that always seemed to be happening of late? Or was it the mysterious work of a booger man, an evil portent? And how come Moon's old man owned so much of the town? Shoot fire, this wasn't any place for him to be hanging out, not with a nestful of red-loving rascals. Bowie Turnbow downed another whiskey and limped away to his room. He slept this night with his boot on, slept uncomfortably as well as uneasily. A moaning wind came up after midnight, eerily rattled the hanging sign below the window, and Turnbow dreamed about haints.

The next morning, Bowie and Harley Frame

didn't waste much time getting out of Bozeman, little reason to tarry too long in a place filled with potential enemies, all of these friends of the Tree family. This was very disconcerting to Harley Frame, discovering there were so many Indian lovers. Worse yet, they had come face-to-face with Moon Tree. They both knew what he looked like now, and even though no suspicion hung over their heads, Moon had seen them, a fact that could prove embarrassing somewhere down the line if he ever encountered them in a less desirable situation. Fate, concluded young Frame, pure and simple fate, meeting up with him that way.

Some distance beyond the gate leading to the Stuarts' main buildings, Harley Frame came to a halt. In a pasture not more than fifty yards from the road, he saw a beautiful stallion, an Appaloosa, calmly nibbling the tender shoots of new meadow grass. Nearby were a dozen or more horses of regular cut, nice stock, but nothing compared to the handsome stud.

"Now, look at that," he said, whistling softly. "There's a piece of horseflesh that would bring more than a few hundred bucks. Mos' likely a thousand. Wonder why they got that boy running way out here?"

"Grass," mumbled Turnbow. "Green grass, I'd say." He gave his companion a curious stare. "Just what you thinking about, Harley? You ain't getting any fancy ideas, are you? We's a far piece from the Ruby."

"Nice herd of horses out there," commented Frame casually. He nudged his own horse ahead and grinned over at Turnbow. "No, just thinking ahead a bit." Nodding toward the river bottom up ahead, he said, "Not too far to the river and all those cottonwoods, not too far to the canyon, either, a good night's ride over to our place."

"You mean we can come back," Bowie said, getting the drift of Harley's reckoning. "Come back when it's good and dark, maybe just help ourselves and cut out."

Harley Frame grinned and stroked his sparse mustache with anticipation. "That's just what I was thinking. Only one thing stopping us far as I can see—that ol' jack fence, and it ain't much bother." His stare settling on the horses, he added, "Gonna come up with some good spring rains one of these nights, ground all nice and soft, everyone tucked in their bedrolls listening to that rain coming down on the roof. Nice sound at night, puts a feller right to sleep nice like. Hell, a herd of buffalo could come grazing through here and nobody's gonna hear 'em." He glanced over at Bowie. "Reckon ol' Dupee would like my idea?"

For the first time since the piano crushed his toe, Bowie Turnbow smiled. "Dupee has a good nose for money, Harley, you know that. Shoot fire, that man can smell greenbacks under a stack of shit, he can."

* * *

Sean O'Grady, aware of Divinity Jones's indebtedness to the Tree family, readily agreed to share in the farewell party for Ruth and Claybourn Moore. The ranch was on the way back to Dubois, and Moon's invitation to stop over and enjoy a few days vacation seemed an excellent idea. Early this Sunday after the conclusion of their successful engagement in Helena, the three entertainers boarded the stage for Bozeman and later were picked up in two buckboards driven by Moon and Robert Peete. By the time they arrived at the big ranch, it was late afternoon, sunny and mild, and the children eagerly ran beside the wagons heralding the reappearance of Divinity Jones. After a few hugs on the porch of Benjamin's house, introductions were made for the newcomers. Sean O'Grady and Beauregard Lincoln were taken to their respective rooms in James Goodhart's and Benjamin's homes.

It wasn't much of a respite for Divinity. She was too excited, happy to be back with Miss Benjamin, and she spent most of her time in animated conversation with White Crane, all the while packing the new baby around in her arms. Others of the family came in for a few words and all left with the same awed impression—Divinity Jones was a new woman.

Everything White Moon had told them was true, but they had no idea how true or how astonished they would be until later that evening.

The patriarch, Ben Tree, had invited a dozen of

his closest friends and their wives to the Moore party, including the Stuarts, the Blodgetts, Lucas Hamm from the big mercantile, and John Borke, president of the Bozeman bank. Since Sad Sam Courtland was back in town for a week or two, Moon asked him out to the festivities. After all, Sad Sam had known Clay Moore for four years, and he was no stranger to O'Grady and Jones, either.

All of these guests were on hand when Molly, Shell, and Little Blue began bringing the large platters of food out to the tables on the porch.

It was difficult for Jessie Stuart to keep her eyes off of the glamorous Divinity Jones, or her vivid imagination from wandering. Jessie was startled by Divinity's remarkable transformation from a penniless waif to a young woman of wealth, and reputedly, fame, all within a year. Quite unbelievable, quite remarkable, and quite disturbing, too. Divinity Jones also was delectable.

Only one person had recognized this a year ago—Zachary Hockett, whose eyes had penetrated the shabbiness and grime to see something no one else had, hidden beauty.

The children, sharing Divinity's exuberance, gathered around her like moths drawn to a flame, prompting another touch of envy from Jessie Stuart.

While Moon Tree didn't join this small coterie of fans, he certainly wasn't oblivious to the blonde charmer, nor she to him. Jessie noticed this, the few fond exchanges of glances, the all-too-obvious twist of satisfaction on Moon's seldom-smiling lips. And when Moon finally joined Jessie near the end of the serving table, she couldn't help but express herself candidly, enviously. "It seems to me, Uncle Moon," Jessie said, "you are no longer the Pied Piper. Miss Divinity is stealing away your nieces and nephews."

Moon Tree, the mask of indifference, merely shrugged and went about filling his plate. "She has a way about her," he said. "She can be just as much of a child as she can a woman. Sort of like a colt in a way. The children understand this, ei. The little ones see things we don't. Maybe that's it."

"There's nothing wrong with my eyes," Jessie said with a grim little smile. "Or yours, either. She's all woman, and she knows it, too, knows right where you are every minute."

"Did you talk with her?"

"Briefly," replied Jessie. "Zachary and I talked with her. He said you were a dear friend of mine, and that sure brought a light to those big blue eyes. She said you were also a dear friend, her buddy, her *mon chéri,* and that's about as far as we got, all the children hanging on her. *Mon chéri,* indeed!"

"Tut, tut," Moon protested gently. "Miss Divinity just feels a little obligated, what with me taking her home last year, helping her with those damned critters, ei, maybe the railroad part, too. I pay it no mind, just did what I could. Tried to teach her to quit all that cussing, things like that."

"*Plenty* obligated, I'd say," said Jessie, playing on one of Moon's habitual words. Nudging him with her elbow, she whispered, "Did you do anything else along the way, teach her anything else, things like that?" She emphasized the "things like that."

"That's plenty good potato salad," Moon Tree said, nodding at a big bowl. "My sister made it, one of Molly's dishes. Never had anything like this in the village. Sometimes I think living like white folks is not so bad, Jessie. You put some on my plate, please, and we'll go over there by the trees, find a place, and spread our blanket."

Jessie Stuart wrinkled her nose, but managed a thin smile at her evasive lover. "Moon, you spread more than a blanket. You know what you're spreading, don't you?" She placed a large spoonful of salad on his already crowded plate. "You're spreading you-know-what, and I don't want to step in it."

"Tut, tut," he repeated, politely ushering her from the porch. "I think I'm plenty hungry."

Zachary Hockett shortly wandered over, balancing a large plate in one hand and a glass of wine in the other. Lowering himself cross-legged like an Indian, he grinned at White Moon and said, "*Hau*," but got no more response than a casual nod. "Do I sense hostility?" he asked, looking from Jessie back to Moon. "Hostility on such an auspicious occasion? Don't you realize, I'm going to be the ramrod around here now? Come on, ease up, you two."

"Yes," Jessie smiled. "Congratulations, but I don't know how you'll ever manage this one."

Moon, emitting a small grunt, pointed his nose toward the crowded porch, in the direction of Divinity Jones. "She really means *that* one."

"Oh, Jesus!" exclaimed Hockett, after a glance at Divinity. "Is this what's cooled off the air around here? Well, well," and he forked into his plate, examining what he had selected. Pausing before taking a sample, he said to Jessie, "I don't think there's much of a problem up there, little woman. From what Mr. O'Grady says, it's going to be a long time before they ever get back to this country again. Our friend Miss Divinity is off to bigger and better things. Now, if she was still a sheepherder, didn't know much better, well, that might present a problem. Pretty face like that, nice figure, could turn any man's head, make any woman a little jealous, I suppose. That's only natural. Most men like to look at pretty women, you know."

"And who says I'm jealous?" said Jessie huffily.

"Just assumed this was the problem," explained Hockett. He munched a bite of baked beans, swallowed, and gave her a defensive look. "Curious? Would that be the word? Curious about Miss Divinity and her old friend Moon, here?"

"Jealous," put in Moon Tree with a slow grin.

"Women get crazy ideas. Divinity always had some crazy notion someone was after her crotchie."

Jessie Stuart promptly thumped him lightly on the head with her fork. "Nonsense! And don't be saying things like that. It's crude."

"Funny, though." Moon chuckled. "This whole thing is funny."

Hockett laughed with Moon. "Anyhow, you can forget it. Couple of days and she'll be gone, a dead duck, and it'll be like nothing ever happened." He took a drink of wine and winked teasingly at Jessie Stuart, "If anything does happen . . . or did . . ."

Moon Tree growled into his plate, "You're both crazy." Crazy but plenty smart, and he swallowed a piece of roast beef almost whole. What a pair of poker players these two would make. The intuition. They could cipher the cards before they hit the felt. As for Moon, without admission, there was no guilt. Certainly they could read nothing in his stoic face, one of his strongest attributes. Of course, if ever Miss Divinity and Jessie got together and made admissions of their own, the issue would no longer be Hockett's dead duck—*he* would.

Sometime later, everyone started to gather around the porch, bringing out a few benches and chairs. This was occasioned by Sean O'Grady, who began riffling up and down the keyboard of the piano that Moon and the men had rolled into place near the back of the porch. And with a big smile, Willie Left Hand soon appeared with his fiddle, tuned up his strings with Mr. Beau. O'Grady, who had recognized Willie's ability several years back in Virginia City, had invited him to play along, at least on some of the tunes he knew, and this was an honor for the Salish breed who had once deplored the very suggestion that Divinity Jones knew anything about the guitar or could hold a tune. Whatever thoughts Willie Left Hand entertained about Divinity Jones's musical prowess quickly came to an end when she, O'Grady, and Mr. Beau teamed up for the opening number, a rousing welcoming piece written by O'Grady, the last part of it duplicated in French by Mr. Beau and Divinity.

Divinity Jones, singing to the heavens, stomped her heels, flaunted her body, and prowled the length of the porch. At the finish, she bowed so low that her long hair almost brushed the floor.

From this moment on, a surprised Jessie Stuart knew that Moon Tree was no match for Divinity Jones. A tryst? Perhaps. But there was no one in the Montana Territory who could harness the energy and talent of this little wildcat.

For the next hour, the guests of Ben Tree sat transfixed as Divinity displayed her versatility, sometimes joyously prancing about, sometimes provocatively shaking her behind, and then in a dramatic transition, hushing everyone with a ballad so lonesome and sad that tears came to the eyes of the women. After the final number, Divinity pleased everyone even more, shouting, "*Merci boucoup!*" She had never known kinder people or a finer audience, she told them, and she was especially grateful to her buddy, Moon Tree. "*Que* Moon Tree *est sympathique!*" How likeable her buddy, Moon Tree.

Later, they moved the piano inside, and O'Grady, Mr. Beau, and Willie Left Hand played for another hour of dancing. Toward nine o'clock, the buggies began pulling away for town, many final farewells being called out to Clay Moore, who was leaving the next day for the Yellowstone with Ben Tree and Rainbow. Inside, the few remaining guests, the Stuarts among them, were engaged in quiet talk in small groups, the excitement of the day finally expended. Off in a corner were some of the Tree family women, young and vibrant, and Jessie Stuart was with them. But it was an uninhibited Divinity Jones who was doing most of the talking, relating stories of her recent trip to San Francisco. Her listeners were doing most of the tittering, because a few glasses of unaccustomed wine had put a small glow on all of them. Comments and assessments were freely passed among the young women, and when Divinity accidentally, in a moment of excitement, used the word "crotchie," everyone shrieked, even Jessie.

This was a memorable night for all of them, perhaps never to be repeated, and they were savoring every minute of it. Divinity's stories were as humorous as they were unbelievable, finally prompting Shell Hockett to ask what everyone had been wondering but that only a little wine had finally allowed to surface.

With a sly look, Two Shell asked haltingly, "You go one moon on trail with White Moon, ei? You find . . . you have no excitement?"

"Oh, yes!" Divinity replied without hesitation. "Oh, it was all exciting. Mr. Moon was a gentleman. He taught me many wonderful things."

Two Shell asked, "Exciting? What you do . . . exciting?"

The rest of the women giggled.

Divinity said with a little smirk, "I learned something new each day. He was a proper man. He never taught me anything about . . . you know, the bunk . . . bedding."

Everyone laughed again, everyone except Jessie Stuart.

Divinity jones understood. She said, "Oh, I think it would be good to have Mr. Moon with me on another long trip, maybe different this time. Who knows? *Mon Dieu,* would a woman lie about this? He's special to me, plenty good, as he would say. But, you see, he already has *beaucoup* ladies in his life, colored ones, two red and two black, the four queens. *Ainsi soit-il!* So be it. *Je le regrette, mais c'est vrai.* I'm sorry, you see, but it's true, and so we go different ways now. My debts are paid, but I'll never forget Mr. Moon, not as long as I live."

SEVENTEEN

Had it not been for the attention Jessie Stuart had been giving to a small split in the Appaloosa's right front hoof, she probably would have never known the young stud was missing. It was White Moon's suggestion to put Hawkeye out to pasture for a while until the hoof improved to the point where it could be filed and the horse shod for the first time. When Jessie rode out this morning, the day after the party at the Tree ranch, she discovered a small section of the fence pulled away. The stallion was gone, as well as four or five other horses. Jessie didn't really know the actual count of this particular herd, but it was obvious from the clutter of tracks going up the road that Hawkeye wasn't the only one stolen. After a few minutes of inspection, she rode back at a gallop to the ranch to find only her mother and brother still at the house.

A pure case of rustling. Ed Stuart allowed after hearing her story, and together, he and Jessie headed for town to report the incident to Sheriff

Bill Duggan. In fact, with the theft of the valuable stud, it was more than rustling—it was outright banditry, and almost in Adam Stuart's front yard!

Jessie and Ed didn't make it into Bozeman. In the distance, coming down the lane from the Tree ranch, was a wagon carrying a piano, and perched on the driver's seat were Moon Tree and Divinity Jones. For once Jessie Stuart wasn't jealous. Too much had transpired the night before, too many revelations, and under the present circumstances, she was more than happy to see both Moon and Divinity.

Moon Tree, after listening to Ed Stuart's explanation, clouded up in anger, cursed several times, much to Divinity Jones's pleasure, and shook his fist angrily, unusual behavior for one who normally reacted in such a way only to yellowjackets and hornets. Without a doubt, this was the work of Dupee Clancy's men, the drifters that Divinity had spotted three weeks ago in Armstead. After all that time and effort that he had put in on the Appaloosa, not to mention the danger of getting caught in Jessie's bedroom, Clancy and his boys had filched Hawkeye. Moon Tree was incensed.

So was Divinity Jones when he mentioned Dupee Clancy's name. She also shook a small fist, shouted at Moon, and not in French, "Go get that son of a bitch, Mr. Moon! Bring him back by his balls!"

This was a painfully emphatic order, and a tall one, too, but Moon Tree allowed that if anyone was ever going to catch up with Dupee Clancy, it would have to be he. Sheriff Duggan never seemed to make any progress unless he had some help from the Tree family, and no one west of the mountains was making any headway, either. Moon decided that Divinity and Jessie should return the piano, and at the same time drop off word at Duggan's office. In the meantime, he took Jessie's horse, and along with Stuart, rode back to the Tree ranch to get organized.

As Moon expected, there was a small amount of bickering over who was going to do what, and by what authority. Zachary Hockett, in his first day as foreman, was reluctant to let Moon go charging off into the hills after a gang of rustlers. After all, it wouldn't bode well for him if something happened to one of Ben Tree's sons on his first day out of the chute.

Complicating this was Benjamin One Feather, who decided his expertise in such matters was essential, mainly to keep an eye on his younger brother, to keep him from falling through another roof, or something even worse. Moon, on the other hand, who for many years had played second fiddle to Benjamin One Feather during the Indian wars, negated any thoughts about his older brother joining the chase. Benjamin, he explained, had a wife and two children to think about. And besides, Moon felt it was his obligation to fulfill his promise to Divinity Jones to avenge her father's death.

"Well," Hockett concluded, "we'll wait for Miss Divinity and Jessie to return, see what old man Duggan has to say, what he wants to do. He's the law. Sure as hell, we aren't."

Ed Stuart pooh-poohed that consideration. "Time that old buzzard gets everyone saddled up, those horse thieves might be all the way to the Idaho Territory . . ."

"Or Canada," Moon Tree interjected with a scowl.

Benjamin One Feather, putting his arm around Zachary Hockett's shoulder, said, "Do you remember a long time ago how we made those wolfers disappear up in Spirit Canyon? Ei, you came up there with the rest of your bluecoats looking to find a wolfer's camp, graves, all of that evidence old Birdwell said was there."

Moon Tree grinned at Hockett, who always got a bit edgy when anyone humorously brought up the old days, his first experience with the Crow, or his love affair with the Nez Perce, Two Shell Woman.

Moon said with a mysteriously foreboding sound to his voice, "Ghosts, spirits of the dead, all gone, nothing, not a trace. Who could forget that?"

Hockett groaned. "Jesus! You two ever going to let that story die? What the hell does that have to do with horse rustling, anyhow? That was a sacred place to your people, a burial ground. Just what are you getting at?"

"We could make those rustlers disappear, too," Benjamin said.

Two Shell Woman had been a part of the Spirit Canyon episode, a captive of the wolfers, and she had savagely burned their eyes out with a hot firebrand after Benjamin and his braves had killed them. Emerging from the kitchen where she had been listening, she gave Benjamin a reprimanding look, spoke to him in Nez Perce. "That was in Indian country, my brother. We no longer live in the old days or the old land. You still have Indian blood. People resent this. You do something plenty bad and get caught, they will hang you on the nearest tree. You be careful. I don't want White Crane a widow so soon. *Sepekuse!*"

Zachary Hockett, aware that his wife was once again talking around him, asked, "Now what's she telling you?"

White Moon replied evasively in a whisper, "She says we should hang those rustlers from the nearest tree . . . something like that. Quit wasting our time with all this talk."

"Well, I don't want them hanged," Hockett said. "Not by my men, and I don't want you to get the notion of making them disappear, either."

"Can't wait for another day or two until Duggan gets his ass moving, either," commented Ed Stuart. "I want my horses back now, before those bastards chase them to another country, blot their brands."

"Agreed," Benjamin said, looking at Hockett.

"What I'm saying is you seem to forget how well we operate."

"How you make people disappear, you mean."

White Moon, shaking his head, protested gently, "No, sometimes we leave their bodies. The coyotes and wolves make them disappear."

When the discussion ultimately ended, it had been decided that White Moon Tree, Benjamin One Feather, and their neighbor, Ed Stuart, would combine talents and track the thieves. When Bill Duggan and his posse came along, all they had to do was follow the fresh tracks and catch up.

Moon Tree, not to be denied, elected himself to "carry the pipe" on the hunt, and after packing a few supplies on their ponies, they rode off, back to the Stuart ranch to outfit Ed and to examine the tracks in the east pasture.

As it turned out, the three were to get no help from Bill Duggan. When Jessie Stuart stopped by his office, he was gone, headed north to Helena to pick up a robbery suspect. Jessie did the next best thing—she sent a message to the sheriff's office in Virginia City. Rustlers were about, maybe headed that way.

It wasn't too difficult to read the sign; there was only one unshod horse in the bunch, the Appaloosa Moon had prevented getting new iron because of the split hoof. From what the Tree brothers could ascertain—and they were experts in ciphering tracks—there were three rustlers running six of Stuart's horses, and they were headed

southwest, at least ten hours ahead. It didn't surprise Moon Tree—Armstead was that direction,
the last-known location of Dupee Clancy.

Initially, the three young men had no trouble
following the trail left behind, particularly in the
bottoms of the Madison Valley where the horses
had cut a clean swath through the high grass. And
the rustlers obviously had gotten their butts wet
fording the high water of the river, for it was
flooding in the lowlands. But once up along the
rolling hills east of Virginia City, the thieves became clever—they split up into two groups,
moved the horses along well-established trails
where the tracks often mingled with other livestock sign.

Ultimately, Moon decided to give up the tracking and head directly for Virginia City, where they
could case the narrow canyons below. They were
losing too much time by slowly picking their way,
their heads always craned to the side trying to trail
Hawkeye's prints. There weren't that many unshod horses in the area anymore, and it was likely
that the rustlers didn't even know they had a Judas pony with them.

Darkness caught up with the trackers at Virginia City, darkness and civilization. No sign of
the missing horses could be found among the dozens of trails, the ruts, and the pocked hillsides,
but Moon Tree, the pipe carrier, wasn't deterred.
Information was often useful, and he knew right
where to find it: the Montana Billiard Arcade, one

of his occasional poker haunts. After checking in at the Virginia City Hotel and enjoying a steak dinner, Moon guided Benjamin and Ed to the card palace. It was a little early for the main game, but Jiggs Dulaney, as usual, was at a table sipping a cup of coffee and reading a newspaper. He gave Moon Tree and his two friends a casual nod, motioned to the vacant chairs, and asked his patented question: "Come to play or just watch?"

And Moon, taking another glance around the room, answered, "No money here. Maybe later." He introduced Benjamin and Ed, and they all took seats. "Truth is," Moon said to Dulaney, "I came to talk."

"Talk never won a hand, Red Man," Dulaney replied with a wink at the others. "What's your game?"

Moon Tree related the reason for their presence in town, and his suspicions about the renewed activity of Dupee Clancy.

Jiggs Dulaney took another sip of his coffee, folded the newspaper neatly, and rested back in his chair, his hands locked behind his head. "Wouldn't know this Clancy if I saw him," he said. "But strangers? Have been a few around lately, cowboy types, and these I always notice. Not any of the locals, in and out, poor stud players for the most part."

"Drifters, you mean?"

"If you will," Dulaney said. "Packing pistols but no wads. Two strangers in here off and on, maybe last two weeks. One, I recall, goes by the name of Bowie." He chuckled. "Now, that one is no poker player. The other one, a young fellow, light hair, peach-fuzz mustache, sits in a game, gets all nervous, usually packs in early."

"That's not our old friend Dupee," Benjamin said. "He's an older man, heavy beard, long nose."

Moon Tree, silent for a moment, pondering, suddenly leaned forward and snapped his fingers. "Bowie! By jingo, I thought I heard that name before!" He glanced knowingly at Benjamin. "Couple of days before Moore's party when I picked up the piano . . . he's the one who got his foot stomped on by the piano. Ei, the other drover called him Bowie, some kind of a nickname, I thought. Same damned two men, I'll wager."

"Spotted my stud, the bastards," Ed Stuart cursed.

Moon asked Jiggs Dulaney, "This Bowie and the other fellow, you think they've caught on with one of the outfits around here?"

"Work?" Dulaney questioned, surprised at such a suggestion. "Drifters, like you said. Mention the word work around men like that and they'd crap their britches." Dulaney stretched once, fluttered his fingers, and pulled out a deck of cards from his vest, casually shuffled, and dealt out a card facedown to each of the men, then took one himself. "Four aces says you get a better fix on this operation from some of Chambers' drovers. They did some tracking last fall, I hear. Didn't come up with much, but they ain't got a lick of red man blood in them, either."

"Thanks, Jiggs," Moon Tree said with a trace of a smile. He knew before he flipped over his card that it was an ace, but nevertheless, did so. It was a red ace, a diamond.

The other three cards were also aces, Benjamin turning up the ace of hearts—red cards to the breeds.

"Be careful boys," Jiggs Dulaney called as they moved away.

Ed Stuart whistled softly as they made their exit. "You play poker with that man?" he asked, staring back in awe. "For crissakes, Moon, how'd he do that?"

"Ei, I play with him once in a while," admitted Moon laconically. "Last time I took him and some others for a couple hundred, went and split it with Miss Divinity. And one of these nights when we have more time, I'll show you how to cut those aces. Just don't ever try it in a game, not unless all of the men are your brothers. Bad medicine, Ed, plenty bad. Most likely get yourself shot."

Early the next morning, Moon, Benjamin, and Ed rode up to Tom Chambers' log house seeking more information. Chambers, after learning their identities, laughed loudly and slapped his thigh as though he had just heard the best joke of the year.

"The Tree boys!" Chambers exclaimed. "By

Gawd, how did you manage to get those sheep down to Utah without getting yourselves shot?"

"Ah, those sheep," Benjamin said with a nod. He looked at White Moon for answers.

White Moon grinned. "The governor's sheep, you mean, eh?"

"One and the same," Chambers said with a wink. "And I sure as hell think someone was laying a big one with that story."

"Well," Moon said, "I didn't tell any story to the newspaper. I wonder who did?"

"Me, goddamn it!" replied Chambers. "And later when I got to thinking about it, I knew I'd made a mistake. Too late to correct it. Damn glad I didn't. Everybody thought it was funny, old man Crosby sneaking sheep over the range."

"We didn't come about the sheep," Benjamin said. "We came to find out if you've been losing stock . . . horses, mainly."

Chambers acknowledged that he had lost a few horses. A couple of his men who had followed the tracks were over behind the barn repairing a mower. He suggested that Moon, Benjamin and Ed go down and have a talk with them. And still laughing, he went back into the house.

As it turned out, the first man Moon Tree met behind the barn was one of the two drovers who had accosted Divinity Jones up in the Ruby Valley in the now infamous "crotchie incident." When he saw Moon Tree approaching, he edged behind the mower and held up his hand in a protective manner.

Moon, likewise, held up his hand in return, more in the manner of a greeting, however. He gave the drover a friendly smile. "Hey, I see you remember me."

"Now, how in hell would I forget you!" was the reply. "Moon Tree, you and them goddamned sheep. The governor got you bringing some more of 'em through here? You clearing it with the boss this time?"

"No, sir," Moon replied. "No such thing. We're over here looking for some missing stock, a few horses."

"Well, that's a caution." The man sighed.

At this point, Moon Tree felt Old Man Coyote's breath against his neck. A gleam came into his dark eyes, and he introduced Ed Stuart and Benjamin. "Yes, this is my brother, Benjamin, the one I told you about that day, ei. He has no sense of humor at all. That was his wife you were fooling around with. Ei, good thing I came along first, maybe your bones would be plenty white by now."

Grinning sheepishly, the drover, who said his name was Charlie, shifted uneasily as he sized up Benjamin, who just happened to have a deep scowl on his face—not from Charlie's behavior, but because of Moon's outlandish story.

Charlie dropped his arms helplessly alongside his baggy trousers. "Like I said, we was only funnin' a bit, that's all, and that woman of your'n started screeching like a banshee. I tell you, that's all it was. . . ."

"No matter," said Benjamin, searching for something plausible to tell the poor man. "No matter at all. Fact is, she was a noisy one at that. Ei, so we got rid of her down in the Idaho country, threw her out of the wagon."

"You did?" Charlie exclaimed. "You did that?"

"Threw her out on her ass, right in the middle of the prairie."

"Oh, Lord," lamented Charlie. "She had such a purty little ass, too."

After several serious nods between Moon Tree and his obliging brother, and an awkward, puzzled stare from Ed Stuart, Moon came to the point: what about the horses that Charlie and his companions had followed the past fall?

Charlie, of course, was mighty happy to be of any assistance he could.

"Yes," he said, "sure as hell there was tracks. They went right up the road heading for the mining camps."

"How far did you follow them?" asked Moon.

"Not very damn far. Snow squall came along that very morning when we discovered the horses missing. Tracks got all blown in, you know. Time we got up to Laurin, we lost 'em."

Moon was puzzled. "This is plenty strange, ei? They were moving the stock right into a town?"

"Looked that way," Charlie answered. " 'Cept

we didn't find a soul who remembered any horse coming through."

Moon scratched his head, then was suddenly struck by the realization that somewhere in between Laurin and Alder, the canyon opened up to the south, the Ruby Valley, cattle drive route. There were so many draws, sage-brush flats, and box canyons down that way a white man could lose himself and never be found. Not an Indian, of course. With a farewell to Charlie, Moon Tree, Benjamin, and Ed went back and retrieved their horses. Moon told the others that he knew where they were likely to pick up Hawkeye's track again, and it wasn't too far.

Dupee Clancy was elated to be back in business again, to be back riding with his two closest friends, his *only* friends. The cabin larder was full of good grub and the hidden corral had some seed in it, a beginning: six good horses, including one expensive stud. Prospects for a prosperous summer looked good. After the theft of Adam Stuart's stock, Dupee Clancy figured they could lay low for a few days, then filch a few head from the Chambers and O'Keefe spreads before making one last sortie over in the Gallatin.

Dupee Clancy and Harley Frame had their sights set on the Tree ranch, partial payments on debts long overdue. In Bowie and Harley Frame's last go-round, they had discovered a line cabin way above the main Tree property, a small corral there with six horses in it, probably stock used by the outriders. Fortunately, it was near the timber adjacent to open range, and two gates were conveniently located at the upper end of the barbed wire fencing. Not much of a trick to get those horses up into the woods and over the hills into the Madison in one night, long before anyone discovered they were missing. And by then, just like the Stuart job, it would be too late. Big plans, one last strike, and ride hell-for-leather to the border up through the Snowy Mountains.

These plans suited Bowie Turnbow: get in and get out in a hurry. Ever since the appearance of that Divinity Jones his luck had been bad, and this had him confused and worried—afraid, actually, but he didn't want to admit it. He wondered why, if this woman had a booger working for her, why she hadn't sicced it on Dupee Clancy. After all, he was the one who shot her old man. Hell, Bowie wasn't even around when that happened. But no, everything was happening to him instead of Dupee. First it was the piano crushing his toes, and the big one now looked like a black walnut, all wrinkled and mangled, so sore that he finally had to cut a hole in the tip of his boot. Subsequently, he burned his hand on the iron frying pan; he was kicked in the shin by one of Stuart's horses; he lost his canteen crossing the Madison River, and the morning after their return from the Gallatin, he broke off a piece of tooth on a chunk of bacon rind. Of course, he lost twenty dollars playing poker in Virginia City, which he discounted because he usually lost anyhow. He figured cards had nothing to do with the curse of a haint or booger. And on this particular evening, just when he thought maybe he was out of the woods, a piece of errant kindling flew up from his ax, poking him below the eye. This was all he could take. Throwing up his hands in despair, Bowie Turnbow saddled his horse and headed down toward the road in the bottom, aiming to ride into Laurin for some whiskey.

Flattened out on a boulder about thirty yards away, Moon Tree watched Bowie thread his way down the trail. It was a temptation to follow, to intercept Bowie along the road in the dark and hogtie him, at least get one of the culprits out of the way, but Moon wasn't in any position to abandon his surveillance of the cabin. Benjamin and Ed Stuart had already departed on foot up the nearby slope, following the tracks of the stolen horses, horses that they now believed were pastured in a pocket or mountain meadow not too far from the cabin. Moon Tree had assigned himself the job of watching the cabin and its three occupants, but he hadn't figured on any of them leaving. Even in the dusk, he had recognized the man called Bowie—his conspicuous limp and slouchy hat. Moon chuckled. That piano of Lacey Tubbs had done a job on the old cowboy's foot, all right.

Actually, Moon wasn't too concerned about Bowie's departure, since he now knew his identity and the direction he was heading. This was a matter of discretion and caution, trying to keep the promise made to Zachary Hockett—no disappearing acts, no killings. This, of course, took some of the fun out of the game, really made it more dangerously challenging. Taking three rustlers alive was going to be a plenty good trick, almost as impossible as dragging Clancy back by his balls, Divinity Jones's choice. But Moon Tree had agreed to give it a try. The chance that Bill Duggan might show up was becoming slimmer by the hour. But this was to be expected. Duggan was always arriving on the scene a day late and a dollar short.

As Bowie departed, Moon heard the low hoot of an owl, his brother's version of the call, and he hooted back, the signal of safety and approach. Directly, Benjamin's head popped up from behind some downfall and Ed Stuart's white face followed. The men sneaked up to Moon. They had located the horses, the Appaloosa included, in a small meadow above.

An easy task, Benjamin said, to reclaim them. What did Moon want to do?

Precisely that, Moon Tree decided. The best thing they could do was get the horses back, probably after midnight. In the meantime, they should find a place along the river, eat, and get some sleep. Clancy wasn't going anywhere this night, and when dawn came, and assuming Bowie had returned, the three rustlers would be trapped inside the cabin. Walking in on them in the black of the night might prove dangerous, someone ending up getting shot. But, truthfully, Moon had not given much thought as to how he was going to entice the rustlers out of the cabin in the daylight, either.

Ed Stuart smiled at Moon and gave him a small barb. "You're not going to try that roof stunt again, are you? Smoke 'em out?"

Moon Tree never had a chance to answer this impertinent question, for coming back, his horse in a trot, was Bowie. Surprised, Moon motioned the others down. "By jingo, here comes that Bowie fellow back! Why, he didn't even get to the bottom!" The men hunkered behind the rocks and watched as Bowie hastily dismounted. Before hobbling back to the cabin door, he stooped low and surveyed the dark, shadowy trees; then, with his rifle at the ready, he crouched low and inspected both sides of the cabin, raised up and surveyed the roof. After this strange performance, Bowie slipped off the saddle of his horse, removed the bit, and picketed the animal close to other men's horses in front of the cabin. With a final cautious inspection of the dark surroundings, he disappeared inside. A lantern appeared at the window, glowed brightly, then vanished.

Moon, Benjamin, and Ed exchanged curious glances. "Now, what was that all about?" Stuart whispered. "You think he knows we're here? How could he know it?"

"Must have heard us hooting," Moon whispered

back. "Maybe we didn't sound so good, out of practice on our hoots."

"Aw, hell," replied Stuart softly, "ain't no man afraid of owls, and I couldn't tell the difference, so how could he?"

"Well," Moon Tree retorted, "something scared him, ei? He came back plenty fast for some reason. That man's afraid of something, ei, and if the other two are as jumpy as he is, they'll shoot at shadows, anything that moves. Probably sitting in there now with rifles between their legs."

"Then how we going to handle them?" asked Stuart. "Mr. Zachary said he didn't want anyone killed. If they start shooting . . ."

"I know." Moon nodded grimly. "Ei, that's plenty bad. This is what we get for talking to Hockett in the first place. We could set fire to the cabin, shoot them when they come out. Easy that way, and maybe better than hanging, throw their bodies back in the fire, and who knows any different?"

"Who in hell cares?" Stuart whispered. "Clancy is a killer, isn't he?"

"*Eeyah!*" Moon said. "No good, white man. Zachary Hocket cares, that's who. So what I propose is this—we do it the Injun way, ei? If we can't make these men disappear, we'll make their ponies disappear." He grinned at Ed Stuart. "You ever steal ponies?"

"Hell, no," Ed replied, offended at such a question. "Why would I steal horses? I got dozens of 'em. I'm no damned horse thief."

Benjamin One Feather, sensing what was coming next, said, "We better get Stuart's stock down to the bottom first before we take those others. Then Ed can lead the Appaloosa down the road and the rest will follow right along. Take them down to Chambers' place for safekeeping until we get this job finished."

Stuart looked surprised. "You mean you're going to steal their three horses and leave them up in the cabin high and dry? Not try and take them in?"

Moon Tree answered with a sly grin, "Hey, it's been a long time since we've stolen ponies from the *shoyapee*. It's a long walk down to the Gulch, ei? And they can't stay up here without their ponies. First thing they'll do is go down below and report it. Well, we'll just sit down there, take a little nap, and wait for them, give them a plenty good ride to the jail in Virginia City." Peeking up over the rocks, Moon cupped his hands, abruptly hooted softly several times, and the eerie call floated up through the trees, echoed faintly across the canyon. A shaft of light suddenly appeared at the cabin door, and a head popped out. The door closed, and Moon Tree laughed quietly.

Inside the cabin, Bowie Turnbow leaned up against the shut door, holding the lantern out in front of him, casting long shadows of his two companions against the far wall.

"Y'see," he said excitedly, "it ain't right. That's three times I heard 'em. Ain't no owls supposed to hoot before the moon's up. When owls do that, go making their ruckus before the moon's up, it's a sign, a bad-luck sign from the haints. Now, you look out there, ain't no moon in sight, neither."

"For crissakes, put that damned lantern back here," Dupee Clancy said disgustedly, thumping the table. "Stop acting up, talking about those haints all the time. You'll get yourself a fit carrying on this way, get Harley so all riled up he's scared to go out and take a piss."

Harley Frame, his head over beans and sausage, and swabbing the perimeter of his plate with a big chunk of bread, mumbled, "Haunts never bothered me. Never saw one in my life. Best thing you can do, Bowie, is shoot those owls, cook their asses right good."

Clancy cackled at that, but Bowie didn't think it was funny at all. Wagging a finger of warning at his two cohorts, he shouted, "Blasphemy, boys, blasphemy! You go shooting a hooty owl and you're pulling the shades. Bad luck for certain, it is."

Clancy scoffed. "Now, where in the hell did you come up with a notion like that? Something your ol' grandpappy told you? That ol' man's got you bamboozled. Sit down and eat your beans, for crissakes, you're making me all edgy-like. Spooks! By damn, if you ain't a caution!"

"Nothin' to trifle with," Bowie Turnbow warned, replacing the lantern. With a dark look, he said, "Once a feller did away with one of those hooters, I hear tell, plucked the feathers, too, makes himself a purty doodad for his hat, one of those fancy trims. Next morn', his ol' lady's fetching eggs from the coop and a whipsnake up and hit her right between the eyes with his tail stingers. She's blind for almost a month, she is, and that same day, the ol' boy lost his best heeler in the mud swamp." Bowie Turnbow clucked his tongue and squinted at the other two. "No, sir, you don't go messin' 'round with hooters or roosters that crow at midnight, not by my book, you don't."

"Look, Bowie," Harley Frame said reassuringly, "there's owls all over this country. Hell, I see 'em all the time snatching up varmints. Never pay me no mind, though, day or night, so quit your fretting."

"First time they've ever been around this cabin," Bowie Turnbow asserted. "You ever hear 'em here before? No, sir, you never did. That's one of those omens, you know."

Exasperated, Dupee Clancy angrily wagged a spoon at Bowie. Enough was enough. "Now, listen here, just because you went and hit your eye with that stick and heard a couple of owls making love calls ain't no cause for heaping your shit on us, so just hush awhile and eat your vittles. We're tired of hearing your goddamned booger stories. If there's any booger 'round here, it's you, for certain."

But Bowie Turnbow wasn't hungry, and he glumly limped away, over to the stove, where he poured himself a cup of coffee. No profit in belaboring the matter, not to these skeptics. He knew more about haints than they did, had grown up with them, had watched his kinfolk make potions and talismans to ward them off. Bowie didn't want to anger ol' Dupee more than he already had, but he knew one thing: it was also bad luck to poke fun at a booger, sort of like provoking the devil. So, misunderstood and without solace, Bowie Turnbow sat on his bunk and sipped his coffee. Later, he played some poker with Clancy and Frame, lost as usual, and when he went to bed, he didn't sleep too well. He heard the owls two more times, and the ominous sound of scratching on the door.

The next morning, Bowie was up bright and early, not that there was any necessity for haste, for there was little on the agenda; blotting the brands on the horses and a ride down to the saloon in Laurin to catch up on the gossip. He was just happy to see the sun and hear a few jays chattering in the pines, looking for a morning handout of leftovers. When he hobbled out to greet the new day, he got as far as the front stoop, and his outcry brought Dupee Clancy and Harley Frame out of their bedrolls in a hurry.

"Our horses are gone!"

It was true. The small clearing where the three horses had been picketed was empty. Clancy's first reaction wasn't one of alarm. He craned his long neck and stood on his toes, searching the bottom far below. "They're down below somewheres, probably at the creek, strayed, mos' likely."

Harley Frame, somewhat more observant, said dryly, "Damned smart horses, then, taking their saddles and blankets with 'em." He pointed at the empty makeshift pole rack where one of the raucous camp-robbers was now perched. "Now, what do you make of that? Took their tack with 'em."

Bowie Turnbow lifted his voice to the sky and shouted, "Horse thieves! We've been robbed, right under our noses." He gave his two companions an angry glare.

Dupee Clancy was scratching the seat of his long johns, and Harley Frame was rubbing his thin blond whiskers.

"I told you those owls was giving us a sign. No, you wouldn't listen, pay me no mind. Now see what's happened."

He started to shove his way back into the cabin only to be greeted by a set of numbers engraved on the door. His ears hadn't been playing him tricks during the night.

"And lookee here," he said disgustedly, "they even had the gall to make their mark."

"Well, leastways it weren't no boogerman," Clancy said. He and Frame stared curiously at the door. "3-7-77." "Now, what the hell kinda mark is that?" Clancy inquired. "Bunch of goddamned numbers. Huh!"

Harley Frame didn't ponder on the deep knife cuts too long. He had a recollection of this particular set of numbers, had seen them once over in Miles City on a placard hung around a dead man's neck, a horse thief, as a matter of fact.

"This is a vigilante sign, boys," he said calmly. "Those are the sizes of a grave—three feet wide, seven feet long, and seventy-seven inches deep. I reckon the rustlers were trying to tell us something, like to get the hell outta here. We ain't wanted."

Dupee Clancy asked hotly, "You mean someone's moving in on our territory? Someone's trying to scare us out of the pickings?"

"What else?"

Scowling at the warning, Bowie Turnbow said, "I don't like the smell of this one whit. We been here since last year, minding our own business. Who's to tell us to get the hell out when we was here first?"

With a shrug, Harley Frame passed on through, back into the cabin. "I don't know, maybe one of your boogers," he called back. "But I'll tell you one thing, I sure hope some of those horses up above in the corral ride bareback, or we're up shit creek without a paddle."

EIGHTEEN

Toward high noon on this day in late May, three disgruntled drovers were nearing the lower end of the Ruby River road, the limping one bringing up the rear, hobbling along with the aid of a big staff. Bowie Turnbow was hurting, but all three of them had a problem—they were cowboys without horses, and with only sixty dollars among them, they had not much of a stake to rectify their poor status.

Down the road, sitting in the shade of a lone pine tree, Moon and Benjamin Tree were patiently awaiting their approach, while to each side, hidden in the tall sage, were two other men, young Ed Stuart and Charlie Simmons, one of Tom Chambers' drovers. Charlie Simmons was happy to join up with his old friend Moon Tree, and he did consider Moon a friend now, although at one time Moon had scared the daylight out of him by firing a shotgun over his head, all because of that crazy Divinity woman and the governor's sheep. Now that Moon Tree had a plan to apprehend some rustlers, one of them with a five hundred-dollar reward on his head, Charlie was going to get a slice of the pie, a hundred-dollar cut just for aiming his rifle in the proper direction, namely at the rustlers' backs. Of course, he wouldn't have to shoot, because with Moon Tree's plan there wasn't going to be any shooting. Charlie saw some sense in this, for he had been a witness to some campside instruction on the use of a pistol, Moon Tree being the teacher. No one in his right mind would attempt to draw down on Moon, and with that other cantankerous breed brother beside him, well, that would be pure suicide. Charlie felt secure in his job, and when he heard the signal, the lone call of a crow, he peered out of his cover of sage and looked up the long flat. Sure enough, here came three men, just as Moon Tree had predicted.

On the other side of the rutty road, Ed Stuart also was feeling secure. The chase was coming to an end; he had his father's stock back; he was bodily intact; and the experience, all things considered, had been a good one. In fact, he rather enjoyed the company of Moon and Benjamin Tree. Ed had the idea that Moon would make a pretty darned good brother-in-law if he could ever get off his poker-playing ass and commit himself to Jessie. Moon's plan was a good one, better than the last one over on the Madison when two of Clancy's boys ended up dead. The fact that Benjamin was down there backing up Moon simplified matters, too. One of those Tree brothers was bad enough, but facing up to two of them, particularly Benjamin when he had his dander up, was sufficient to make a man faint of heart. Young Stuart heard the call of a crow, took one quick look up the canyon, and hunkered down. Three men were approaching. When Stuart checked the other direction, he saw Moon Tree walking out to one side of the road, Benjamin positioning himself on the other. Sliding a shell into the chamber of his rifle, Ed Stuart crouched on one knee and waited.

As soon as Dupee Clancy saw two men standing in the road directly in front of him, he thrust his arms to the side, halting Harley Frame and Bowie Turnbow. He had no idea who these strangers were, or what their business was, but he wasn't about to get any closer until he found out. He didn't have to wait long.

"Nice day for a walk, ei?" Moon tree called out.

Clancy thought this was a peculiar type of greeting. He glanced around suspiciously. Strange, these men didn't have any horses, either. This was his first observation, his first thought, and he ventured a reply, saying, "Someone steal your horses, too? We got rustled last night, been on the trail for more'n two hours."

"No," Moon replied, "we got ours, over in the willow there. Tough luck, I'd say, for you boys."

This was as far as the conversation between Dupee Clancy and Moon Tree progressed, for

Bowie Turnbow, recognizing Moon, blurted out, "What the hell you doing way out here!" He gave Dupee a shove in the back. "That's that Tree fellow, Moon, goddamn it! Something's going on here, something goddamned crazy, I'll tell you!"

Moon Tree tipped his hat once to Bowie Turnbow. "Hello, there, Bowie, how's that foot coming along? By jingo, that piano almost did you in, ei? I thought I recognized you, that limp."

"What's this?" Clancy asked, glaring at Moon and Benjamin. "What you men up to?"

Moon Tree calmly replied, "Came to meet you, Dupee, see what you looked like." He motioned to the nearby sage. "Some of our friends are over there. Rifles on you, so it's probably best you take off your belts, just drop them in the dust there. Ei, I almost forgot—your horses are over there, too, all ready to ride."

All the while, Harley Frame had been silent, his eyes riveted on Benjamin Tree, who because of his hat and ranching attire appeared considerably less savage than when they had first met long ago on the buffalo grounds, when Benjamin One Feather set him afoot on the prairie. Frame, hearing Moon's order, stepped to the side, saying, "I'd rather take my chances right here with your brother, the one they used to call Benjamin One Feather." He took several more steps and glared at Benjamin. "You don't remember me, do you? Don't even know me, a piece of shit's all I was, me and

Birdwell, the boys you left to die over on the Yellowstone."

"Hold it!" commanded Clancy, ever hopeful of resolving the stand-off. "We ain't through talking here yet. Not until we see all the cards."

Both Benjamin and Moon were astounded by this sudden twist but had no chance to reply to Harley Frame.

"Game's over, Dupee," Harley said grimly. "If I'm going, I sure as hell ain't going alone," and with that, he jerked out his pistol and fired at Benjamin.

It was an errant shot only because Harley Frame was hit first, and his bullet kicked up some dust to the side of Clancy. Frame's sudden move had caught the usually quick Benjamin Tree by surprise. His revolver was out, aimed directly at the tumbling Harley Frame, but it was Moon Tree's pistol that had already belched out a cloud of smoke, not Benjamin's. Harley Frame flopped over on his back, hit full in the breast. He didn't move.

Moon Tree was temporarily devastated, and he cursed aside, "By damn, he didn't have to do that, *Eeyah!*"

"Ei, he had to." Benjamin sighed. "Had me, too. Had me hands down."

Dupee Clancy, his jaw slack, threw away his pistol, and Bowie Turnbow, his rugged face ashen, did likewise. Bowie hovered above Harley Frame's body. Looking up at Moon Tree, he said, "He was a good boy, he was. Had this itch all the time, this itch. Never paid no mind to owls, either."

Sheriff Bill Duggan wasn't too happy about having to ride all the way over to Virginia City to pick up Dupee Clancy and Bowie Turnbow. But he had to, and without much delay.

Divinity Jones was leaving in several days for Denver. It was much easier for her to identify Dupee Clancy as her father's killer than to make a trip to the territorial prison in Deer Lodge for testimony and identification from Gabe Arbuckle, one of the original members of Clancy's gang. Finding Stuart's horses near the cabin site was evidence enough for the rustling charge, and Bowie Turnbow readily admitted stealing the stock, even though, as he explained, he knew all the time the "signs" advised otherwise. There was no doubt in his mind that Divinity Jones had a booger working for her.

Later, when Miss Jones came to the jail to identify Clancy, Bowie refused to even look at her. He thought she might queer his plea of leniency, a prison sentence instead of hanging.

Divinity Jones did, however, get a look at Clancy, her fourth and final. "That's the son of a bitch," she said, and she walked away, swirling her tight skirt and dabbing her forehead with a silk handkerchief.

Sean O'Grady, Divinity Jones, and Mr. Beau were treated to a sumptuous feast their last night at the ranch. In fact, it was a dual celebration, shared by Adam Stuart and the Tree family. Everyone thought that Moon, Benjamin, and Ed deserved some honor, so along with the farewell to O'Grady and Jones, tribute was also paid to the three drovers.

Adam Stuart, happy to have his horses back, was appreciative that the two Tree boys had brought his son home safely. After he'd listened to Ed's account of the Ruby Valley incident, his faith in the integrity and courage of Moon Tree was once again confirmed. Here was a young man who know how to handle himself in dangerous situations.

Jessie, overhearing this, quite agreed. Moon Tree really knew how to play his cards.

And this, explained Moon Tree to Jessie one night a week later, was what life was all about— life was like a card game, poker, if you will. They were sitting in the Stuarts' kitchen, alone at the big table. As promised, Moon had shown Ed Stuart the trick of cutting aces from the deck, and Ed, still thoroughly mystified, had gone to bed scratching his head. Now, placing the deck in front of Jessie, Moon told her that no one could successfully play the "great game" without a full deck. The deck in front of her was fresh, yet Moon said that he knew a card was missing. As Jessie watched with an amused smile on her pretty face, Moon Tree swiftly threaded through the suits. When the shiny cards were all spread out, what he said was true—the queen of hearts was missing from a brand-new deck.

Moon looked at Jessie's surprised face. "I need another lady," he said. "Can't play this game without a queen, can I? You care to fill in? Give me a complete deck?"

A joyful cry rang out through the stillness of the house.

In the Stuart ranch kitchen the next morning, Mrs. Ellie Stuart didn't cry out with joy. Mrs. Stuart's reaction to Moon Tree's unique marriage proposal was more of an agonized shriek. Wham! She banged her spatula against the big iron skillet, jolting young Ed out of his chair.

"He's an Indian," she cried. "Adam! Adam, you get in here!"

But Adam Stuart who, along with his son, heard the news late the previous night, had already made himself scarce. However, he did hear his wife's outcry from his refuge in the barn. He came up with a deaf ear. He sneaked out the back of the big barn and rode off toward the river bottom. Strays down there, work to be done.

Jessie said defensively, "Moon's only part Indian, you know that. You wouldn't even know he had Indian blood unless you knew the family."

Mrs. Stuart exploded. "Everyone hereabouts knows the family! Breeds, the lot of them!"

"Aw, Ma," Ed pleaded. "Hell, they're the most respectable people in these parts."

"Well, that surely doesn't cover much ground, does it? Outside of us, who else is 'round these parts?"

" 'Sides," Ed continued, "Moon has given us a hand more'n once. He's one of my best friends. Good reputation, not a bit of gossip about him."

"He's a gambler," retaliated Ellie Stuart. "One of those shooters, too, and I'm not having your sister marrying up with that kind of man. Indians!"

Jessie thrust out her chin defiantly. "Mama, will you please listen! You don't understand. He's the son of a very prominent rancher. He's a rancher himself. He's no gambler, either. He just likes to play cards sometimes. He's a card player, a good one, too."

Ellie was astounded. "Gambler? Card player? There's a difference?"

Ed said, "Moon doesn't make his living playing cards, Ma. He don't need to. The Trees got all the money they need. The old man owns half of the town. Hell, to my notion, Moon's a damn good catch for Jessie. He's a handsome cuss, and he's rich."

"Ye gods!" Mrs. Stuart whipped off her apron and strode to the back door. "Adam! Adam, I want you here right now!" Whirling about, she said, "We'll settle this once and for all. That boy won't get any permission from us. It's nonsense, pure nonsense. All the white boys out there and . . ."

Ed Stuart sat alone at the table. His sister had fled. He stared at an empty plate. "It don't make much difference, Ma," he said with a weary sigh. "Don't make much difference what you think. Ain't a man in Bozeman City any better than Moon Tree, white or red—part red."

"I'm her mother," declared Ellie Stuart. "And you shush. A father and mother makes the difference."

"No, Ma, I'm sorry," replied Ed. "It's what they call after the fact. I think Jessie's already been sorta consorting with Moon. If you understand. Sparking."

"Consorting? What do you mean, 'consorting'? And this 'sparking'?"

Ed shrugged. He hadn't even had a sip of coffee. He shook himself from the chair and went to the stove, calmly poured from the big porcelain pot.

Hands on her hips, Ellie said, "Are you meaning sneaking 'round romancing? That kind of consorting?"

Ed knew breakfast was not forthcoming. He also knew his father thought a marriage between Moon and Jessie was a very good idea, not only for Jessie but for the Stuart ranch. "Get our operations closer together," he had said. Balancing his hot mug, Ed headed for the screen door. "It's like this. I think it's best Jessie gets herself hitched and damn quick. Best you make up your mind to it, too. You see, you might have a grandchild running around here. Other way, might be some little bastard playing on the floor. Reckon that's what always happens when it's after the fact."

"Adam!" screamed Ellie Stuart. "Adam!"

NINETEEN

Early morning, a Sunday. The Antler Saloon was almost empty. Lacey Tubbs was arranging bottles behind the long bar. Two men were at a round table near the front window: Moon Tree and the silent partner of the Antler, Sad Sam Courtland.

"Thirty to one."

Sad Sam grunted. "Good enough. How about that one?"

Moon brushed an unruly lock of hair away from his eyes. "It smells. About as bad as drawing to an inside straight. Should have folded on the third draw."

"Not bad, my boy, not bad." Scooping up the dummy hands, Sam shoved the cards in front of his sometime poker partner. "Deal 'em," he said. He plucked his cigar from the tray and watched Moon shuffle. Moon shuffled and shuffled. He idly riffled the cards, broke the deck, and stacked, pop, pop. He riffled them again.

Annoyed, Sad Sam said, "If you don't put those little boards into play, you're going to wear the spots off. What you doing, son, trying to crimp a few?"

"Sorry." Moon began to deal out seven hands of five-card stud. This was idle time, practice, a way to keep the fingers in shape, the mind sharp.

Sad Sam had come into Bozeman City the previous night for a friendly game or two. He played, then slept in one of the rooms upstairs. Moon Tree had played, too, not his usual best. He went back to the ranch, slept a few hours, and returned for a visit. Sam was leaving for Helena on the noon stage. As Moon turned the first face cards, Sam said, "You're ailing. I know it. Last night, you played on a cloud, 'least your mind was up there. I know it's not booze. That leaves the second worst sin, a woman." His heavy lids blinked lazily. "Which one?" Sweet Divinity or Jessie?"

Moon was evasive, in no mood for confessions, so he didn't answer that question. But as for last night, why, he hadn't been off track that much. He wasn't a loser, anyhow. He said, "I didn't play that badly, Sam."

Sad Sam tutted. "Four pigeons in the game, regular simpletons. By rights, every one of them should be in hock today. I think you let a couple of them off the hook on purpose. That's the trouble playing in your own backyard. Too damned much sympathy for your friends. You don't like to cut throats. And like I told you, you were sitting right between the fools."

Moon groaned. "In all these months we've been

together, you never once told me about that seating business. Never, goddamn it!"

"Then you sure as hell never pay much attention to where I plant my bottom."

"Never gave much thought to it," Moon admitted. "Cards are cards. You play your hand no matter where you sit."

"Oh, that's true, my boy, that's true."

Moon stopped dealing and grinned. "I like to sit across from you so I can watch you blink, maybe pick the side of your nose when you pair up a buried picture."

Sad Sam asked innocently, "I do that?"

"And come to think of it, you do sit to the right of the dealer most times." Moon held up a hand. "And you don't have to tell me why. I'm not that stupid, Sam. Ei, you got a plenty good shot at the crazy ones, get a chance to size 'em up."

"Well, I damn well get a better idea of when to stay, raise, or fold where there are three or four idiots shoving chips ahead of me, that's for certain."

Moon set the cards aside. "I'm not up to this. Out of sorts, I reckon."

"Did you give Divinity a good send-off?" asked Sam with a sly smile. "Ask you to go tour with her a spell down Denver way?"

"Hell, no," said Moon. "They left two weeks ago, right after she identified Dupee in Duggan's jug. Trial last week didn't last more than a half hour. Guilty. Clancy's getting the rope, and ol' hop-along Bowie twenty years. Duggan's taking them over to Deer Lodge in a few days."

Sad Sam measured the stub of his frazzled cigar. With careful aim, he tossed it expertly. It landed in the nearby spittoon. "No man's going to put a halter on Miss Divinity, Moon. She's going for the big time. She sings up a storm and she knows how to wiggle her little butt, too. Your legs aren't long enough to keep up with her, not anymore." He chuckled. " 'Course you never had much truck with her when she and her old man had the woolies. I figure that would have been your best chance."

Moon glowered. "I never did try to keep up with her. Never looked for a chance, either."

"Hmmm," mused Sad Sam. "Now I do recall something about a little to-do up at the Placer one night. Yes, I do recall that. Seems like—"

"Not my doing," Moon cut in. "Fact is, I went up to play cards. Second fact is, you had your long fingers in that, too. Eeyah, You helped set me up!"

"That was her idea, not mine," replied Sam. He flexed his fingers. "So this leaves our little Miss Stuart, eh? Did she finally tell you to go to hell? Is that it?"

"Nope, I asked her to marry me."

Sad Sam blinked. "Oh, Lord, Lord," he moaned. He eyed Moon Tree closely, then his head tilted back. He momentarily stared at the beamed ceiling before shuttering his heavy lids. "I know when you're bluffing, son," he said sleepily.

"You always get a little wrinkle in your forehead. You surely ain't putting the bluff on old Sam now. Lord, Lord."

Moon Tree gave the table leg a kick. "By jingo, you should at least wish me luck. I need it. That's the least you could do. It's not like I'm shooting myself in the head. What kind of a friend are you?"

Sad Sam was motionless. He muttered, "Why should I congratulate you? Son, I thought you were ailing. Why, you're feeling downright miserable." One eye slowly opened. His Adam's apple rolled once. "Figure you made a mistake, eh? Feel like crawdadding, is that it?

Moon said sourly, "No, but I started a war. Mrs. Stuart's on the warpath. The Red man got her dander up. She's dead set against my marriage. Adam and Ed think it's plenty good. They all had a row about it. Jessie flew the coop. Mrs. Stuart didn't like them taking up against her. She quit cooking."

Sad Sam's eyes opened. His head lowered, and he managed a small, devilish smile, its sardonic effect helped by the black, pointed goatee and his thick, arched brows. "Figure she'll starve them into submission?"

"It's a mess."

"Where did your sweet little fig fly to?"

Moon Tree sighed. "Over to our place."

"Ah, yes, refuge. Women always do that. Misery loves company. Always look for another woman's shoulder to weep on. You've got a passel of them at the ranch, all right."

"Not their shoulders, damn it! My shoulders. "She came up to the line cabin for a few days."

"Lord, Lord."

"Our women took her back, tried to patch things up with Mrs. Stuart. She called our place 'the reservation.' " Moon heaved another sigh. "If you can imagine that . . . my sister Blue, Shell, and White Crane. One Indian starts the ruckus, and three go back and try to settle it. Yah, that was like sending Sitting Bull to make peace with Custer!"

"Custer's dead and gone, son."

"So am I."

"No wonder you've lost your touch."

"There's nothing wrong with my touch. I can't concentrate, that's all."

Leaning across the table, Sad Sam said, "It's like I first told you. You just can't mix liquor and women with cards, son. Get your butt whipped every time."

Moon fell silent. He thought maybe that's what he really did need, a good belt of whiskey. Of course, he knew better. Whiskey had never been a part of his life. His father hated liquor, had polished off whiskey drummers like flies when he was a young man, so the legends told. And he certainly didn't need a woman. His hair was full of them. After a while, his face brightened. He looked over at Sad Sam. "Say, you in a rush to get back to the Gulch?"

Sad Sam drawled, "I don't have anyone sweet to come home to like you, Moon. Just why you asking?"

Moon placed his hands flat on the table. He proceeded to lay out a plan, one by which he could kill two birds with one stone. Work at the ranch, he explained, was presently slack. Both Benjamin and Zachary Hockett had urged him to get away for a week or two, as Hockett said, "to get out of the line of fire." Benjamin suggested a trip over to the Stillwater to see Ben Tree and Rainbow. Father might have some good advice on all of this wrangling. Moon doubted this. By his reckoning, his father never had known anything about women, except how smart they were. He had mentioned this. How could his father know anything? He had no experience in such matters. As he told it, he and Rainbow took each other for man and wife out on some prairie in the Idaho Territory. There were no cranky mothers, fathers, or relatives with whom to contend. They didn't even need a preacher man or church. And Ben Tree was more white than red, at least by blood.

"We can ride the train over there," Moon went on. "Get off at the new Stillwater siding and hike up to my folks' place. The mountains, the brooks. The fresh air."

Sad Sam's mouth dragged. "Good Lord, there's mountains and fresh air all around us! I might go getting funny in the head out in the sticks like that. Oh, I can see your point, getting away and waiting for the dust to settle out at the Stuart spread. Hell yes, but you don't want to take me along to share your misery. Bawling on another fellow's shoulder isn't manly, you know."

Moon Tree growled, "By jingo, I didn't plan on bawling on your goddamned shoulder! Fact is, I was thinking we could get out of there after a night and move on to Billings. I've been over to see Clay once, look over my father's new operation, but I've never played poker in that town. Never played in Miles Town, either. So I was thinking—"

"Poker? Did I hear my favorite tune?"

"Yes, poker."

"That's a lovely word," drawled Sad Sam. "At times it makes me feel like singing."

"You've never sung a lick in your life."

"The song is in my heart. Yes, deep within my heart, son."

Yes, Moon Tree thought, clean country for a spell. Benjamin and Zachary's idea was brilliant. The women of the Tree ranch thought otherwise. Running away was dishonorable, no way to resolve a matrimonial crisis. They sympathized with Jessie Stuart. Two Shell, the most vociferous of the lot, chastised her foreman husband, Zachary, for allowing Moon to leave in such an ignoble manner. She called it the "pull-up-pants-and-run" ruse, a common trick among irresponsible, conniving men. The Tree ranch, the Stuart spread as well, were houses divided.

Dispute notwithstanding, Willie Left Hand hitched up a buggy and drove Moon into Bozeman City later this day. Dark looks from the women followed.

Moon and Sad Sam Courtland, carpetbags in hand, their money belts fat with greenbacks, boarded the train for points east, first to visit Ben Tree, and then to test the felt tables of Billings.

The Stillwater siding was not a scheduled stop on the new line. To most folks it was in the middle of nowhere, about halfway between Billings Town and Bozeman City. However, to the knowledgeable it had significance. Somewhere up the little green Stillwater Valley, somewhere in the rolling foothills below the Great Bear's Tooth, was the residence of a very influential man called Ben Tree. And a small part of the railroad belonged to him; he had invested money in its construction. When the flag was up, the train stopped. When anyone asked to get off, the request was granted. Toward dusk, Moon Tree and Sad Sam Courtland stepped off. The brakeman gave them a farewell, wagged his arms several times, and the engine huffed and slowly moved ahead.

A small but sturdy shed somewhat larger than a privy was tucked away in a path of aspen fifty yards up the narrow road. A wire attached to the top of a nearby pole went into it. Except for a bench, a small, potbellied stove, and a red box nailed on the wall, it was barren.

Sad Sam, not particularly impressed with the primitive surroundings, eyed Moon curiously when he opened the side of the little red box. Inside was another box, a small brown one. Sam's tired eyes widened. "A telephone?"

"Communication," Moon said with a grin. "A talking wire, ei? My father's idea. He has friends who know these things. He has old enemies, too. Always best to crank this thing to let him know who's coming up the trail. Safer this way. No boom-boom."

Sad Sam placed his bag to the side, removed his natty gray fedora with the wide brim, and sat on the bench. He sighed. "Yes, I understand. Mr. Tree takes the necessary precautions. Intruders, that sort of thing."

Moon gave the handle several cranks. He smiled again. "He never has liked intruders. All of this land around here as far as the eye can see used to belong to his people. Now he has a few hundred acres up there, a plenty good lodge. Hard to find, too."

Sad Sam said softly, "Isolation."

Another few more cranks. Moon had an ear to the receiver. Shortly he spoke a few words in one of his native tongues, nothing Sad Sam could understand. Moon laughed, said a few more words, and replaced the receiver on a hook. "My mother," he said. "She says my father will come with a wagon. Not too long. We don't have to walk. Plenty good, all right. Three miles to that place up there."

Sad Sam nodded. "Yes, son, plenty good."

Later, the buckboard rattled down the trail, and the usual bear-hug greeting between father and son took place. Sad Sam had met Ben Tree at the party in honor of Claybourn and Ruth Moore. He was now welcomed with a very hardy handshake and a wry grin.

Ben Tree said, "Sam, how did you let this young fellow drag you away from civilization? By jingo, don't you know these hills are swarming with redskins?"

"Ah, you have friends about?"

"Ghosts," returned Ben Tree. "Spirits of the dead."

Sad Sam tossed his carpetbag in the wagon box. "This, good friend, wasn't my idea of a short vacation. I seek more than communion with the spirits." He plucked a packaged deck of cards from a suit-coat pocket. With a glance at the dusky sky, he held up the cards. "I trust some of them understand the great game."

Moon said to his father, "We'll be leaving for Billings in a day or so, test our game with the squatters."

Ben Tree, flipping reins, replied, "Oh ho, then this is a card trip, is it?"

Sad Sam drawled, "Your boy is on the run, Ben.

He's renewed hostilities, started another one of those Indian wars. Boys at your big camp told him to take a week or so off. Might help the peace parley."

"*Eeyah*," groaned Moon. "No war, damn it, just a little misunderstanding."

"You yourself called it a war," countered Sad Sam.

Ben Tree looked across at Moon curiously. "The women? The women, I'll wager." He chuckled.

Surprised, Moon asked, "How did you know that?"

"Women always get the pot boiling. When things get a little dull, they stir up the fire. I know damn well it isn't rustling. You wouldn't be here. You'd be out chasing instead of running."

"I'm not running."

"Which one?"

"All of them."

Ben Tree and Sad Sam laughed.

Ben Tree listened while his second son discussed the "war" and what had caused it. After Moon concluded, his father was silent for a moment. They were approaching the homestead, what Moon and Benjamin referred to as "the fort." The great log structure had a huge covered porch and only one entrance, a door at the front. High windows were placed on three sides. The back of the building was solid logs. Set among a few towering firs on a small bluff, the house had a commanding view. Inside were two fireplaces, one in the kitchen, another in the parlor, and there were two bedrooms. Tucked back against the wall of the porch were two bunks for summertime comfort.

Ben Tree finally spoke. He asked, "Did you come for advice or to see your parents?"

Moon replied politely, "It is always an honor to see my parents. Ei, and since I was a child, I've listened to your words, when you spoke as a chief as well as a father. I honor you."

Ben Tree smiled at his son's politeness. "First then," he said almost in a whisper, "don't mention this to your mother. Such matters always grieve her. She's had enough of that in her life, always worrying because of our problems, fighting for honorable causes. Wait until you can tell her something happy, like the wedding date."

"Who said anything about a wedding date?" Moon looked up ahead. Rainbow was on the porch, waving. He waved back.

Ben Tree said, "If you love Jessie, you marry the woman. Isn't this what it's all about? You're living in the whiteman's world, son. The Stuarts are God-fearing people. They helped build that first church."

"So did we," Moon retorted. "So did we, and the only times I remember being in it was the first day it opened and when we buried old man Jones, and Divinity went to wailing and shouting right in the middle of the sermon."

Sad Sam lamented, "Lord, Lord."

"What's the point?" asked Moon.

His father swung the wagon toward the porch. "Let me put it in terms you understand," he said. "Let's calculate the odds on this hand. You have, say, four of our women—that's counting Molly—and you have three men, all on your side of the table. Throw yourself in the pot, ei? Sweeten it with Adam, Ed, and Jessie. By my calculation, that's eleven-to-one odds. I just don't think Ellie Stuart's hand is big enough to win this game."

Sad Sam chuckled.

Moon looked askance. "Judas priest, Pa, what kind of solution is that? Everyone piling on her like that she'll buck like hell. Damn it, this is no poker game!"

Ben Tree said, "Sometimes life is a poker game. Poker is a cutthroat game. There's no more room for bluffing. You have the deck stacked, and the way I see it, she can't do a thing about it. Ellie's the joker, and in five-card stud, the joker is out of the deck. Best you and Jessie be setting the date. You have my blessing."

TWENTY

The prospect of the gallows awaiting him at the territorial prison in Deer Lodge dismayed Dupee Clancy. It upset his innards just thinking about it. For several days, he barely touched the rations brought in by Sheriff Bill Duggan and his young deputy, Carl Drescher. However, the victuals, usually beans, ham, sourdough, and sometimes a Mulligan stew, never went to the hog trough. Bowie Turnbow had no superstitions about jailhouse grub. He chucked down anything his cellmate buddy left untouched. Bowie's twenty-year sentence hadn't affected his appetite one whit, but he continued to blame his present plight on Dupee Clancy and the deceased Harley Frame. Had they only paid attention to the omens!

It was impossible for Dupee to escape Bowie's continual harping about ignoring the signs. His partner's references to the hooty owls were particularly irritating. That a few squawking bug-eyed birds had landed them in the hoosegow was hogwash. Dupee hated to 'fess up to it, but it was there as big as a wart on his honker—a little shank-bone woman and two smart-ass breeds were responsible for this unpleasant incarceration.

By the day, Dupee Clancy grew more sullen and hostile. Bowie Turnbow was the real boogerman in this deplorable turn of fate. He told him to keep his big mouth shut. Dupee took to playing cards between the bars with another unscrupulous character in the adjoining cell. The man's name was Loco Talley.

Talley had a first name, Thomas. Few people in Bozeman City knew this. Frequently Loco himself forgot it. Ever since his childhood in Kansas, he had been called Loco. He had a habit of borrowing other people's property, anything from hardware to clothing, roast'nears to chicken, the last two of which he readily shucked, feathered, and consumed. He was also a good pickpocket, which explained his present occupancy in the cell next to Dupee and Bowie.

Until recently, Loco had a woman and two children sharing his dilapidated shanty behind the new freight yards. This always made for good conversation with the villagers. When some wag asked him how the little bastards were doing, he always had a glib reply: "Whose, yours or mine?" Loco was a funny man. He was also a pole cutter and a very poor poker player.

A reprieve for Dupee Clancy and Bowie Turnbow on this Monday in early September—

Sheriff Duggan left to testify in a rustling trial in Livingston. Dupee's last journey had been postponed until Thursday. The usually morose Dupee was elated. He saw a glimmer of hope; his appetite suddenly improved. He had been nesting a devious plot; he thought there was some chance he could hatch it.

After Duggan's houseguests dutifully slid their empty tin supper plates under the cell doors, Dupee hunched up and began his palaver and card playing with Loco. "Loco," he said, "you ain't got a Chineeman's chance this time 'round. You see what the judge done to me? I'm dead meat. By next week, I'll be resting in potter's field."

"Back luck," Loco said. He blew on the cards once and kissed the deck.

"What you always doing that fool stunt for?"

"It's for good luck."

"Humph! Well, you're damned well gonna need it when you meet the judge. You better be thinking on that."

"I ain't no killer like you." Loco began dealing.

"Way I see it," Dupee continued, "they'll rack you good this time, send you up. Boys 'round here tired of feeding your ugly face. By Gawd, you own the place by now. It's not your second home, man, it's your first." Clancy cackled.

From the side, Bowie Turnbow grumbled, "Better'n the place we're headed, Dupee."

Clancy turned and craned his neck toward the jail office. Deputy Drescher had disappeared with the dirty plates. Dupee said in a hushed voice, "I ain't planning on going to the big hotel . . ."

"The big hotel in the sky, y'mean?" Bowie asked.

"No big hotel anywhere, goddamn it!"

With a trace of annoyance, Loco said, "Play your cards."

"I'd damn sight rather get shot in the head than get my neck throttled," Dupee said. "Y'know, give a man a fighting chance. 'Least that's the way I look at it."

"Y'had your fighting chance once, Dupee. Those Tree boys done scared the shit outta you." Turnbow grinned. "For a fact, me too."

The light was fading. Dupee squinted and momentarily studied his cards. He glared through the bars at Loco. "Man, can't you ever give me something to play with? This ain't low ball, is it?"

"Jacks or better," said Loco. "How many you need?"

"Five."

"Five! For crissakes, you only get three!"

"I need the whole deck, that's what."

Curious, Bowie Turnbow sidled over and hunkered next to Dupee. Bowie, by experience, knew when his partner was leading up to something. Dupee always did a little testing, sort of like old man Smithers back home at the creamery used to do. Smithers stuck a finger in the cream and licked it before he set a price on the can.

Bowie asked, "Something on your mind, Dupee? If you ain't going to the big hotel, just where you aiming to go?"

Dupee's grin behind his black beard was yellow. "I was thinking we could all go"—he pointed his nose—"outside, if Loco here has a notion. I figure it'd be right easy now with Duggan out of here. That is if Loco wants to throw in with us."

"I ain't looking to get shot," Loco said.

"Why, we can fly like birdies in the sky. Skedaddle down and get all that loot we got cached. Hell, we might even go on down to ol' Mex, get us some of those *señoritas.*"

It was Bowie's turn to squint. He did so, almost in Dupee's black beard. "Loot . . .?"

"Damnation!" Dupee cried, one big eyelid flapping. "You been in here so long you done started forgetting? And keep your voice down."

Bowie Turnbow rested back on his heels, a sickly grin on his face. "Yessir. Yessir, I almost forgot . . . forgot about that little secret." He pressed a finger to his lips murmured, "Shush," then looked warily toward the office.

Dupee Clancy looked, too. His dark eyes suddenly sparkled. "Say," he said excitedly, "we could cut the kid, Carl, in. Why, he'd likely turn the key and ride out with us for a few thousand bucks. Now, what you think about that? Hot damn, that's a scorcher, ain't it?"

Bowie slid into the charade like corn syrup. He glowered and said in a hushed voice, "To hell with the law! He don't get no share of the pie, not in my book. Law's what got us in here in the first place. Piss on that deputy."

"Law had nothing to do with it," Dupee hissed. "It was those stinking Injuns." His eyes narrowed and he added menacingly, "Have to come back from ol' Mex one of these days and take care of some unfinished business, partner."

Loco, his nose poked through bars, followed the conversation from one man to the other. Loot? A big pot hidden away somewhere? He finally whispered, "How much you got in your box?"

"No box," Dupee quickly answered. "Big ol' canvas bag. Nigh on ten thousand, I reckon."

"Mebee eleven, I'd say," Bowie interjected.

Loco Talley gripped the bars. His knuckles turned white. "Holy moley, and it's going to rot!"

Dupee lamented, " 'Less we get outta here, 'tis for sure."

Silence. Dupee and Bowie, their faces racked with despair, stared at Loco. Loco shot another furtive look at the office. Deputy Drescher had returned from the little commode. He was wiping the plates with a towel. Loco whispered, "You figger foxing him some way? This it?"

"You want in?" asked Dupee. "Split the pot three ways?"

Loco Talley gulped. "Hell yes, deal me in!"

Another day passed. Working double shift, Deputy Carl Drescher was a tad weary. He had to make the usual rounds by day, check on complaints, and order meals for his three prisoners. By night, he rousted a few unruly drunks from the three saloons, and kept an eye out for trouble in general. By midnight, he was happy to wash up and hit the sack in the back room.

The routine this Tuesday night was no different. About midnight, Drescher made his last stop at the Antler Saloon. He chatted briefly with Lacey Tubbs, then went back to the long street. It was empty. He walked down the boardwalk checking doorknobs at a few of the stores, hesitated at Lucas Hamm's mercantile to peer in the window. Everything was in order, so he headed for the sheriff's office.

Inside the jail, he saw that the place was in an uproar. Shouts and groans bounced off the walls. Deputy Drescher rushed to the cells. In the first, Dupee Clancy and Bowie Turnbow had their hands and arms through the bars of the adjoining cell. They had Loco Talley locked in a death grip. Loco's eyes were bulging, his face was distorted and florid, and his throat was gurgling.

"Stop it, you idiots," Drescher screamed, "you're killing him!" To little avail. In fact, Dupee and Bowie went to their task with more intensity. Drescher drew his revolver and fired a shot into the floor planking. Once again, to no avail. In desperation, he grabbed the key from the wall peg and hurried over to Loco's cell. In one swift move, he turned the key and threw open the door. Cursing, Drescher frantically tore at the arms and hands of the two men. Suddenly, Loco went limp. Dupee and Bowie released their grip and began shouting triumphantly.

Drescher was horrified. As Loco slid down between his legs, the deputy yelled, "You crazy bastards! You killed him! Now you'll both swing. I saw the whole thing!" But before he could move away, Loco Talley adeptly flipped over and came up behind the startled officer. Loco was laughing like a loon. Loco Talley was a pickpocket, and a very good one. In a flash, he ducked to the side and passed Drescher's revolver to the outstretched hand of Dupee Clancy. Without hesitation, Dupee fired point-blank. The slug smashed Deputy Drescher in the chest, and he was dead before he crashed against the opposite wall.

"Get us out of here!" roared Dupee.

Moments later, Loco had the cell door open. Bowie Turnbow bolted to the gun rack and seized a rifle and a shotgun. He scooped up a few shells, yelling with delight, "Oh, sweet charity, we did it!"

When he turned, Dupee had Drescher's forty-five aimed at Loco Talley.

Talley cried, "Hey, what's going on? What the hell you doing, pard? I thought we had a deal . . . ol' Mex . . ."

"You don't talk their lingo, *Loco*." Blam!

Six doors down at the Antler Saloon, Lacey Tubbs was wiping the bar. He heard two faint pops. He went out to the boardwalk to investigate. It was dark and silent. He saw nothing amiss. He returned to the Antler, pulled the shades, and bolted the door.

TWENTY·ONE

When the train slowed at the Tree Livestock Company siding, Moon and Sad Sam jumped off. It was late afternoon, still sunny and bright. The men were anticipating an equally pleasant night under the glow of a hanging lamp.

But for the present, the stockyard's odor was horrendous. Sad Sam sniffed and coughed.

Moon smiled and said, "Ripe, ei?"

"Yes, son, the sweet smell of progress."

Moon said reflectively, "You know, when I was out on the prairie with my people, I used to think the smell of buffalo was plenty bad. I tell you, Sam, that was a good smell compared to these critters."

They hopped across several sets of tracks, circled the new sheds and a series of long, freshly painted corrals. Several hundred cows and steers were milling about inside. Beyond the corrals, the brick walls of the packing plant were partially up. A few workers were moving about, some carrying the last loads for the day.

Directly, a lanky frame appeared in a distant small building, then a wave and a friendly shout. "Hey, Moon . . . Sam!"

Moon waved. Sad Sam ambled along, a white handkerchief to his nose. Ultimately, the men met on the small porch and exchanged handshakes with Claybourn Moore. Moon and Sad Sam were surprised that Moore had anticipated their arrival. The explanation was in a lengthy telegram that Moore picked up from his cluttered desk. He handed it to them.

Slumping in his chair, Moore said, "Not the best of news for a greeting. It came in the morning. Hockett figured you'd hop off here to get a couple of horses. I don't think you'll be needing the horses now."

Moore and Sad Sam read the message in painful silence. Moon's usually stoic countenance slowly turned to livid outrage. He cursed, and hit his fist on the desk. "By the Great One Above," he moaned, "we should have made these men disappear when we had the chance. I told Hockett. No, he didn't want them killed. Justice! What kind of justice is this? How did they manage to pull this off?"

"Maybe Zachary will have a clue," Moore replied. "Looks like he's a deputy. Reckon the city council didn't have a choice, old man Duggan somewhere in the sticks and a dead deputy on its hands."

Sad Sam tutted. "Poor Locco. The old pole cutter never could manage a winning hand."

A short discussion followed. Moon agreed there was no need for the two horses. He wasn't going into town to play poker. His brain was afire. He was going home to search for two killers. Likewise, Sad Sam had lost his urge to play the great game. But transportation back to Bozeman City appeared to be the problem. The west-bound had long since departed. Then Clay Moore snapped his fingers. He had a solution.

"What?" Moon asked.

"Freight," Moore said with a smile. "Every Wednesday and Friday night. Catch it right over there." He nodded toward the tracks. "I have four empties going over to Johnny Grant's spread in the Deer Lodge Valley. They'll hook 'em on around midnight. Why, hell, you boys can be back in town early in the morning."

Moon's angry face mellowed. "By jingo, Mr. Clay, that'll do it!"

With a touch of apprehension, Sad Sam asked, "Cattle cars, I presume?"

"Well, of course," Moore answered.

"A pity."

Clay Moore laughed. "Oh, you don't have to ride 'em, Sam. Hell, there's a caboose. You and Moon can ride with the crew. I'll arrange it."

"Most kind of you, Claybourn." Sad Sam removed his fedora and wiped his forehead with the white handkerchief. With a weary sigh, he said,

"It's going to be a long night. I wonder if those good fellows play the game."

The "good fellows" were Archie and Hooks. They played the game, but without proficiency. In between a few delays, and by the light of a flickering lantern, Moon and Sad Sam dealt cards and drank coffee until dawn. It was a learning experience for Archie and Hooks, but at a limit of a quarter, not too painful.

A night of playing poker in dim light never seemed to tire Sad Sam's eyes. He was his usual observant self. As the freight began to slow in the Bozeman City's yards, Sad Sam saw Loco Talley's tattered shack come into sight. The old place was sandwiched in between a stinking slough and a line of golden willows, a mosquito hellhole if there ever was one. The early September air was chilly, and a misty film hovered over the cattails.

As Sad Sam reminisced about the grizzled pole cutter's poker shortcomings, a strange sight began to unfold. A man jerking at his suspenders ran from the outhouse toward the shanty. He disappeared. Sad Sam squinted in the hazy dawn and tried to penetrate the mist floating over the slough. Directly, another man appeared on the little porch. He crouched like a monkey preparing to leap a stick. The "stick," from what Sad Sam could make out, was a rifle. Then the first man reappeared, also brandishing a rifle.

Sad Sam turned and said to Moon Tree, "Son,

it appears squatters have moved into Loco's cabin. From what I deduce, they're preparing to attack our position. They're armed, so it leads me to the conclusion these gentlemen are your old friends, the very ones you seek."

"What!" Snake-bitten, Moon leaped forward and pressed his head to the windowpane.

"Up ahead there," Sad Sam said. "Can you identify them from this distance?"

"Not yet," Moon whispered.

Sad Sam said, "I doubt they can hear from this distance, either."

"By jingo, if it's Dupee and ol' hippity-hop, they must have holed up there waiting for this rig. They didn't rustle up any horses."

Sad Sam replied dryly, "They probably didn't want to ride out and have a posse on their tails. Clever fellows, sneaking away on a freight."

Hooks, the brakeman, was leaning out the door on the other side of the caboose. Archie came close to Moon and Sad Sam. "What's so damned interesting out there?" he asked.

"Nothing in particular," said Sad Sam. He got up from the window seat and carefully brushed a few cinders from the shoulders of his coat. "Might be ducks coming across the water in a few minutes. Moon wants to identify the species."

Archie elevated his nose. "That's Shit Creek over there. I wouldn't touch a duck outta that place. Whew!" He turned and took up a position behind his partner. Moments later, both of them hopped off.

"Damn, Sam!" Moon exclaimed. "Look there! It's Dupee, all right. He's in front, and here they come, plenty fast! They're making right for those empties up ahead."

Removing his fedora, Sad Sam shared the window with Moon. "Getting their feet wet, aren't they? Hightailing it. I don't suppose they'll master the art of flying."

Moon jerked around. "This is bad medicine, my brother."

Sad Sam began removing his coat. He carefully draped it over the back of the seat, then pulled out his revolver and examined the chamber. He drawled, "Let them settle, son. Tell one of our friends to uncouple that first empty and move on ahead." His little smile faded. "I think we can do the rest if we play our cards properly. Dead or alive, Moon?"

"Ol' Red Nose never took prisoners."

The freight screeched to a halt. "Red Nose?" asked Sad Sam.

"General Gibbon, the bastard!"

"Ah, some of your illustrious past."

As they stepped down, Moon said, "I'll duck under and have the cars split off. Meet you on this side."

"We surround them?"

"Hell no! We sneak up like Injuns, shoot 'em through the slats."

"Very unsportsmanlike."

"By the power, Sam, what do you think they'd do to us!" Moon crouched. "If you're behind this car, I'll give a little hoot, sorta like an owl. That's the sign when we're ready to close in, ei?" He stared up at Sad Sam's fancy fedora. "And you better take that thing off. Might get a hole through it."

Sad Sam shook his head. "Better the hat than my head, son."

Moon ran off in a crouch, caught up with Hooks, and quickly explained. In turn, Hooks made a few signals with his arms. He uncoupled the first cattle car, made another signal, and with several jolts, the engine moved ahead.

Moon looked cautiously around the boxcar. He was ready to move, so he hooted softly. At this point, his plan went awry. He saw Sad Sam bending low in a careful approach from the caboose. Drawing his pistol, Moon moved toward him. Moments later, as he peeked in between the slats of the first car, he heard several heavy thuds, then the sound of feet pounding away. In a flash, he knew what had happened. Dupee and Bowie thought they had been stranded on the siding. They were on a dead run back to Loco's shanty.

Moon Tree leaped the coupling. The two fleeing men were at the edge of the shallow water about fifteen yards away when he shouted. "Ho there, you bastards! Hold it!"

Bowie Turnbow stopped, whirled around, and

shouldered his rifle. But Moon touched off his revolver first. His shot was true. Bowie flew backward, his reflexive shot whining away over the top of the boxcars. Dupee Clancy's shotgun roared, and the peppering shot splintered the boards next to Moon. Moon fell and scrambled beside the wheels, a stinging sensation in his shoulder.

Dupee's second round never came. Instead, Moon heard a roar to his right. Dupee flipped over into the cattails. Only the heels of his boots were showing. One car behind Moon, Sad Sam stepped out. He wagged his revolver once. "Are you hit?"

"Ei, I think a couple pellets nipped me in the arm somewhere." Moon got up and dusted himself. He fingered his shoulder. It was nothing. Holstering his pistol, he flexed his arm, then walked slowly toward the stinking pond.

Sam called, "Any movement?"

Shaking his head, Moon turned away. "No, my brother, they're dead . . . two dead ducks in the pond."

Archie and Hooks came on the run. After a short explanation, Moon thanked them for their cooperation. By then, Sad Sam was retrieving the carpetbags from the caboose. He finally stepped down. He shook hands with Archie and Hooks, told them he had enjoyed their company.

Adjusting his fedora, Sad Sam said, "Sometime we'll play the game again, boys." He smiled. "Under better circumstances, I trust."

The resounding shots had stirred some of the townspeople. Moon saw four riders galloping across the adjacent field. In back of him, the locomotive whistled once and began to move slowly backward to couple the boxcars.

Sad Sam commented, "That's the only thing I enjoy about a train, son, the way it whistles."

"Ei, I like it better at night," Moon Tree said. "Reminds me of wolves on the prairie, lonely sound." He looked at Sad Sam. "You saved my hide back there," he said. "That second barrel. If Dupee . . . well, I owe you for that, Sam. I know you're a card sharp. I didn't know you could shoot, too."

A trace of a smile crossed Sam's sad countenance. "Your father said it, Moon. Sometimes life is like a poker game. When the stakes are high, you can't make a mistake." He chuckled and put his arm around Moon Tree. "Of course, I don't deny it . . . sometimes a man gets lucky, too."

The first two of the men from town approached and reined up. Zachary Hockett. The early-morning sun reflected brilliant shards from the shiny badge of the second man.

"Moon! Sam!" said Hockett. "Where in the hell did you come from? How did you manage . . .?"

Sad Sam said, "We came in on that freight back there. Not the most pleasant accommodations, I assure you."

"Good morning, Sheriff," Moon said with a

touch of sarcasm. "It was a very short vacation. You spoiled our card game."

"We were just getting up another posse," Hockett said. "The telegram? Well, I'm damn sorry about that. The women. They were worried, bushwhacking, that sorta thing. They insisted I send it." He shrugged.

"That does not surprise me."

Robert Peete was the second rider. He nodded toward the train. "What was all the ruckus . . . the shooting?"

Moon Tree replied, "Ducks. We caught some ducks over there on the Loco's pond. Fact is, they couldn't fly. We got two of 'em." He gave Zachary Hockett a dark look. "You better get on over there and fetch 'em, Mr. Hockett, before they disappear."

TWENTY-TWO

October came dressed in yellow, red, and orange, and the great trees around the little church radiated this warmth. Peace had come to the valley, with it concession and reconciliation.

Inside the church, beautifully dressed women and gentlemen attired in their Sunday-best waited expectantly. The sweet scents of bouquets and delicate perfumes mingled. There were hushed voices and gentle laughter. This was a happy occasion; this was the wedding of Jessie Stuart and Moon Tree.

Sad Sam Courtland quietly observed from a pew near the front door. Next to him sat Claybourn Moore and his wife and son. To the side of the flower-decked altar, a prim little woman with a lace-trimmed bonnet played the piano, a variety of hymns with which only a few in attendance were familiar. This was irrelevant. These were beautiful and understanding people. They knew the significance of a blessed union between a man and a woman.

A momentary disturbance at the rear door caused a ripple of excitement. A pretty woman dressed in a shimmering gown entered, followed by two gentlemen wearing tailored black suits. All three were smiling. The little man to the rear was partially hidden by a glistening bass fiddle.

"Good Lord," whispered Claybourn Moore. "It's Divinity Jones!"

Ruth Moore chimed in, "What a pleasant surprise!"

"I thought she and those boys were in Colorado," Clay said. "A big tour of some kind."

Sad Sam whispered, "They were."

Clay glanced suspiciously at Sad Sam. "You . . . you knew about this?"

Sad Sam stared directly ahead. The prim little piano player had vacated her seat. Sean O'Grady took her place.

Sad Sam whispered again. "This is a big game, Clay, the biggest one the Red Man is ever going to play. For the big game, you need a royal flush, all hearts, the big red one."

Suddenly, the church was filled with joyous music. The beautiful voices of Divinity Jones and Sean O'Grady blended in melodious harmony. Beauregard Lincoln's smile was broad and pearly. His big bass echoed through the long room, thug, thug, thug-a-thug, thug.

Paul A. Hawkins's bold new trilogy begins with *The Shooter*, the epic journey and adventures of a reluctant young gunfighter who became a frontier legend. The following is the beginning of Hawkins's new novel, which will appear in stores in April 1994.

FOREWORD

I knew Hardy Gibbs. Most often, he was a quiet young man, yet very personable. I was the only writer on the frontier who witnessed his prowess with a handgun. In the more than twenty years I worked as a reporter, I saw many gunfighters, and many who claimed to be, but were not. I never saw one with the quickness and the accuracy of Hardy Gibbs. What set him apart from all others was that he was a marksman. Yes, I would honestly say that Hardy Gibbs was the ultimate gunfighter.

—Henry Burlingame
Harper's Weekly

PROLOGUE

Lusk, Wyoming Territory, July 1878

The few onlookers along the rutted street, were a be-draggled lot of drifters, hopeful miners, and drovers, and not a single one of them was aware of what had precipitated the stand-off. But, to a man, they quickly ducked for cover along the small boardwalk when the shooting began—three shots in rapid succession, two from the young shooter standing alone in the middle of the ruts, and the last one a misdirected bullet that splintered one of the posts in front of the Yankee Dollar Saloon. The lone gunfighter in the middle of the street still stood; two of the three near the saloon door lay flat on their backs, and the third man was edging toward the hitching rack, his hands elevated in surrender. The spectators, those who weren't slack-jawed by this shocking display of gunplay and sudden death, were whispering among themselves, some moving cautiously back toward the saloon, wondering about the fate of the third man, barely a man, with his hands high in the air. Several other witnesses weren't interested in anything more than getting back to the watering hole and washing the cotton wads from their mouths with a good belt of redeye. They had witnessed an unnerving spectacle.

The buckskin-clad gunfighter offered up only several brief words of explanation to the curious and the stunned who were still staring back and forth at each other and down at the two forms on the planking before the saloon. Waving the long barrel of his revolver across the scene, he said simply and quietly, "Horse thieves . . . rustlers."

The brief conversation that followed, the bystanders couldn't hear. But the young fellow with his hands in the air quickly lowered them and unbuckled his gun belt, hurried over and began stripping the saddle from a black Morgan. He then went over to his fallen companions, frisked their pockets and vests, and along with his own wallet, promptly deposited them in a pile directly in front of the street shooter.

The shooter's next words to the trembling man were clearly audible.

"You ride back up the road and tell Mr. Bullock there's more than one way of skinning a cat. Tell him I'm taking your profit back to the army and the Crow at Fort Custer."

As the youth turned and walked toward the hitching post, the shooter quickly came up behind him and gave him a sound kick in the butt. "Yes, and one other thing . . . in case he or any of your thieving friends take a notion to follow, just tell Mr. Bullock I have good eyes in the back of my head, too. I'll drop him or anyone else who dares to follow me just like I did those two over there."

The young man made a weak protest. "Have a heart, mister," he said pleadingly. "That's a two-day ride. I can't make it by myself . . . hostiles . . . Sioux. They're all around the road."

"Well, that's your good fortune," said the gunfighter. "Fetch yourself a couple along the way and make up your losses you have here. I hear they're paying two hundred fifty dollars for the head of Indians in Deadwood. And consider yourself lucky. If you had whiskers on your chin, I'd have killed you." Pointing his revolver, the man added, "Now, get riding before I change my mind."

Visibly shaken, the youngster did as he was told. Fumbling at the looped reins on the pole, he finally managed to mount his horse and kicked away, up the worn wagon road to Deadwood.

The shooter, after holstering his revolver, wiped his brow with his sleeve, scooped up the loot from the street, and led the black horse over to the livery and disappeared inside. Five minutes later, he came out riding the Morgan and trailing a brown and white Indian pony. Edging up to the porch, he tossed out a ten-dollar gold piece. "Cheaper than Indian heads . . . only worth five dollars each. Bury them and have a drink on Charlie." With a casual wave he rode off down the road to the south.

All of what had transpired in ten minutes puzzled most of the motley group of observers, more particu-

larly several who knew who the man Bullock was—
Seth Bullock, Sheriff Bullock, head of the law in the
recently declared county of Lawrence, Deadwood, Territory of Dakota. Why anyone, especially a killer, was
ordering a horse thief back to Deadwood to a sheriff
was more than puzzling—it was confounding and in-
comprehensible, and one observer, Charlie Rollo, an
old-time high plains drifter and drover, knew no explanation for it.

His companion, Red Lockhart, another destitute
trail hand, staring at the departing shooter, wheezed,
"Well, in all my born days, I've never seen the likes of
that one, never! Thought he was one of us, just a drover, waiting around to catch on with some outfit coming down the valley. Strange kid, always playing on one
of those harmonicas, sad like . . . made you feel like
something was going to happen, something not too
good. Said his name was Charles. Poof, and just like
that, slicker 'n a whistle, he pulls the shades on those
two and runs the other one out of town. And back up
to Sheriff Bullock? Now, what do you make of that?"

Though Charlie Rollo couldn't comprehend this either, he did shed some light on the identity of the mysterious gunman. In his dozen years on the frontier,
Rollo had seen only two or three men who wielded a
handgun with any proficiency at all. At twenty-five
paces, most couldn't hit the broad side of a barn, and
that was a fact. But this particular man, he allowed, he
had seen before, somewhat different in appearance,
now with mustache and long hair. Rollo hadn't forgotten that snaky stance, though, the little bend in the

knees, and that quick, outward thrust and direct aim of the weapon. "I don't know what to make of it . . . that Bullock business, but I'll tell you this. That feller's name ain't Charles no more than my name is Abraham." He carefully stepped around the two bodies, hesitated briefly, glancing at the foamy holes in their breasts. "Look at that, would you?" he said. "Right properly placed, both of them, directly in the middle of the chest."

Red Lockhart didn't care to look. "Said his name was Charles . . . that's what he told me last night. Waiting to catch on with an outfit trailing to Kansas."

Charlie Rollo said, "Charles, my ass! He's a goddamned gunfighter, wanted in Missouri, but that ain't his real handle. His name is Hardy Gibbs. I saw him take down a feller in a card game down at Hays. Bang! That one was smack-dab in the head. Thought his name was Charlie there, too, Charlie Parsons, only later it turned out he was Gibbs."

"Hardy Gibbs!"

"One and the same," replied Rollo.

"Why, he's the Shooter!"

"That he is, one of the best around, they tell me, maybe the best. Probably put a dozen men in the sod, that one."

"Well, what the hell is he doing up in this country? . . . and how do you know it's Gibbs? And consorting with Sheriff Bullock? Now, come on, Charlie, it don't make a lick of sense. Not a lick."

"No, it don't, I reckon," answered Charlie Rollo. "But it's Gibbs, all right. Oh, hell, I don't know about his face all that well . . . two summers ago, maybe, I forget . . . clean-shaved then, but I don't forget his style, that little goosy step forward, the way he's hunched. He ain't standing loose and hanging like a scarecrow. You saw it yourself. He's a goddamned cat."

"Can't say I did. Happened too fast."

"Well, I saw it," countered Charlie Rollo. "And another thing. That revolver. I suppose you didn't notice that, either."

"Hell, yes, I saw it," Lockhart said. "I saw it belch twice, I did."

"Seven-inch barrel. No Colt, either, no Navy piece, no stubby Frontier Six. It's a goddamned Gibbs Special, and there just ain't many of those pieces around. Damn things cost a fortune."

As they walked into the bar, Rollo glanced knowingly at his companion. "Gibbs Special, a five-shooter, hand-made, a two-pounder forty-four . . . ?"

"Gibbs." Red Lockhart clucked his tongue.

"That's right," Rollo said with a grim smile. "Gibbs. That feller's grandpaw makes 'em . . . Amos Gibbs."

"And the boy shoots 'em," sighed Lockhart. In a brief musing, he nodded several times. "Hmm, must be a good thousand riding on his head . . . Missouri, Kansas."

"I reckon so," replied Charlie Rollo. And pointing his nose to the south, he said, "Well, there he goes, Red, a heap of swag in his bag and a thousand or so on his head. You want to follow, take a chance? Get some bounty?"

"No-siree-bob," Red Lockhart replied. "No, I just want a drink, that's all."

"You hear what he said? Said he was taking profit up to Fort Custer. That'd be up the Bozeman Trail, and I reckon I know that country . . . places to hide along the trail."

Red Lockhart stared at Rollo. "You suggesting—?"

Rollo winked. "I reckon we oughta have a drink, all right, sorta talk things over. Let that boy get on the road aways, then, mebee mosey out real easy-like."